THE ROAR
OF DEATH

I'm sure I'd have heard the rumble of the rock slide had it not been for the roar of the river rushing in and out of the rocks against the side of the bank. But suddenly the rocks came down with a roar, striking me in the back. My feet flew out from under me, and I screamed as the bush I was holding onto came loose. A boulder struck me and flung me sideways. I slammed into the wall of rock beside me, my hands flailing, trying to grip something. My left side struck the ground with such force I once again cried out in pain. I looked up and saw more boulders crashing down. I was directly in their path, yet I couldn't move. **I could only lie there helplessly as death rained down upon me. . . .**

Other SIGNET Gothics You'll Want to Read

IN
THE
SHADOWS

by
Dorothy Daniels

Ⓢ
A SIGNET BOOK
NEW AMERICAN LIBRARY
TIMES MIRROR

SIGNET TRADEMARK REG. U.S. PAT. OFF. AND FOREIGN COUNTRIES
REGISTERED TRADEMARK—MARCA REGISTRADA
HECHO EN CHICAGO, U.S.A.

SIGNET, SIGNET CLASSICS, MENTOR, PLUME AND MERIDIAN BOOKS
are published by The New American Library, Inc.,
1301 Avenue of the Americas, New York, New York 10019

FIRST PRINTING, SEPTEMBER, 1978

    1 2 3 4 5 6 7 8 9

PRINTED IN THE UNITED STATES OF AMERICA

IN
THE
SHADOWS

◆ One ◆

Our dining room was small and the oak furniture inexpensive. Yet tonight it took on a look of opulence, made so by the exquisite lace cloth that covered the round table. Crystal candlesticks, containing lighted candles, flanked a matching bowl that was filled with short-stemmed roses I'd gotten from the neighborhood florist. The crystal was the best and so was the china. The only other light in the room came from the candles in the sterling candelabra which sat on the sideboard. I suppose such luxury looked incongruous in a flat otherwise furnished with only the bare essentials. Papa could never have purchased even one of the aforementioned items. They were gifts given to him and Mama by her sister, my Aunt Emma von Linden.

Aunt Emma, whose wealth was fabulous, had lived the life of a recluse since Mama's death. After that sad occasion, she had kept in touch with Papa. She even paid for my education in a private girl's school, where I learned to appreciate the better things in life. The more I saw of it, the more I longed to be a part of the upper strata of society. It was a life of excitement, travel, and parties that gave one an opportunity to meet interesting and famous people. However, I didn't expect the opportunity to enter that life to come so soon. Yet when Aunt Emma issued an invitation to visit her and to remain as long as I wished, I accepted even before consulting Papa. Something I'd not have done had I known he would be so against my going.

Since this was to be my last night with him, I prepared his favorite dinner. Roast chicken with giblet dressing, mashed potatoes, and carrot mousse. I'd baked a cake that morning for our dessert. I prided myself on my cooking and I could see Papa was enjoying it. We ate slowly, our talk light and cheerful, yet each aware that after tonight we would be separated for some time. I was eager, even

1

impatient for it. So much so, I didn't feel the slightest pang of guilt that Papa had lived alone for most of my growing years, which had been spent at a finishing school.

He went to the sideboard and poured us each a glass of sherry. I was surprised to see his hand shake as he tilted the Waterford crystal decanter. He had seemed quite composed during our meal, making me believe he'd dismissed the uneasiness he felt about my visit.

While not handsome and of only medium height, he commanded attention with his prematurely white hair and warm, alert blue eyes. He was still trim of figure and dressed neatly, though inexpensively. His carriage was so majestic that he could easily be mistaken for one of those gentlemen I had seen pass in and out of the portals of the exclusive clubs that were housed in elegant buildings on Fifth Avenue. However, Papa was employed as a floor-walker for a department store. He had worked up to that position from a clerk and I was proud of him.

He broke into my reverie. "Shall we drink our wine here or in the parlor?"

"In the parlor." I blew out the candles on the table. "You can light the gas burner in the fireplace and we shall sit before Mama's portrait."

"Another gift from your aunt." Bitterness tinged his voice. "It was painted during your mother's stay there."

"It was dear of Aunt Emma to send it to you."

"Dear of Aunt Emma," he said contemptuously. "Your mother would be alive today if it weren't for her."

His sudden change of manner puzzled me. "I had no idea you resented her."

"Why shouldn't I?" he demanded.

I went over to him. "Papa, you sound childish. Did you begrudge Mama the luxuries Aunt Emma bestowed on both of you when you married?"

"Begrudge isn't the proper word. I was embarrassed by them, knowing I could never purchase anything to equal them."

I picked up both glasses, handed him his, and kissed his cheek. "I'm sorry. I didn't know your feelings toward Aunt Emma were so bitter."

"There was no reason for you to. At least, not until now."

"Let's go in the parlor and talk this over. We don't have to sit before Mama's portrait."

He managed a smile and his tone softened. "I want to—after I light the gas in the grate."

Though it was June, we'd had five consecutive days of rain, so the flame sent out a welcome warmth. Papa settled himself in one of the two maroon velvet chairs he had reupholstered and eyed Mama's portrait thoughtfully. Her eyes seemed to be smiling down at us and once again I noticed how closely I resembled her. Our hair was the same shade of auburn, our eyes hazel. Our mouths were large, but our lips well-shaped. Papa often told me Mama was more slender than I, but while she had been a scant five feet, I was six inches taller.

Papa broke into my reverie. "Do you remember your mother? You were only three when she left."

"I remember a lady whose laughter was soft."

He looked pleased. "Like yours, Celeste."

"Thank you, Papa. I also remember she had a delightful fragrance when she held me close." I switched back to the subject uppermost in my mind. "Papa, don't you think I have a right to become better acquainted with Aunt Emma? After all, she is Mama's sister. And certainly, she must have cared a great deal for Mama when she insisted on sending me to a very expensive girls' school."

His mood changed again. "And made you scorn the only kind of life I could give you."

I set my glass on the table, went to him, and knelt beside his chair. My hand reached up and I turned his head so he had to look down at me.

"Papa, you don't really believe that."

"I do, Celeste," he said sternly, "because it's true."

I returned to my chair, disheartened by the change in him. "I must be a great disappointment to you."

Papa spoke with quiet determination. "I love you, Celeste. Never doubt that. However, I'm still bitter because of what happened to your mother at Linden Gardens."

Linden Gardens was the name of my aunt's estate, located in upper New York State. Her husband had been an immigrant, but he seemed to have been blessed with a magic touch, for shortly after his arrival in America, he quickly amassed a fortune and acquired a beautiful estate. Tragically, he had not lived long enough to enjoy it, but my aunt had remained loyal to his memory and never remarried.

I said, "Mama's fall down the stairs, though fatal, was an accident."

"Yes," Papa agreed. "But I still say she should never have gone there. I was as much against her going there as I am against your going."

"Why didn't you want her to visit Aunt Emma?"

"I felt her first duty was to you, a mere toddler. Your aunt was wealthy and could afford the best medical care. Instead, she wrote, begging your mother to come to her. That she was ill and frightened."

"If I had been in Mama's place, I would have gone. After all, Mrs. Marley took excellent care of me."

"She was a good friend of your mother and she consented to look after you during your mother's absence. She was like a second mother to you."

Until her death four years ago, I thought, remembering the kindly lady.

"Then your aunt entered the picture." Bitterness again tinged Papa's voice.

"She always maintained contact with us, Papa," I reasoned. "She sent me lovely gifts and purchased all my clothes."

"I'd have liked nothing better than to have been in a position to forbid it." He paused and sighed wearily. "To have done so, would have made me a martinet. Each year I prayed that once your education was completed, she would let you alone. Instead, she invites you to visit her, hoping you'll like it enough to remain forever. Do you wonder I'm resentful?"

I tried another angle in an attempt to win his approval. "Papa, I'm not trained to do anything practical. I couldn't make my way in the business world."

"You could have," he argued. "I'd intended for you to go to business school and learn to be a typist. You could still do that. The money is in the bank for it. It's an honorable profession. I've even been promised a position for you at the store. It's still available."

I made no answer.

Papa said, "I know. The thought is appalling after having mingled with the daughters of wealthy families."

I tried to keep the irritation out of my voice as I spoke. "Such a thought never occurred to me. The simple truth is that I would love to visit Aunt Emma. Is it so wrong to want to be a part of beauty and elegance and riches for a little while? I was taught to admire and appreciate those things. I've learned all the social graces so that I can move into such an atmosphere with ease. I know Aunt Emma's home must be magnificent and I want to see it. Don't be too harsh on me, Papa. I'm young. I don't want to disobey you. In fact, I won't. You need only forbid me to go."

"I would never forbid."

"Then ask me not to go." Though sorely disappointed at the turn our talk had taken, I managed to hide it with a smile. "Say you need me more than Aunt Emma."

"And have you resent me forever after?"

"I swear I wouldn't."

"I know Emma is lonely. She's been a recluse since your mama died. I won't deny it was a terrible shock to her, coming so soon after the death of her husband."

"Was she aware of the resentment you bore her?"

"Possibly—since she never came here. Also, if she ever found the letters I wrote your mother, she'd know."

"Weren't they returned to you?"

"No. I suppose they're stuck away in some drawer."

"I'll see if I can find them and send them back to you."

"I'd rather you didn't." He stood up. "You have an early train to catch tomorrow. I'll do the dishes."

"We both will." I was already on my feet and I picked up the glasses. We'd scarcely touched the wine. The magic of the evening was ended.

Papa followed me to the kitchen. We completed our chores, our talk once again light. To my delight, he told me he was not only resigned to my departure, but I could remain as long as I wished.

I flashed him a smile of gratitude, then asked a question that had crossed my mind for the first time.

"Am I a snob, Papa?"

He chuckled softly. "Let's say you still have a little growing up to do."

"Which is a nice way of saying I am." I kissed his cheek, took the towel from him, and spread it on a rod behind the kitchen stove.

"You'll grow up," Papa said kindly. "Just be careful."

"I don't know what I have to be careful of," I said lightly. "But I'll remember that you cautioned me."

"That's all I ask." He glanced at the kitchen clock on the shelf over the sink. "Almost ten o'clock. Your train leaves at seven tomorrow morning. I've ordered a hack to pick you up."

"Thanks, Papa. Will you come to the station with me?"

"Yes. Now run along. I want to read the evening paper."

I had packed and repacked my baggage, but once again I checked everything. Satisfied, I undressed and slipped beneath the covers. My excitement was so great, I doubted I'd sleep. But I did—the entire night.

I had to contain the excitement within me while bidding Papa farewell, though I suppose I didn't fool him. He smiled, joked a little, and waved until we could no longer see each other. Though the train was almost full, I felt as if it were my own private car. I kept my eyes trained on the scenery, marveling at the beauty of the countryside, made more beautiful by a brilliant sun. Even Mother Nature seemed to want my journey to be a pleasant one.

I was the only one who left the train at Wilmot Depot. The ride had taken about three hours.

I had met my aunt only once, when she attended my recent graduation. I was both surprised and delighted that she wished to attend. She was a quiet woman, short of stature and quite timid. Or perhaps it was shyness. It didn't matter. I loved her, not only because she was Mama's sister, but for her many kindnesses during my growing years. I held no resentment because Mama had answered her request to come and stay with her, following the death of her husband.

I wondered if she would be at the station and secretly hoped so. The conductor helped me alight, then swung my three pieces of baggage down from the platform. He tipped his hat, smiled a farewell, and boarded the train. It left with a burst of steam and was soon chugging on its way.

I turned my attention to the platform and for a moment my spirits fell. No one was there. I started toward the closed door of the depot, but before I reached it, a lady in a red satin suit with matching slippers opened the door and moved briskly toward me. Though not thin, she was trim of figure and as tall as I. Her head was swathed in what seemed like yards of black veiling, some of which covered her brow and tied under her chin. Her eyes were the most striking thing about her. Even through the veil, I could see they were a dark brown and deep-set. Though her hair was still jet black, I judged her to be in her mid-fifties. She approached me with a smile and I heard the tinkle of bells. I thought it was caused by the many bracelets she wore, visible when she extended a hand and spoke my name.

"I am Wanda Vargas," she said. "I live with your aunt. I suppose you could say I'm her companion."

"How do you do, Miss Vargas," I replied.

"It's Mrs. But call me Wanda. It would please your aunt as well as me. We are very close. I am happy you consent-ed to come."

"Thank you, Wanda. How is my aunt?"

"Lonely. I hope you can do for her what I could not."

"Is something wrong?"

"Yes," Wanda said. "Though I was against mentioning it just now. Especially since your aunt is hopeful you will like it here so well, you will remain. So do I."

"Thank you again. I am indebted to my aunt."

Mrs. Vargas—or Wanda—slipped her arm around my waist and guided me toward the interior of the depot.

"My baggage." I spoke with a touch of concern.

"Zeffrey Innis will come for it. He oversees the garden-ers and is also the coachman. I wanted to greet you alone. Should you see him, you might wait for the next train back."

She laughed at my sobering features. "Don't fear him, Celeste. I'm only joking. When you meet Zeffrey, you will understand."

We walked through the depot and came out on the side where the carriages could pull up and await their passen-gers. Ours was a lovely surrey with green satin upholstery and matching fringe. The driver was standing alongside it.

"Zeffrey, this is Miss Celeste Abbott." Wanda's tone be-came formal. "Her baggage is on the platform. Please get it."

He acknowledged the introduction with only a curt nod, then took out a pocket watch. "Train's ten minutes late."

"So were we," Wanda replied. "And I apologize, my dear."

"It didn't matter," I replied.

Zeffrey had already entered the depot. We got into the carriage and awaited his return. Despite the warmth of the day, he was wearing a long overcoat that age had faded to an ugly green. Atop his head was a derby that had also seen better days. His features were bony, almost to the point of emaciation.

"Is Zeffrey ill?" I asked.

Once again, Wanda laughed. I had the feeling laughter came easily to her and thought she must be a cheerful influence for my aunt.

"No," she replied. "He has a voracious appetite. As for his appearance, he refuses to wear a uniform. I told your aunt she should insist, or discharge him. But she is a very compassionate lady. And I wouldn't try to influence her because Zeffrey has a very sick wife and your aunt feels they need his wages. At least, that's what she claims."

"In that case, I should think he would carry out my aunt's wishes."

"Not Zeffrey. He's rather old and doesn't hear too well. Also, he worked for your uncle and your aunt feels it's her duty to keep him on. I suggested pensioning him and she mentioned it to him, but he was offended. That was the end of it."

Zeffrey reappeared with my baggage, placed it in the back of the carriage, settled himself in the front seat, and urged the horses into motion. There wasn't a sign of a house or a building of any kind. Nothing but wilderness. I expressed my puzzlement and Wanda informed me that the village was in the opposite direction and I would see it soon enough.

"Wilmot is like most villages," she continued. "A large green, a church at either end; on one side a courthouse, library, and stores; on the other, residences enclosed with picket fences. The village is much older than the depot. Though that's old enough. Would you like to see the village before we return to Linden Gardens?"

"Oh no," I exclaimed. "It's Linden Gardens I'm excited about."

"You have reason to be," she replied. "Your uncle did himself proud. He loved flowers and was determined to have every type of garden imaginable, despite the rugged climate. He was successful." She paused, then added, "You'd have seen them long ago except your Papa refused to bring you here."

I quickly came to his defense, though I'd not known that. "Papa works, you know."

"Of course, my dear. I meant no offense, though I can't

help but ask if he objected to your accepting your aunt's invitation."

When I made no answer, she said, "He did."

"He still hasn't gotten over Mama."

"It's understandable," she said quietly. "It was a dreadful tragedy."

"Did you know about it," I asked.

"My dear, I was there. Your aunt almost lost her sanity. She still blames herself for your mother's death."

"Why should she when it was an accident?" I discovered that the tinkling sound came from Wanda's hoop earrings, which had tiny bells attached to them. They were in constant motion, for she emphasized her statements with gentle nods of her head.

Her manner became confidential. "She said she should never have written to your mother, asking her to come."

"Papa said the same thing," I replied. "I don't feel that way."

Wanda flashed me an appreciative smile. "I'm sure you don't, or you wouldn't have come. Yet, I should think you would resent her death as much as your father. After all, it deprived you of a mother."

"Perhaps if I had been older, I'd have felt differently. I was not quite three when Mama died."

"Killed by a fall down the stairs," Wanda said quietly. "She wasn't the first."

"What do you mean?"

"A servant had fallen down that stairway three months prior to your mother's fall."

Her statement shocked me. For the first time I understood the reason for Papa's resentment, though I wondered why he hadn't told me.

"Are the steps waxed so heavily they're unsafe?"

"No. But they are made of the finest marble. Your uncle put the best of everything in that house."

"It seems strange that after one person suffered a fatal fall on the stairway, they weren't carpeted."

"I don't suppose anyone ever thought it would happen again. A pity, since three have met their deaths by a fall down that stairway."

"Two were killed before Mama?" I asked in dismay.

"No. The third fell six months ago."

I was certain Papa had no knowledge of that or he would definitely have forbidden me to come.

Wanda said, "I didn't mean to put a damper on your visit, but it's something you have to know. It was I who urged your aunt to have you visit her in the hope you could take her mind off the tragedy."

"Does the house have a curse on it?"

"It would seem so, though I never thought of that before. Are you superstitious?"

"No."

Wanda regarded me carefully. "You have the same direct manner of speaking your mother had. Your aunt may talk a great deal about your mother. I was hoping your presence would have a healing effect on her. Yet I wonder. You're the image of her."

I was too appalled by what I'd just heard to express my thanks. I said, "Please tell me about the third accident."

"Nora Martin came to the village about seven months ago," Wanda began. "A charming young woman quite active in helping the poor. Your aunt took a liking to her when she called to collect a check for the church and. . ."

I broke in on her conversation. "It would seem that if Miss Martin came only to collect money, there would be no need for her to go upstairs. Unless my aunt was ill."

Wanda's eyes chided me for the interruption. "As I was saying, your aunt took a liking to her and asked her to return. She did—several times because she liked your aunt as well. Also, she was as fascinated by the occult as your aunt."

"Are you saying my aunt believes in spirits?"

"Not the way she used to. She tried to contact her husband many times through mediums, but Calvin Rosby exposed them for the frauds they were."

I had no idea who Calvin Rosby was, but at the moment I was more interested in Nora Martin since she had met her death in exactly the same manner my mother had.

I said, "If not mediums, what area of the occult does she indulge in?"

"Occult is a poor word to use in regard to your aunt. I'll state it more plainly. Emma is a great believer in palmistry. Also tarot and astrology, as they relate to human destiny, interest her. Though most of all, I would say she favors the crystal ball."

I voiced my disapproval. "I didn't know my aunt could be taken in by charlatans."

"I am a gypsy, Celeste. Not a charlatan."

I wondered if there was no end to the surprises I'd be confronted with. "I thought you were my aunt's companion."

"I'm that too. But I read palms, I study the stars, and I tell the cards. I do it because I believe in it. I will read your palm, my dear. With your permission, of course."

"It would be a waste of time," I said, rather primly, I suppose. "I don't believe in it."

She gave a little sigh. "I'm not offended. We'll just forget it. Would that we could forget the death of Nora Martin. It has had a devastating effect on your aunt."

"When did it happen?"

"Six months before your graduation."

"Please tell me more about Nora Martin."

"Nora came to Linden Gardens to accept a check that your aunt wished to donate to a church bazaar. It is given annually to aid the poor of the congregation. People from miles around attend. It has rather a carnival-like atmosphere. Your aunt also pays for that, though no one but the pastor knows."

"You were saying that Miss Martin—or was she married?"

"No. Unfortunately, the day she came, I made the mistake of reading her palm. Nora was fascinated and asked if she might return."

"To have her palm read?"

"If she wished. But what she really wanted was to see the Zodiac Room. She didn't have time to see it that day. Your aunt invited her to come the following evening when I would gaze into the crystal ball to see if I could catch a glimpse of her future."

"You really believe in that?"

"Completely. And so did Nora. She had recently returned from a prolonged journey to Europe. That night I saw things in the crystal ball no one could have known unless they had been with her."

"Did you foresee her tragic end?"

She chided me gently. "My position with your aunt is that of a companion. I've never abused what I consider a gift."

"You mean your ability to look into the future?"

"Yes."

"But with Miss Martin, you saw her past?"

Wanda smiled. "She sat with me only once before the

crystal ball. She asked me to tell her about her past. In fact, she dared me."

"If she was a local girl, that shouldn't have been difficult. You could have acquired such information from the villagers."

She smiled at my skepticism. "The villagers fear me and have little to do with me. Miss Martin's family maintained a summer residence here some years back. However, her parents died two years ago and the house hadn't been occupied until she came back up here."

"That was seven months ago."

"It was the first time she had been here since she was a child. She told us her parents preferred travel. And so did she."

"Was she healthy?"

"Very. I'm sure her fall wasn't due to weakness. It was an accident."

"Were there witnesses?"

"No. It happened at night. She was staying here as a favor to me."

"Did she sleepwalk?"

"Not that I know of. You see, in all the years I have been with my aunt, I've never had a vacation. Since she and Nora got along so splendidly, I asked your aunt if I might take a brief vacation, provided Nora would stay at Linden Gardens. Both your aunt and Nora agreed." Wanda paused and gave another sigh. "That's why I wasn't here."

"Please tell me more."

"There's no more to tell. Please don't question your aunt about it unless she brings up the subject. She gets spells of melancholia. Sometimes she refuses food for days. I hope your being at Linden Gardens will raise her spirits."

"I'll do my best."

The carriage gave a sharp turn, knocking me slightly off balance. I might have fallen out if Wanda hadn't caught hold of my arm, steadied me, and drawn me back onto the seat.

"There is no more time for talk. You will hear about it soon enough. But at least you will be prepared for the change in your aunt's manner. She has spells."

I turned my attention to the grounds—or estate would be a far more appropriate term. Linden Gardens was aptly named, for the grounds were a mass of color. The sweep of lawn leading up to the gray stone dwelling was edged with rose bushes in full bloom and the air was heady with their fragrance. The three-story dwelling was impressive, made more so by the sweeping drive that sloped upward rather steeply. The windows were mullioned and recessed. Most impressive were the fountains that lined the entire front of the entrance. The sun's rays fashioned rainbows in the air from the moisture, giving the entrance a fairy-tale quality.

I couldn't help but exclaim aloud at its beauty. Wanda laughed at my elation.

"I had no idea it was like this," I said.

"I take it your father spoke little of your aunt," she said.

"Very little. Be assured, though, I wouldn't be here if he objected."

"I doubt he would deny you anything, though your aunt feared he would not allow you to come."

"Because of what happened to Mama?"

She nodded.

I thought of Nora. "He probably wouldn't have, had he known there was a third tragic death. I'm surprised he never mentioned the first. Did he know about it?"

"I would imagine your mother wrote him. That is the reason your aunt sent for her. Emma had a complete breakdown. Your mother worked wonders for her in the brief time she was here. Of course, when she suffered that fatal fall, Emma went to pieces. Your aunt feels she is cursed."

"Perhaps it's the house that is cursed."

"Don't say that to your aunt. She's very proud of it. She blames only herself for what happened here."

"Was your crystal ball able to foretell the tragedies? Or didn't you consult it?"

Wanda was stung by my words. She lowered her eyes as she spoke. "I am very fond of your aunt. I am also very loyal to her. That's why I was in favor of your coming here. I hope you can brighten her spirits. She thoroughly enjoyed attending your Commencement."

"I was both proud and happy for her to be there with Papa. And I was thrilled to be invited to Linden Gardens. Of course, I didn't know its tragic history at the time."

"Perhaps your aunt feared you would not come if you knew about Nora."

"I probably wouldn't have, but I want you to know I meant no offense when I referred to your crystal ball. It's just that I thought you referred to it constantly. It does sound intriguing."

Her eyes took on a faraway look. "In recent years, I go to it only when I am drawn to it."

"In that case, I do owe you an apology. Please forgive me."

She placed her hand over mine which rested in my lap. "There is no need. Perhaps I did wrong in telling you the bad news before you saw your aunt. But she felt you should be told so that if you wished to return, you could do so without seeing her."

"Why did she invite me here?"

"She needs you. I was supposed to tell you about the tragedy at the depot since there is a train that will come by in about an hour."

"Why didn't you tell me at the depot?" I asked sharply.

She looked confused. "Because—because you seemed so self-assured. So like your mother. She was most competent. And in the little time she was here, your aunt showed great improvement. Your mother also won over the villagers."

"Are they difficult?"

"Most of them think this house is cursed and refuse to set foot in it."

"Perhaps it is."

Wanda gave me a knowing look. "Then you do believe in spirits and omens and such."

"I never did—up until now."

"Shall I tell Zeffrey to continue around the drive and bring us back to the depot?"

"No." I answered without hesitation. "I don't know how long I'll stay. But my aunt was most generous in clothing and educating me. It would be ungrateful of me to turn my back on her."

"Especially now that she needs you."

"Did Mama know about the first accident?"

"Certainly. That was one of the reasons your aunt sent for her. It happened less than two months after Eric von Linden died."

"Strange that Papa never mentioned the first accident to me."

"It happened so many years ago, I can't be certain. But it may be that your aunt didn't tell her about it until after her arrival. I did not see the letter your aunt wrote your mama."

"Perhaps Mama didn't tell him, knowing he disapproved of her coming here. He felt I should have taken precedence over her sister."

"It may sound strange, but I thoroughly agree with him."

The happiness I'd felt when I started my journey had abated. I was glad Papa had no knowledge of a third fatal accident, resembling Mama's. I had known only of Mama's falling down the stairs. Now I learned she was the second and Nora Martin, the third. I had scoffed at Papa's concern for me. I'd even scolded him. I remembered his saying I still had some growing up to do. Some intuition told me I had better accomplish it quickly.

Zeffrey stopped the carriage and, to my surprise, assisted Wanda and me to the ground. I followed her into the castle-like building.

Wanda whisked me through the entrance hall and up the stairs to my aunt's suite so swiftly there was no time to observe either the reception hall or the stairway, which was long and wide and curved slightly in its ascent. Certainly it didn't appear dangerous. But our echoing footsteps gave me an eerie feeling, as if I were walking through a vast tomb. Marble, heavily veined, was everywhere. Its coloring was beautiful. Even some of the walls were marbled. Those that weren't, were mirrored. But it was cold. It needed people—lots of people—to bring it to life. A ball, perhaps, with music everywhere. The edifice needed both music and people to lend a spirit of merriment and joy. I sensed only sadness here.

Halfway along the corridor, we paused before a heavy door of dark wood, highly polished. The doorknob was gold. The opulence was frightening. It must have been evident in my face, for Wanda gave me a reassuring smile and knocked lightly.

My aunt bade us enter. To my surprise, she was in bed, propped up with many pillows. She smiled wanly, but extended her arms to embrace me. I went to her, greeted her warmly, and kissed her cheek.

She seemed a completely different person from the one who had attended my graduation ceremonies. I stepped away from the bed and she settled back on the pillows, emitting a sigh of exhaustion as she did so.

"Thank you, my dear, for coming." It seemed an effort for her to speak.

"I didn't know you were ill, Aunt Emma," I replied. "Are you certain you want a visitor just now?"

"I want you here." Her glance switched to Wanda.

Wanda nodded reassurance. "I told Celeste about the recent tragedy. It didn't dissuade her."

My aunt seemed dubious. "If your father had known, I'm sure he would have forbidden you to visit me."

"Perhaps," I admitted. "And had I known, I may have been reluctant to come."

"Thank you for your honesty, Celeste," my aunt replied. "And for your information, I am not ill. These spells come on me. They go as quickly."

"You do see a doctor?" I asked.

She nodded. "He tells me my condition is brought on by nerves. I sometimes think I will lose my mind because of the tragedies that have occurred in this house. First, a maid. Then your dear mother. And six months ago, poor Nora. A brilliant girl. She had a very inquiring mind. I suppose that is why she was so fascinated by meeting someone like Wanda, whose knowledge of the unknown fascinated her."

"Your niece is not fascinated by it." Wanda spoke as she moved about the room, lowering the shades, filling the room with shadows. It was understandable, for my aunt had been shading her eyes against the light with her hand.

"I'm glad you're not, Celeste," my aunt said. "Perhaps you can break the curse that has enveloped this house since the death of my beloved Eric."

"Don't you believe the deaths were accidental?" I asked.

She nodded slowly and lowered her lids.

"Then why do you say the house is cursed?" I asked.

"It is in the cards," she replied quietly. She was tiring, for her voice was barely audible.

Wanda was aware of it. "You've talked enough for now, Emma. Have you decided which suite Celeste should use?"

"The one across the hall if she wishes." Aunt Emma

spoke without opening her eyes. "Your mother used it, Celeste. Does that make it less appealing?"

"More so," I replied.

"I still mourn your mother," Aunt Emma said. "I have never forgiven myself for beseeching her to come here."

"That happened long ago, Aunt Emma. She'd not want you to feel that way. Papa said she wanted to come. He tried to dissuade her, but to no avail."

"Because of you." Her eyes opened to regard me. "How right he was. I know he hates me."

I quickly corrected her. "Papa hates no one."

"Come, my dear," Wanda said. "Your aunt is exhausted. I think the excitement of your arrival was too much for her."

"Perhaps I shouldn't have come."

"Perhaps," my aunt agreed. "But I'm pleased you did."

One of her hands raised. I stepped back to her bedside and held it lightly. Despite the warmth of the day and the gentle breeze flowing into the room, her hand was cold. I raised the covers and placed it beneath. Her eyes closed again and she spoke without opening them. "It's already after noon and you must be starved. Wanda will see that you have lunch."

I made no answer, for Wanda had alfeady gripped my arm lightly, urging me from the room. "Zeffrey will bring up your baggage," she told me. "Kate will help you unpack."

"I don't need any help," I replied. "We were taught travel etiquette at school."

"You attended the best," Wanda replied. "Your aunt insisted on that."

She closed my aunt's door noiselessly and we crossed the hall to the door opposite. She opened it wide and we entered.

"It pleased Emma that you were willing to take the rooms your mother used. She was fearful you would object."

"Why should it please her?"

"I can think of only one reason. Because you will be close to her. She worshiped your mama. In the short time I knew her, I did also. And, as I told you, she captivated the villagers."

"How could she have had time to do that when my aunt was so ill?"

"Your mama made the time."

Before I could question her, she was out the door and had closed it quietly. I didn't mind. There would be plenty of time for questions. And from what I'd learned in my brief conversation with Wanda, several were already forming in my mind. I better understood Papa's disapproval of my visit. Not that I felt there was any foul play. If that had been so, a police investigation would have taken place. Papa would have informed me of that.

I turned my attention to the suite, a combination sitting room and bedroom. The two rooms were joined by a wide archway hung with soft lavender draperies, held back with a thick gold cord that slipped over porcelain cupids attached halfway up the wall on either side.

The sitting room was tastefully furnished with delicate French furniture, upholstered in green satin to match the color of window draperies. A table in the center of the room held a crystal vase of pink roses whose fragrance filled the room and an oil lamp with a frosted globe that was circled with a garland of painted rosebuds. Both sides of the fireplace were decorated with potted plants, lending further color to the attractive room.

I stood in the archway and observed the bedroom. Here, the French motif also prevailed, giving the room a dainty feminine air. Twin night tables flanked the bed. On each sat a lamp and a silver tray on which were a glass and a silver carafe. One table also held a Bible; the other, magazines and bound books to help lure sleep.

A light knock sounded on the door. I went to it and admitted Zeffrey. He was now wearing a brown corduroy jacket over a turtleneck sweater. He placed my baggage in the bedroom and informed me that Kate would be up shortly with a tray of food.

I removed my gloves and hat and placed them on a chair beside the bureau. There was a smaller archway that led to a dressing room, mirrored on one side. Opposite was a wide shelf on which were colognes and perfumes. None were open, making it obvious they had been purchased for me. The opposite wall had sliding doors that opened to reveal a long closet. There were racks for shoes, shelves for handbags and hats. The shelves were covered with padded fabric and perfumed with lavender. The place had an air of luxury. How sad, I thought, my aunt did not have the good health to enjoy it. I opened another door, which revealed a bathroom, also well-mirrored.

I washed my hands, splashed my face with cold water, dried it, and returned to the sitting room, just as Kate entered. She had no trouble handling the large tray, but she almost dropped it at sight of me.

"You're Miss Celeste," she said when she found her voice.

"Yes. You are Kate."

"Kate Corcoran," she replied with a trace of a brogue. "I knew your mama. You startled me for a bit. I thought she'd come back."

"You've been working here a long time," I said.

"I came a month before your mama had the accident," she said. "A dreadful thing. Everyone in the village loved her."

"Are you from the village?"

"No one from the village would work here," Kate said, disgust edging her voice. "They say the place is cursed. And it could well be. Myself, I think it's the room. But your aunt . . ." She gave a quick shake of her head.

"My aunt what?" I wanted to hear the sentence completed.

"She doesn't dare make a move without going to that room. She swears by it."

"What room?"

"One fit for the devil. Stay out of it, Miss Celeste. If your mama had lived, she'd have had it done away with, I'm sure."

"Why?"

Kate set the tray on the table and lifted the silver covers off the dishes. The plate contained a colorful fruit salad. There were hot biscuits, a dish of pudding, cookies, and a pot of tea.

She eyed me with amusement. "You're as curious as your mother was. She was always questioning people. She loved to ask questions."

I laughed. "I guess I take after her in that respect. It's the best way to learn things."

"The only way," Kate agreed. "Now I must be running along. Miss Wanda asked me to tell you they dress for dinner."

"Is my aunt well enough to go downstairs?"

"Oh yes. Though not tonight," Kate replied briskly.

"She gets these spells. She's very morose. For a while, she was cheerful and even seemed happy. Part of it was due to the lovely letters you wrote her. Part of it was because of Miss Nora. She was young and cheerful. Good for your aunt."

"Don't you think Wanda Vargas is good for my aunt?"

"Oh yes," Kate said briskly. "She's a cheerful person. And so is Mr. Calvin. They've been loyal."

"I'm sure you have also."

"Thank you, Miss. Now I must get back to my kitchen. I have more to do since I'm the only one here every day. Help comes from a village about ten miles north of here. We have five come in once a week. They come early and leave in time to get home before sundown."

"Isn't that an odd arrangment?"

"Not when no one from the village will work here."

"Was Nora Martin from the village?"

Kate sobered. "You know what happened to her?"

I nodded. "It seems strange three should have met their deaths in the same way."

Kate spoke with concern. "It's the room. It has a crazy name. I wouldn't even try to say it. Don't go in it. I swear that's what killed your mama. Also the young Miss Nora. A lovely girl. She was a little older than you. Your aunt said you are nineteen."

"Yes." I eyed the luncheon and sat down. "It looks delicious."

"Enjoy it," Kate replied. "And enjoy your visit."

"I'm sure I will." I was already seated. "Even more so when my aunt recovers."

"She has these spells from time to time. Melancholia, the doctor says. Because of what happened here. She'll never move, though. Won't even take a vacation. Miss Wanda has given up trying to get her to take a voyage to Europe. Would do her good. This place has too many unhappy memories for her."

"I wonder why she continues to live here?"

"Because of your uncle. He built this for her."

"It is beautiful," I said.

"A showplace," Kate agreed. "Only nobody comes, so the rooms are all closed up. Well, my dear, I must be off."

She gave me a wide smile, said she hoped I would enjoy my lunch, and left. I liked her. Her face was round, with rosy cheeks and dancing blue eyes. She was rotund, but her gray uniform was well-tailored to fit her figure. Her lace cap covered thick black hair that was braided and wound about her head. I judged her to be about forty.

I ate slowly, my mind filled with what I'd learned since my arrival. I'd not tell papa about the latest death in this house. I knew he'd summon me home immediately. If I refused, he would come up here and bring me back. I understood better now his resentment toward my aunt. I almost wished he had told me about the first tragedy and I wondered why he hadn't.

I cautioned myself to stop thinking selfishly. Certainly my aunt was deserving of my loyalty after all she had done for me.

After eating, I brought my baggage into the bedroom to unpack. I noticed two closed doors in the bedroom I hadn't checked. I opened the nearest door and stepped into a closet. A brief inspection revealed it contained clothes from another era. I selected one dress, carried it from the closet and held it to the light. It gave off a slightly musty odor, the result of being in that closet for years.

It was a Dolly Varden, popular in the 1870s. In the polonaise style, it had a short, bunched-up overskirt attached to a bodice that was made of green chintz. The skirt was a deep orange silk with rows of ecru lace covering it. I assumed it was Mama's. How elegant she must have looked in it.

I returned it to the closet and opened the other door. It was also a closet, though much deeper than the first. One side was empty, but hanging from the bar were several pomanders that gave off the faint fragrance of lavender. The bar opposite held a complete wardrobe of dresses. Beneath them, shoes were placed in orderly fashion almost the length of the floor. I picked one up and studied the sole. It had never been worn. A further check revealed it was my size. I set it down and selected a gown. It was a soft, flowing green chiffon. I brought it over to a standing mirror and held it to my figure. It was also my size! My aunt had purchased a complete wardrobe for me. I knew better now what Wanda meant when she said they dressed for dinner.

It was so beautiful, I laid it across the bed to admire as I went to work filling the drawers with my undergarments, gloves, and other accessories. I had worn a straw toque, not expecting to remain here beyond the summer. However, I noticed hats of straw, velvet, and even one of fur on the shelf. Obviously, I was welcome to remain as long as I wished. The thought pleased me. I closed my bags, fastened the straps, and set them at the far end of the closet on a wide shelf.

I went over to the window and feasted my eyes on the gardens, which were a riot of color. The rear of the estate sloped to the Hudson River, though there seemed to be a sheer drop to the water. I decided to take a stroll, lured by the beauty of the grounds. Standing at the window, I noticed that the silence was broken only by songbirds. Even the impressive section of formal garden, which was rectangular in shape, with shrubbery well over six feet, was inviting. Topiaries were evident, their shapes ranging from those of animals to what resembled benches, complete with backrests. I doubted they would be very comfortable to sit on, though two figures, that of a male and female, seemed to be approaching one, for just that purpose. They appeared to be so real, one could easily forget they were topiaries.

◈ Two ◈

I left my room and went down the stairs, studying them carefully. They seemed quite safe and I turned my attention elsewhere. Not a sound, other than my echoing footsteps, drifted through the house. Two windows of stained glass broke the solid expanse of wall and sent a flood of color onto the stairs and the hall below. I noticed an enormous cabinet, heavily filigreed in gold leaf, with bronze statues of nude females seeming to support the sides. The doors were decorated with porcelain plaques of cherubs. Beyond it was a sofa, the frame of which was ornamented with inlaid mother-of-pearl and painted garlands. Viewing just those two pieces was sufficient evidence of my aunt's wealth. It was almost too ostentatious. I wondered if she wouldn't be happier in less elegant surroundings.

I had no idea of the arrangement of the rooms, but I could explore them later. Just now I wanted a breath of air. I suddenly felt resentful that Mama's clothes had been left in the closet to rot and absorb the musty odor. I wished they had been given away. At least then they would have served a purpose. It seemed strange that they had been ignored even though the suite had been kept up.

I opened the heavily carved front door and crossed the porch. I walked around the side of the house to the rear, inhaling deeply of the roses in full bloom that lined the fieldstone path.

Just beyond the house there were larkspur, gladioli, petunias, nasturtiums—just about every flower imaginable. To the left of the house there was a large greenhouse. That meant there would be flowers the year round. My uncle had thought of everything. He'd planned well, yet had not lived long enough to enjoy it.

I decided to inspect the grounds behind the high hedge to get a closer view of the topiaries. It was hotter than I thought and I was beginning to feel slightly uncomfortable. I found an opening and stepped into refreshing shade. A more welcome sight was a marble bench with a back, gently curved to fit my spine. I sat down and feasted my eyes on the topiaries. Directly in front of me were the two leafy figures. At this close range, I could see they seemed to be holding hands.

"Aren't they clever?" The voice, deep and masculine, startled me.

I stood up quickly. A gentleman of indeterminate age was standing in the opening I'd just entered. He was easily six feet in height, with black hair that had a loose curl. A recalcitrant lock fell on his forehead, which he brushed back, but it fell forward again. He had dark eyes and bronzed skin, attesting to his love of the sun. A thin line of mustache above an almost sensual mouth gave him a rakish look. His smile revealed white, even teeth. He was lean and muscular and dressed in white trousers and a shirt.

He said, "I'm sorry I startled you. Please sit down. I'm Calvin Rosby."

"How do you do, Mr. Rosby. I'm ..."

"Celeste Abbott." He motioned with a casual wave of his hand toward the bench. Once I was seated, he joined me.

I relaxed and smiled. "Now I remember. You're the gentleman who exposes mediums who dupe innocent women like my aunt."

"They dupe members of my own sex also, Celeste. I hope you don't mind the seeming familiarity."

"I don't, Mr. Rosby, since you seem to be quite at ease here."

"I live here. I'm your aunt's secretary."

I couldn't help but smile. He seemed much too sophisticated for that.

He betrayed no trace of self-consciousness as he said, "You find it humorous."

"Oh no," I declared. "I didn't mean to sound rude."

"You didn't," he said lightly. "I have to work for a living. I answered an advertisement in the newspaper for a typist who would not object to employment in a rural area. Your uncle was so amused when he discovered I was a man, he hired me. After his death, your aunt kindly kept me on. She insists I have served her well and she has never had any regrets."

"Didn't my uncle know you were a man from your letter?"

"He did not. I signed the letter with only my first initial. And since I write backhand, it's not always easy to know if the writing is that of a man or a woman."

"True," I admitted. "Have you been here long?"

"Eighteen years," he replied.

"You don't seem . . ." I paused, compressed my lips and felt my face suffuse with color.

"That old?" he smiled. "I'm thirty-eight. For you, that would be old."

"I didn't think you more than twenty-five. I'm sure I'm not the first to tell you that."

"No," he replied frankly. "Though if you look close, you will see a few gray hairs."

"I shan't look that closely, Mr. Rosby."

"Calvin, please," he urged gently. "Since I work for your aunt, it would be more natural."

"I disagree," I said. "You're poised, intelligent, and blessed with charm."

His laughter was pleasant to hear. "You're the one with charm, Celeste. You're always very frank. Your mother was too."

"You knew her?" I was astonished. Also, pleased.

"Certainly. As I told you, I've been here eighteen years. Her accident occurred sixteen years ago. She loved to tell us about you."

"I don't remember her, though we have a portrait of her."

He nodded. "There was an artist living just beyond here at the time. Your aunt commissioned him to paint her portrait. That was his specialty."

"Papa said it's a beautiful likeness."

"It is," Mr. Rosby said. "Though she was here briefly, she made friends wherever she went."

"Papa said she was here six months."

Mr. Rosby nodded. "I suppose you know what happened."

"Only that she had a fatal fall down the stairs."

"I heard her scream and reached her before she died."

"She lived after the fall?" I asked in amazement.

"Only a few moments. Kate was here, but on the third

floor, and heard nothing. I wakened Wanda and asked her to look after your aunt, who was standing at the head of the stairs in a state of shock. I went for the doctor."

"But if Mama was dead . . ."

"The doctor had to issue a death certificate," he said remindfully. "I covered her before I left. It would have been thoughtless to do otherwise."

I nodded. "It's puzzling how Mama could have lost her footing. The stairway looks quite safe. And at night I think mama would have used the marble banister to make her descent."

He nodded agreement. "No one understands. It's as strange as when the maid fell the month before. And Nora Martin six months ago."

"A pity Wanda couldn't have seen that in the crystal ball and prevented it."

He looked incredulous. "You mean you believe in that stuff?"

"I don't. But Wanda does. My aunt does also, if I can believe Wanda."

"You can believe her. I don't, though I'm tolerant." He gave me a knowing look. "I work here."

"Wanda said she tried to get my aunt to travel, hoping to erase her tragic memories."

"That's true also," he replied. "But your aunt worships her husband's memory. And unless the weather is too inclement or she has one of her spells, she makes frequent visits to the mausoleum to pay her respects to her husband's memory."

"Where is it?" I exclaimed, astonished at such news.

"Beyond the greenhouse."

"I saw that from my window. Beyond it, there is nothing but forest."

"True. There is also a stone path free of weeds and brush that leads to it. The area around the tomb is cleared."

"And the grounds cultivated?"

"Yes. Though not ostentatiously, like this."

I smiled as I nodded.

"We think alike, Celeste," he said.

"What do you mean?" I would brook no disloyalty to my aunt.

"Tell me honestly, wouldn't you like to live in a less pretentious abode?"

I couldn't refrain from smiling. "If you had asked me

that question last night, I would have replied negatively. However, now that I'm here, I do find it a little overwhelming."

"Very much so. The art objects in the house are worth a king's ransom."

"I haven't been through the house. But the little I saw bears out what you say."

"Your uncle was an art collector. He made a fortune in gems. Your aunt has a room full of stock certificates in gold and diamond mines."

I was aware of the sources of my uncle's wealth, having heard of it from Papa, in answer to my endless questions, so the subject held no further interest for me.

"Did you know my uncle well?"

"I knew him as a man of high moral and ethical standards. He had a brilliant mind. Your aunt was completely ignorant in regard to business affairs. However, she has a most capable attorney who comes up from New York City periodically. His name is Luke Aarons."

"I suppose he must be in close contact with you."

"Somewhat," he replied. "He sends up a sum of money each month and maintains that your aunt is somewhat profligate. I have told him on more than one occasion that since it is her money, it is her right to spend it as she wishes. She is a most philanthropic lady."

"How well I know."

He appeared embarrassed. "I didn't mean it that way. You're her niece."

"I know you didn't, Mr. Rosby."

"Thank you. She is generous with me also. However, she wants her money's worth. Both Wanda and I see to it that she gets it."

"When I saw her today, she didn't seem capable of making even a simple request, much less giving an order."

"She's having one of her spells."

"Just what are her spells?"

"What causes them, you mean?"

I nodded.

"Fear of the unknown."

"Spiritualism?" I'm sure I showed my dismay.

"No. I cured her of that by exposing them."

"Are you versed in that?"

"My father dabbled in it, as an amateur. He entertained at social events. He used to regale me with tales of his experiences. He told me about the mediums and their tricks, and how they did them."

"How lucky for my aunt you answered her husband's advertisement."

He frowned thoughtfully. "I'm not so sure."

"What do you mean?"

"Well," he spoke slowly, "she still swears by Wanda. So she isn't cured."

"How did my aunt happen to meet Wanda?"

"Your aunt attended a soiree at which Wanda read palms, told the cards, and gazed into her crystal ball. Your aunt was so impressed she begged your uncle to hire Wanda as a companion. Eric von Linden never denied his wife a thing. However, much as I frown on that sort of mumbo jumbo, I must confess Wanda has foretold many things that have come true."

"A pity she couldn't have foreseen the deaths in her crystal ball. She might have prevented them."

"I think Wanda is a little frightened of that crystal ball. She claims she doesn't go near it anymore unless she feels an urge so strong she cannot ignore it."

"She told me she read Nora Martin's past in the crystal ball."

"It was uncanny," he admitted. "But I'm wondering if she may have overheard Nora relating her past to your aunt."

I regarded him with new interest. "Are you saying Wanda is a faker, too?"

He stood up and looked down at me. "I am saying no such thing. She's a loyal friend of your aunt. I respect both ladies. Sometimes I think Wanda reads the crystal ball as she believes your aunt would want her to. And there are times when she will see things in it that give me a start."

"Can you mention something specific?"

He seemed amused. "She predicted your visit here."

I said, "I wouldn't call that startling."

"Your aunt was certain your father would refuse you permission. Wanda was of the opinion you might not wish to come here because of what happened to your mother."

"So she consulted the crystal ball."

"At your aunt's request."

"Were you a part of it?" I asked.

"No. I'm much too realistic—and practical. I told them both you would come."

I eyed him curiously. "How could you be so certain?"

"I told you I was practical. If I were in your shoes, I wouldn't miss an opportunity to come here."

"I know what you mean," I said coldly.

"I've offended you," he said, not at all concerned about it.

I stood up. "Yes, Mr. Rosby, you have offended me. I'm not seeking any part of my aunt's fortune."

"There's no need for you to seek it since you're her only heir."

I turned abruptly and headed for the opening in the high shrubbery. Before I reached it, he grasped my arm and spun me around to face him.

I struggled to free myself. "Let me go."

"Not until you've listened to me."

"I don't wish to hear another word. You're impudent."

"I'm outspoken, yes. I didn't mean to be nasty. I apologize."

I ceased my struggles, for I was no match for him. He towered over me and his grasp was so tight, pain shot up and down my arm.

"You're hurting me, Mr. Rosby."

He released me then, but moved swiftly to block my path should I try to slip around him. I didn't. I had no wish to feel his fingers again pressing into my flesh.

"Please hear me out, Miss Abbott. I did not mean you were a fortune hunter. Only that you must have been a little curious about viewing Linden Gardens. You'd be less than human not to want to."

"I thought I detected a note of disdain in your voice."

"You're wrong," he said. "I think you're very levelheaded."

"If Papa were here, he would be the first to disagree."

A smile touched his handsome features, giving him a boyish look. "Why?"

"He says I still have some growing up to do. I laughed at him yesterday when he said that. Now I'm not so sure."

"Has something I said changed your mind?"

I nodded. "You think I came here to inveigle myself into my aunt's good graces."

"I think no such thing. You wouldn't even need to. The fact remains that one day you will be an heiress."

"I don't care to discuss it. I feel ashamed of myself for coming here."

"Celeste, you puzzle me."

"I shouldn't. I think I'm exactly what you said I am."

"Whatever I said, I did not mean it in a derogatory sense."

I was touched by the humility in his voice. Impulsively I rested my hand on his arm.

"I'm glad you said it, Calvin. I deserved it. I've grown up a snob. I know it now. Perhaps in the back of my mind I always knew it. What hurts is that Papa knew it. I only hope he didn't know I always yearned to come here."

"Had your aunt known, you'd have been invited."

"I'm glad she didn't know. At least, I was with Papa during vacations."

"Your aunt's been lonely too," Calvin said.

"She had Wanda—and you," I replied.

"It's different. Despite the fact that the three of us have grown close with the passage of time, Wanda and I are still employees. A blood relative is something different. I know because neither Wanda nor I has anyone. I hope you will remain here awhile. At the risk of making you angry again, I'll say it. You do owe your aunt something after all she has done for you."

I withdrew my hand. "You're right. I'll stay for a few weeks. After that, if my aunt wishes to see me, she'll have to come to New York City. I know Papa will welcome her warmly."

"I doubt you will convince your aunt so easily."

"Papa will. Once he knows my head hasn't been turned by all this"—I raised my arms and spread them outward—"he'll be glad to see Aunt Emma. I now understand his fearing that my private schooling had turned me into a snob."

"If so, it's no longer true."

He joined me in laughter when I said, "I'm not so sure the change could be that abrupt, but at least my eyes are open."

"Speaking of eyes, mine are about to shut. The sun makes me sleepy. I'm going to have a nap before dinner. May I walk you back?"

"No, thank you. It's so beautiful out here, I want to stay a little longer."

"Watch out for the sun. I don't think your fair skin will take kindly to it."

I walked slowly along the flagstone path, observing the beds of flowers framed by low hedges. Halfway along the walk there was a circular pool. In the center was a fountain from which streams of water rose and lowered alternately. It was very effective and was made more so by the water lilies that floated majestically on the surface. I could see why my aunt was reluctant to leave this place. Certainly her husband had put a great amount of money and planning into it to make it the showplace he desired. I wondered how a place of such beauty could harbor such tragedy.

My thoughts returned to Papa and I wondered why he hadn't told me about the first accident that had occurred at Linden Gardens. I was glad he hadn't, for even thinking about it made me feel depressed. I decided to explore more of the grounds, for I knew the acreage must be vast.

I had a sudden desire to view the mausoleum. Since I was more than halfway down the rectangular enclosure, I continued on and exited at the far end. I was quite a distance from the house, and the roar of the swiftly flowing Hudson River was quite audible.

I crossed the vast expanse of lawn to the edge of the forest. There was no sign of an opening at the far end of the property and so I started to climb the slope. About halfway up, I found the entrance, which was made more visible by the sunlight filtering down between the overhead branches that formed an arch over the pathway. It was made of slate and was very easy to follow, for it seemed to move in a straight line. It was pleasantly cool and I moved with a brisk step. Suddenly, the path took a sharp right turn. I made the turn and stopped dead in my tracks. Directly ahead, bathed in sunlight, was a large mausoleum of pink marble, flanked by two angels, each holding a trumpet to its mouth as if sounding the call to Judgment Day. It was breathtakingly beautiful. I could understand my aunt's making a daily visit. One could scarcely feel melancholy here.

I resumed my walk, but moved slowly. It was just as Calvin had described it. The area was cleared, but was protected by pines, which formed a shield around the

three sides. A low hedge bordered the flagstone walk leading to the three steps one used to enter the tomb. I wondered if the iron door was unlocked. Still curious, I
ascended the stairs and pushed gently on it. It moved back
on well-oiled hinges. Not surprising, since my aunt visited
it whenever her health permitted.

There was a narrow walkway leading to the entrance of
the tomb itself. The fragrance of freshly cut roses was evident—even before I stepped into the crypt proper and saw
the large bouquet. Someone else was visible also and eyeing me with amusement.

He was seated on a marble bench. Certainly there was
more than enough room for a bench. A marble table sat in
the center of the space. On it was a large urn holding a
bouquet of pink roses.

"Pretty, ain't it?" Zeffrey said. He was hatless, and
though it was cool in here, his gray hair appeared moist.
So did his face. I sensed he had been observing me from
the house. When he saw where I was headed, he'd taken a
shortcut to get here first. Even so, he'd had to make haste
to do so.

"It's impressive," I replied.

He stood up and rested the palm of his hand on a
marble slab on which was chiseled the name of Eric von
Linden. Below it were the dates of his birth, 1810, and his
death, 1874.

"This is where the master lies," Zeffrey informed me.
"There are those who say he did well in this country. He
did well in the old country, too. He didn't come here
poor." He eyed me speculatively, then said, "You didn't
know that, did you?"

"No."

"And you didn't know until now that he was much
older than your aunt."

"I know nothing about Eric von Linden."

"Not many do. He didn't live long after he built this
place. He was going to adopt my niece. He and your aunt
took a fancy to her, even though she was a maid here."

"Why didn't they?"

He scratched his head and pulled on a lock of hair as
he pondered my question.

"The master died before he could do it."

"Why didn't my aunt adopt her?"

"You'll have to ask her."

I was surprised at how little I knew about my aunt and her deceased husband. I was also surprised at the loquaciousness of Zeffrey and more than a little puzzled by it. I was also intrigued by his desire to talk with me. It seemed as if there were something he wanted to tell me. Something he felt I should know. Or did he resent me? Perhaps I could find out by encouraging him to talk.

I said, "I should think my aunt would have wanted to adopt a young girl after her husband's death. She must have been lonely."

He nodded. "That she was. But she didn't."

"What happened to your niece?"

"This is what happened to her." He walked to my side and placed his hand on the marble behind me. I had to move to look at it. There was a name and two dates engraved on it.

Libby Innis
1857–1874

"She's buried here?" I exclaimed in surprise.

His tone became belligerent. "Why shouldn't she be? She served them both well, from her fourteenth birthday. She was a rare beauty. Fair-skinned, blue-eyed, long, blond, curly hair. She could have been real class. She was the first."

"The first?"

"The first to get killed falling down those stairs."

I understood now why my aunt put up with Zeffrey's idiosyncrasies. She must have thought a great deal of the girl to have had her buried here.

"What about her parents?"

"She was an orphan. My sister's child. My wife and I raised her. My wife was housekeeper here until the accident."

"I'm sorry." I didn't know what else to say.

"You'll be sorrier that you came here." He seemed almost to derive a malicious glee from his statement.

I eyed him coldly. "What do you mean?"

"You'll be the fourth to have an accident."

"I don't believe my aunt would approve of you talking to me in such fashion."

"Why don't you tell her what I said and find out if she approves?"

"You're quite sure of yourself, aren't you?"

He nodded slowly, a smile of triumph on his features.

"I will discuss this with her. I will also discuss the accidents." I contained my annoyance and asked a question that suddenly came to mind. "Or don't you think they were accidents?"

"Don't much matter what I think. Everybody else thinks they were."

A strange sadness crept into his voice. "And Libby ain't here to tell us what happened."

"Was your niece happy?"

He nodded. "She was. She was a good girl, too."

"I'm sure she was. And I'm sorry about what happened. As for the stairs, they look quite safe, but I will take care when I use them."

"You do that, Miss Celeste," he said quietly. "You do that."

I turned and left the crypt, almost sorry I had come here. Then I thought of Mama and her fall down the stairs. And of Nora Martin, the third victim.

I returned to the house, my mind a jumble of questions, none of which I could answer. I thought of Papa and wondered if he knew more than he had told me. If so, I could understand his reluctance to have me come here.

Dinner was served in the formal dining room. The china was gold-rimmed, as was the crystal. The silver glistened and so did the facets of the enormous chandelier that hung above the table. Only candlelight illuminated the room, but some of the wall panels were mirrored and caught our reflections so that it seemed there were more than just Wanda, Calvin, and I at the table. I wore the gown I had taken from the closet and spread across the bed. Certainly, I was dressed for the occasion and indeed that's what it seemed like, for everything cried out of wealth.

I didn't mention my meeting with Zeffrey at the mausoleum. If I discussed it with anyone, it would be with my aunt. Wanda had informed me that she would not join us tonight, but felt she would be herself tomorrow. I hoped so. The journey on which I had started out with such a light heart had not proven to be what I'd dreamed about. I'd thought of a house that, though quiet, would have a vestige of happiness in it. The elegance I'd dreamed about

was here. But it no longer excited me. I felt burdened with
the tragic news I'd learned on my arrival. My confronta-
tion with Zeffrey in the mausoleum hadn't helped. Yet one
couldn't feel dismal amidst such elegance. Calvin looked
handsome in evening dress. So did Wanda, in an emerald
green satin, draped beautifully about her voluptuous figure.

After dinner we adjourned to my aunt's library. I'd been
informed at dinner that there were two libraries. This
particular room was quite small, but it had great appeal,
with its walls lined with shelves filled with books of every
size and subject matter. The chairs were leather and
gleamed with the care they received. We sat before the
fireplace, which glowed with a low fire and sent out a welcome warmth, for the thick walls of the house kept it cool
and gave off a chill at night.

Calvin poured us each a glass of sherry. I wondered
what we would discuss. I hoped nothing dismal. I'd had
enough of that today. I thought about the village and wondered if they went there often. I voiced the questions and
was told they did not, though I would be free to go whenever I wished. Either Calvin or Zeffrey would take me, or
if I could manage a surrey or buggy, I could go alone.

"I'm not certain I could handle two horses," I said. "A
buggy would be more to my liking."

"Then it will be a buggy," Calvin said.

My spirits lifted at the thought. "It will be fun driving
around, exploring the countryside. I wonder how I will
take to a life of such idleness. If Papa were here, I'm sure
he would say—quite well."

Wanda's laughter was throaty. "Is that how he regards
you?"

"No. I kept up our little flat and I am a good cook. I
suppose because I enjoy it."

"That is usually true of things we enjoy." Calvin
downed his sherry and stood up to pour himself a glass of
brandy. He resumed his seat and cupped his hands around
the sniffer to warm it.

"My dear," Wanda said, "your time will be your own
the entire summer or longer, if you wish to stay. However,
there is one little chore you will be asked to perform. It is
your aunt's wish that you do this for her."

"She need only name it," I said, pleased that I could finally do something to show my appreciation for all she had done for me.

Calvin took a sip of his brandy, let it roll around his mouth, appeared pleased with the taste, and swallowed it. Wanda watched him, seemingly intrigued.

I must confess, I was also, though I forced her attention back to me with a question. "What is it my aunt wishes me to do?"

She flashed me a smile of apology. "I think Calvin should be the one to tell you. He is her secretary."

I couldn't see how it mattered, but I sat patiently while Calvin repeated the ritual with the brandy.

Finally he turned his attention to me, though he still held on to his glass. "First of all, Celeste, I must warn you that this is no ordinary request. What you must bear in mind is that your aunt is a very generous person."

"I'm well aware of that," I replied curtly. "If you don't know I'm appreciative, Wanda does."

"I've irritated you," he said and laughed.

"What do you find so amusing?" I asked testily.

"Your display of temper," he said.

"Calvin, stop teasing Celeste," Wanda urged.

He was sprawled comfortably in his chair, but he straightened and set his glass on the table. "I'm sorry, Celeste. But you look most attractive when anger flushes your face."

I ignored his compliment. "Please get down to business."

"Very well. Your aunt wishes you to make a trip to New York City every other week."

It was my turn to smile. "There's nothing difficult about that."

"Oh, there's more to it than just the train ride," he said.

"Then tell me."

"You are to bring a sealed envelope to a hotel on lower Fifth Avenue."

I laughed aloud. "You make it sound as if it were intrigue."

"It is, really," he replied, not sharing my laughter.

"So long as it isn't dishonest, I shan't mind."

"You may think it is when I tell you what you are to do with the envelope."

"I can't make that decision until I hear you out."

Calvin said, "There is a large, upholstered chair in the

far corner of the lobby. It is almost entirely concealed by potted palms. You are to sit in that chair for about fifteen minutes or until you are certain you are not being observed. At that point you will slip the envelope down the side of the chair, making certain it cannot be seen or be discovered by a guest or visitor like yourself."

I was no longer smiling. Wanda looked worried.

She said, "I knew Celeste would object. I don't blame her. It's nothing for a young girl to do."

"I haven't refused yet," I said.

"But you don't like the idea of it," Wanda said. "You look quite tense."

"I'm puzzled. It does sound like intrigue."

"It isn't, though." Calvin spoke as he reached for his glass. "The explanation is simple. It's a philanthropic gesture your aunt makes every two weeks."

"For someone she knows?" I asked.

He nodded. "Someone who is very proud and in dire need. A gentleman who was once a very important figure in New York City. He came on hard times and your aunt has seen that he does not lack for the necessities of life."

"That's good of her. But why the secrecy?"

"As I said, He's very proud."

"How long has this been going on?"

"For almost as long as I've been working for her," Calvin replied.

"Who delivered the money before I came?"

"Wanda and I alternated," Calvin said.

"Why does my aunt wish me to do what you have been doing for years?"

"Please remember, Celeste, I am an employee of your aunt," Calvin said. "I don't question her instructions."

"May I ask her?"

"Certainly," Calvin said. "Both Wanda and I would like to know the reason."

"Doesn't either of you know her well enough to ask?" This whole thing seemed ridiculous. Even childish.

"Oh yes," Wanda said. "However, Calvin is an employee; so am I. There are times when your aunt has us do things that seem strange, perhaps even foolish. But we've never questioned her."

"Why not?" I couldn't refrain from asking the question. The fact that they were employees didn't seem sufficient.

Calvin's lips compressed tightly and he gazed into the

fire. Was he embarrassed, or had I made him angry? I almost felt a mild triumph.

The answer came from Wanda. "My dear, it just so happens neither Calvin nor I has any living relatives. Nor could we ever find a situation so perfect as this. Though empoyees, we are treated as members of the family. Your aunt has been very kind to us. We hold her in esteem. She knows that and has never questioned our loyalty. There was never any need to. So it isn't that she is displeased with us that she wishes you to perform a little chore formerly assigned to us. I think it is just her way."

"Perhaps," I agreed. "Nonetheless, I shall question her. It seems absurd. It would be much simpler to mail the envelope."

"Much," Wanda agreed. "But it would have to be a check. You will find the envelope quite thick. Calvin told you the gentleman who receives the gratuity is very proud. This is the way he wishes it done."

"You mean my aunt let him state how he wished to receive the money, when it happens to be hers?"

"Apparently," Wanda said. "We've never met him. Nor do we have any idea of his identity."

"Has he never been a guest here?"

"Not since we've been here," Wanda said.

"And you've been bringing an envelope to a hotel, stuffing it down the side of the chair for a gentleman to retrieve all these years?"

Calvin finally broke into the conversation. "You can understand why this individual wouldn't want a check. Sooner or later, gossip would uncover the fact that he was the recipient of your aunt's charity."

I nodded agreement. "When do I start my journey of intrigue?"

"This is Friday," Calvin mused. "Though your aunt hasn't said so, I believe she will want you to go to the city on Monday."

I brightened at the thought of seeing Papa again.

Wanda eyed me curiously. "What is it, Celeste? You seem pleased by something."

"I am. I'll be able to see Papa."

"I think not. You'll leave on an early morning train. The only train back in daylight leaves shortly after midday."

"How early is the morning train?"

"Six o'clock from here. And it makes many stops."

"Then I can stay over and return the following day."

Calvin and Wanda exchanged smiles. "Your aunt would either be pacing the floor until you returned, or she would have another spell like the one she is having now."

"Why?" I exclaimed, more puzzled than ever.

"That's the way your aunt is." Calvin spoke in a measured tone, as if I were straining his patience.

"I'm sorry, Calvin." I spoke his name for the first time. "I shan't ask you questions you can't answer. But I will question my aunt."

He stood up and smiled down at me. "Thanks, Celeste. If you learn anything, let me know."

Wanda laughed softly. "I'm too old to be that curious. Perhaps it's because I'm so grateful to your aunt for treating me as beautifully as she has you, Celeste. And you, Calvin."

"Oh, yes," he agreed. "Though I'm as curious as Celeste as to why she has to deliver that envelope of money. It doesn't seem right for one so young to be carrying such a large sum of cash."

Wanda sobered. "I didn't think of the danger involved."

I said, "I thought the only danger to me was the stairway."

"God forbid we should have any more of that," Wanda said.

"If Zeffrey is right, I will be its next victim."

Wanda looked indignant. "Has he been rude to you?"

I decided to make light of it. "I took a walk this afternoon. I even sought out the mausoleum. He was there. He showed me where the young girl—the first victim of the stairway—was buried. She was his niece."

"Yes," Wanda said. "Your aunt and uncle were going to adopt Libby. She had a fragile beauty."

"I got the impression Zeffrey was hurt because Aunt Emma didn't adopt her."

"I believe she would have—given time. The death of her husband devastated her." Wanda reached forward and lifted one of my hands, which had been resting palm upward in my lap. She studied it. "You have a long palm and long, tapering fingers. In palmistry, it is known as a sensitive hand. Did you ever have your palm read?"

"Once. In school. By a gypsy who was passing through. So nobody took it seriously."

Wanda's voice took on a mocking note of doom. "What dire prediction did she make?"

I traced the lifeline from the base of my thumb to my forefinger. "She said my life would be cut short by an accident."

Wanda said, "Because of the break in the line, I suppose."

I nodded. "Would you give that kind of reading?"

"Never. The break could have been due to an illness you suffered as a child."

"Don't you believe in reading palms?"

"I have made a study of hands. I collect drawings and pictures of them. I find them fascinating. However, I am a sensitive and I place great belief in my crystal ball. I looked in it before I came downstairs and I saw your face. It was most unusual to have a face or object or anything appear so suddenly."

"Did you attach some significance to it?" I asked.

"I did. However, since you don't believe in it, I'd rather not tell you."

"Please do," I exclaimed. "I think there might be something to the crystal ball. Also, to teleportation."

Wanda looked surprised. "I thought you were a disbeliever."

"I think I am. But you seem sincere. And you didn't try to play a mumbo jumbo game with the palm of my hand."

She smiled. "Most gypsies would. And I am a gypsy. But an honest one."

"Please tell me what you saw."

"You're certain you want to know?"

"Absolutely."

Calvin started to protest, but Wanda raised a staying hand.

"You were frightened," she said. "You seemed to be in danger. There was another figure above you. It was vague. So indistinct I couldn't determine the sex. But it seemed to be menacing you."

My eagerness to know, quickly abated.

Calvin spoke impatiently. "Why frighten the girl?"

"I didn't want to tell her," Wanda replied quietly.

"It's bunk anyway," he replied, making no attempt to hide his irritation with Wanda. "I wish you'd give up that crystal ball. You frighten Emma with it too."

"I don't mean to," Wanda said. "I can't help what I see."

"I'd like to smash it," he replied. "Or throw it in the river."

"She'd insist I get another," Wanda said.

"Yes," he admitted, somewhat reluctantly. "I just don't like Celeste being frightened by it."

"I won't think about it," I said.

"Good." He flashed one of his magnetic smiles. I could think of no other word for it. He was the handsomest man I had ever seen. "I think we'd better retire. Emma will be up and about tomorrow—now that she knows Celeste will stay."

"She hasn't told us she will," Wanda said.

"What do you mean?" I asked.

"Will you deliver the envelope?" she asked.

"Yes," I replied without hesitation. "Though I will certainly have a talk with my aunt about it. I think it's foolish. I also think that since she is so generous with this mysterious gentleman, he should let her decide how to deliver the money."

"You're right," Calvin said. "I think it's been going on much too long. I doubt she even knows if his fortunes are as debilitated as he professed."

"Is my aunt obligated to him in any way?"

"I'm sure she isn't."

"Don't you know anything about him?"

"No. And after all these years, I don't want to," Calvin said.

And on that statement, we retired. It had been a strange day. I could better understand now why Papa had not wanted me to come here. Yet he couldn't possibly know about the mysterious gentleman who received sealed envelopes of money from my aunt. Despite the strangeness of the day, I slept soundly the entire night.

◆ Three ◆

I wakened early, eager for my new day. I selected a pale green cotton dress with a cream lace fishu. It was one I'd brought with me. I met Kate in the hall. She complimented me on my appearance and told me she had been sent up to see if I was awake. My aunt was already in the breakfast room and was awaiting me. Kate told me to go downstairs and walk to the rear of the house. To one side was an arch that led directly into the room.

It was a most attractive circular room, with several French doors that were now opened, though they were screened for protection against insects. Green-and-white striped awnings sheltered the room against the rays of the sun and gave a softness to the light that filtered through.

My aunt was standing by one of the doors, but turned when I greeted her. I closed the distance between us when her arms extended. She kissed my cheek and held me at arm's length to study me.

"My dear Celeste, I am blessed to have you with me." Though she smiled, her eyes brimmed with tears.

"I'm the one who is blessed, Aunt Emma," I said. "I'm happy I will finally get to know you."

"We can talk while we breakfast." She motioned me to a round wicker table, which was covered with a snowy white cloth. A small bouquet of daisies made an attractive center ornament. My aunt removed the silver covers from the dishes, revealing melon, crisp bacon, fried eggs, and warm rolls. There was also a choice of butter or marmalade and a pot of coffee. The melon was sweet and succulent, and I devoted my full attention to it for the first few mouthfuls.

I wasn't aware of it until I glanced over at my aunt, who was regarding me with open amusement.

"I'm sorry, Aunt Emma. I didn't realize I was so hungry."

"Country air does it," she replied, still smiling. "I'm sorry I was indisposed yesterday when you arrived. I hope Wanda and Calvin kept you company."

"They did. So much so I haven't even investigated the house, though what I've seen is quite overwhelming."

"I hope not to the point where you feel uncomfortable."

"Should that happen, I'll come in here. It's very homey."

"Eric and I spent a great deal of our time in this room when the weather permitted. The view of the gardens and river is beautiful."

"Yes," I agreed, observing both, then glancing around the room. The furniture was wicker, painted white, with green floral chintz cushions and plants in wicker stands placed at measured intervals. There was even a chaise longue, which added to the comfort of the room.

Kate seemed to know when we had finished our first course. In contrast to the bare floors in the rest of the house, this room was carpeted, so we couldn't hear her coming.

My aunt told her she need not return for the other dishes. That we wished to talk. Kate nodded, her features good-natured, and departed.

I said, "Kate is priceless."

"Yes, indeed," my aunt agreed. "I'm extremely grateful, especially since no one in the village will work here."

"At least, they aren't superstitious in the next village. Kate told me help comes once a week."

"I pay well. Perhaps that's why."

I noticed my aunt's appetite was as good as mine. She was wearing a morning gown and a lace cap on her hair, which was generously sprinkled with gray. Her fingers were ringed with diamonds, rubies, and pearls.

"I'm so happy I will at last get to know you," my aunt said. "Your resemblance to Ruth is uncanny. It's almost as if she is alive."

Since she had brought up the subject of Mama, I thought it a good opportunity to bring up the past. "I visited the mausoleum yesterday. Zeffrey was there. He told me about his niece, Libby Innis. It was good of you to allow her to be buried there."

"Since she was killed in this house, and her aunt and uncle worked here, I felt it only right."

"I know what you mean. Zeffrey said you and your husband intended to adopt her."

"That wasn't my reason for doing it," she replied hurriedly. "Was Zeffrey rude?"

"Oh no." Hoping to learn what her reason was for burying Libby in the mausoleum, I said, "I got the feeling he thought a great deal of Libby."

"Both he and his wife did. She was the daughter of Zeffrey's sister. He and his wife raised the child when her parents were killed in an accident. She came to work here as soon as she was the proper age."

"Please don't think me rude, Auntie, but I am curious to know why you didn't adopt her after your husband died? His death must have been a great loss to you."

"It was. One I have never completely recovered from. I fully intended to adopt Libby, but she died before the period of mourning for my husband ended. I'm referring, of course, to the tragic accident."

At least that question was answered for me. I asked another. "Do you think the house is cursed because of what happened here?"

"I hope not, though I am very superstitious. Wanda will tell you that. She is my mainstay. Since you came, I have more reason than ever to trust her."

"What do you mean?" I helped myself to a second hot biscuit, and switched from butter to marmalade.

"Her crystal ball revealed you would come. She didn't think your father would allow you, nor did I, but the crystal ball said you would come."

"Papa didn't want me to come."

"Wanda told me. What caused him to finally give his permission?"

"He never forbade me. It was just because of what happened to Mama."

Aunt Emma nodded. "He fears the same will happen to you."

"Zeffrey assured me that I would be the fourth."

My aunt's face flamed. "I should discharge that man."

I wondered why she hadn't. "Is he always as outspoken?"

"Always. My husband told me that if he preceded me in

death, never to discharge Zeffrey. I have kept my word and will do my best to continue to do so."

So that was why she put up with Zeffrey's impudence. And so must I, along with Wanda and Calvin.

"It would be cruel of me to do so anyway," she went on, "since his wife is an invalid."

"Wanda told me she used to work here."

"That is true. Until Libby's death. She has never set foot in the house since. She scarcely could, since she is confined to a wheelchair."

"Was she in an accident?"

"No. I brought doctors up from New York City to examine her. They can find nothing wrong. But she has never walked since her niece fell down the stairs. It affected her mentally. A psychiatrist . . ." She leaned forward slightly. "Are you familiar with that term as regards the medical profession?"

I nodded. "It's comparatively new. Or it is to me. I read that it's that part of the medical profession that deals with mental disorders."

She looked pleased that I knew. "That's correct. I can see you applied yourself well."

"I'd be less than grateful to have done otherwise. You educated me at the best schools."

"It was my duty," she replied.

Her reply startled me. "Is that why you did it?"

"I deprived you of a mother. I loved my sister dearly. She came to me when I was in desperate need of help. I couldn't get over the shock of Libby's death. Especially so soon after Eric's."

"You've eaten very little, Aunt Emma." I had emptied my plate, so I couldn't say I had suddenly lost my appetite. However, I was deeply hurt by her words regarding me. "Perhaps that is why Papa resented you," I said. "He knew you cared nothing about me. I was vain enough to think you cared a great deal. Otherwise, you would never have spent the vast sums of money on me that you did."

She smiled. "They weren't vast."

"So far as Papa and I are concerned, they were."

Her eyes held a look of apology. "I expressed myself poorly, Celeste. As for loving you, how could I since I scarcely knew you? I saw you only when I came to New York City with Wanda for your mother's funeral. Your father would barely speak to me. You were not quite three. I meant nothing to you at that time."

"You came to mean a great deal to me through the years. You were like a fairy godmother. You saw to it that I had everything. What I didn't realize is that you spoiled me."

"Please don't be angry with me, my dear. I brought you here so that I could get to know you. I want you to be a part of this house. One day it will all be yours."

"I don't want it, Aunt Emma. I know now I was happier with Papa. I only thought I wanted to come here—to be a part of the kind of life that only wealth makes possible."

"That is what I want you to have. I want to love you, Celeste. But first I must get to know you. Please don't deprive me of that privilege. I'm lonely and I'm not young anymore."

"Papa's lonely too. I never thought of that before. You have Wanda and Calvin."

Her head moved slowly from side to side. "They're not family."

"They're very loyal to you."

"I know that. And I pay them well for it. I pay Zeffrey well too, for despite his cantankerous nature, he oversees the gardeners and is always available whenever I wish him to drive me about."

"Do you go out much, Auntie?"

"Usually just for drives. Very infrequently."

"What about New York City?"

"No. There is nothing there that interests me."

"That isn't quite true," I said, turning the conversation in the direction I wanted.

"What do you mean?" Her surprise seemed genuine.

"Wanda and Calvin told me why you invited me up here."

"I invited you here because I wanted you." To my surprise, sternness crept into her voice.

"It wasn't merely to deliver an envelope to a hotel on lower Fifth Avenue?"

"Of course not." She displayed neither surprise nor embarrassment.

"What I don't understand is why you want me to do something Wanda and Calvin have been doing for years."

"Your puzzlement in understandable. Since you question me regarding that, I suppose you are also questioning why I would be a party to what seems almost like a conspiracy?"

"Intrigue is the word I thought of."

"Intrigue then. Though there is no intrigue attached to it. I am merely helping a gentleman retain his self-respect by maintaining his position in society."

"I should think a gentleman would not take money from a lady. A matter of pride, so to speak."

"That is your way of looking at it. Yours is the modern way. Mine is the old-fashioned way."

"If you'd been born to wealth, perhaps I could understand your thinking. But you were as poor as Mama. She was employed as a saleslady in the department store Papa works in. That's how they met. You were a typist in the firm owned by your husband."

"You are just like your mother. Everything had to be spelled out for her. She used to have more tiffs with Zeffrey. And yet she would visit his wife Hester and bring her baskets of food. Zeffrey could have brought it home, but she insisted on doing it. She just liked meeting people."

"So do I. I would like to meet the mysterious gentleman who has been the recipient of your generosity."

She sobered. "You must promise me you will never linger at that hotel with the purpose of doing such a thing."

"I promise. Though I would still like to know why you wish me to deliver the envelope of money."

"Because he has asked me to do so."

"He wrote you?"

"Yes. I think it is because he feels Wanda and Calvin have been coming too steadily and may attract attention."

"It's possible," I agreed. "I still wonder why you don't insist on sending him a check. Why should you be so concerned about his feelings?"

"Because he is a gentleman. Now please, Celeste. No more questions. Either you will do it or you will not. But it must be done my way. I am sure Wanda and Calvin told you that."

"They did."

"Would you like more coffee?" I knew she didn't wish to pursue the subject.

"No, thank you. Two cups are sufficient. It was a delicious breakfast."

"Kate will see that you don't go hungry." Aunt Emma

set her napkin on the table and arose. "I would like to show you the ballroom. Then I will go upstairs and dress. You may amuse yourself in any way you wish this morning. I'll take you for a drive this afternoon."

"I'd like that very much, Aunt Emma," I said. "However, there is one more question I would like to ask."

My aunt eyed me with disapproval, but gave a nod of permission.

"Suppose I refused to deliver that envelope."

"I would ask you to pack and leave." My aunt's reply came without a moment's hesitation.

I was too stunned to reply, for I certainly hadn't expected such an answer.

"Don't feel hurt, Celeste." My aunt moved around the table and placed an arm about my shoulders. "I hope I won't have to. After all, there is nothing dishonest about what you must do. Your mother did it for me and never questioned it. She was the first. After her tragic death, Wanda and Calvin became my emissaries."

"Did Papa know?" I asked.

"I have no idea. I know your mother wrote to him. I consider correspondence between two individuals very private."

"So do I," I said. "Did Mama know the reason she was delivering the envelope?"

"Indeed, yes. She knew the gentleman was a close friend of Eric and helped immeasurably when he first came to this country. Not financially. Eric always had money. This gentleman helped him invest it wisely."

"Very well," I said. "If mama saw nothing wrong in performing the errand, I could scarcely refuse you. When do you wish me to go?"

"Monday morning."

My aunt kissed my brow. I wished she hadn't. Her lips were cold and it was all I could do to repress a shudder. I didn't wonder why I had consented to perform this strange errand. I was curious. Perhaps as curious as Mama. I wondered if Libby Innis had ever had to take an envelope to the Fifth Avenue hotel. Or Nora Martin. I shut out such thoughts and turned my attention to my aunt.

We left the room and moved toward the front of the house. Midway she paused between two doors that were closed. When she opened them, the light filtering through the stained-glass windows slipped into the room and touched one wall that was completely mirrored. Shafts of color bounced around the room, for the opposite wall was also mirrored. To one side as we entered was a dais on which were chairs and stands for the convenience of the musicians and their music. It was carpeted, as were the steps leading up to it. At the far end of the room, French doors were visible. They would open on to a terrace. It being on the same side of the house as the breakfast room, one would have a superb view of the gardens and the river.

"How beautiful," I exclaimed, knowing my aunt wished my approval. "Was it ever used?"

"Only twice," she replied with a tinge of sadness.

"Do you believe your husband would have approved of your living the life of a recluse?"

"Who said I was?" she asked indignantly.

"No one. But you never came to see me. You told me you never go to New York City. You don't travel."

"How do you know that?"

"Wanda told me. She said she has encouraged you to travel, feeling the house has a depressing effect on you."

"What happened here depresses and saddens me. But I once knew love here. No one can take those memories away from me. Without them, I doubt I could have retained my sanity. Perhaps you might understand a little better why I sent a gratuity to the gentleman who was such a good friend of my husband. In a way, I feel by doing something good, it helps to soften the horrible memories of the three tragedies that happened here."

I wasn't sure I did, but I answered affirmatively. It seemed to satisfy my aunt. She excused herself, suggesting I take a walk by the river.

"It's quite a drop to the water," she cautioned. "Also, there is a cliff above the pathway. If you're not surefooted, don't take it."

"I am," I assured her. "We took long hikes at school."

"Then you know the perils," she said. "Let's get out of this room. Though it's clean, it has a stuffy smell. It's cold too."

"You should have a ball, Auntie," I said.

"No one in the village would come," she said. "They believe this house is cursed."

"Don't you have friends from the city who would? It could be a gala affair. I'm sure you would enjoy it too."

Her laughter surprised me. "I'll think about it, Celeste. Until this afternoon, enjoy yourself. Kate will bring a snack to your room. We usually dine separately at midday."

"I doubt I will want anything after that breakfast. I really gorged myself."

"Good. Though you're a little heavier than your mother, you could use a few more pounds."

I thought my aunt a very strange woman. Perhaps living in such splendid isolation had made her so. Certainly her moods changed with lightning-like rapidity. Also, she was extremely frank. Perhaps it was a family trait. I'd not given it much thought until now, but suddenly I realized I was as frank as she.

Once I reached the edge of the property, I found a white fence almost entirely concealed by a heavy growth of ivy. I walked along it and discovered a stairway with a railing leading down to the narrow path. I paused briefly at the bottom to observe the swiftly flowing Hudson River. Because of the many days of rain, it was partway up the bank and made a roaring noise that was almost deafening as it pounded the rocks and boulders that edged the base of the precipice.

I wondered if I would be foolish to explore the path. Its narrowness didn't frighten me because vines and bushes grew out of the earth and stones on the cliffside, giving me something to grip should I need it. The other side dropped down to the rocks below. It was far enough down so that if I made a misstep and slipped, my fall might be a fatal one. Yet I felt my aunt would not have suggested it if she thought it was perilous.

I started along, taking care to move cautiously, noting that the small stones were treacherous; even more so was the moss that was sometimes hidden beneath them. The view of the other side of the river was awesome. At first, I thought it was solid rock, though I knew it couldn't be, since tall conifers grew there also. I paused and looked up on my side, but I could see little, for there were rock overhangs. I liked it. It seemed protective and gave me a feeling of reassurance.

I found myself moving faster. I had no idea how far this footpath extended, or where it led. I wondered if Mama had walked here, or Libby Innis, or even Nora

Martin. If so, how ironic they had met with no disaster here, yet in the safety of my aunt's abode, their lives had ended so calamitously.

I was so immersed in thoughts of the three women, I didn't notice that the rock overhang I had considered a protective covering was no longer there. Nor did I pay much attention to the few pebbles that bounced down from above, though I did glance upward. Nothing was visible except a wall of rock and stone laced with scrub and shrubbery.

I was becoming careless and twice almost lost my footing on the moss, one foot sliding completely over the edge. I might have gone over also, but I had sense enough to grab the scrub with my left hand. I stopped then, deciding I had had enough. I turned sideways to face the other side of the river and take a last, lingering look at it before returning to Linden Gardens. The sun was dazzling on the river, sending reflections up the wall of rock, even penetrating the darkness of the firs. I caught sight of a red fox standing motionless. I wondered if he found me as intriguing as I did him. What a sight for a painter. A play of light and shadow, along with the gray of rock and green of fir.

I'm sure I'd have heard the rumble of the rockslide had it not been for the roar of the river rushing in and out of the rocks against the side of the bank. I know that all that saved me was my grip on the brush at shoulder height. For suddenly, the rocks came down with a roar, some striking me in the back. The ones that reached the ground and bounced against my legs and ankles were the ones that proved the most dangerous. My feet flew out from under me and over the side. I screamed as the bush I was holding onto came loose.

A boulder struck me in the buttocks and flung me sideways, then back on the path. I slammed into the wall of rock beside me, my hands flailing, trying to get a grip on something.

I wasn't successful, but I fell onto the path. My left side struck the ground with such force I once again cried out with pain. Somehow I was flung on my back. I looked up and saw more boulders crashing downward. They were of varying sizes, but some were as long as my torso and twice as wide. I thought I caught a glimpse of a face looking down at me, but I couldn't be sure. I covered my face and head with my arms as best I could. I was directly in their path, yet I couldn't move. My body was filled with pain from being struck with rocks of varying sizes. One rock struck my elbow, sending a sharp jab of pain to my shoulder.

Once again I cried out, though not because I was struck. Someone had grabbed my ankles and pulled me out of the path of the second avalanche.

A voice commanded sternly, "Don't move!"

I felt a strong pair of hands cover a part of my head that was exposed. I opened my eyes to see a man—a stranger. He was sheltering me with his body. He grunted once. I knew why. He had been struck by a rock. I heard the thud as it hit his body.

As suddenly as it began, it stopped. I opened my eyes and tried to move my arms. I couldn't because he was still lying over me, using his body to protect me.

"Be quiet," he commanded. "There's someone up there. This avalanche was man-made."

"How do you know?" I asked, though I too had seen someone. Or thought I had. Fear might have made me think so.

"I saw someone peering down."

"I thought I did also."

"Who would want to kill you?"

"I hope no one," I exclaimed, horrified by the thought.

"Someone must," he said. "What were you doing here?"

"Taking a walk," I replied, thinking the question stupid.

"Even without a man-made avalanche, it's treacherous here."

"My aunt suggested it," I said. "I'm sure she wouldn't have, had she known I would be in danger."

"Who's your aunt?"

"Mrs. Emma von Linden." I was hurting all over and tired of lying on the sharp stones.

"Oh," he exclaimed. "Linden Gardens."

"Yes. Don't you think we could converse more easily if we were standing?"

"I just wanted to make certain the avalanche was over. I'd like to get up there and try to track down the culprit."

"I wish you would," I said.

"I doubt he'd still be around. If I saw him, he saw me."

"Could you identify him?"

"No. I couldn't really see a face. It was more a movement of a body. A swift one, meant to escape detection."

He moved agilely and was on his feet, looking down at me. I tried to raise myself and cried out with pain.

He knelt and rested an elbow on his knee. "Are you sure nothing is broken?"

"I don't believe so. Just bruised. I was struck hard by several rocks."

"And a boulder," he said. "It was undoubtedly meant to hit you so that you would be thrown over the side. Instead, it hit you in such a way that it flung you sideways and back against the bank, saving your life."

"How do you know?"

"I saw it happen."

I knew I had to get to my feet, yet I dreaded the thought of moving even a finger.

"You can't lie here, you know. Water trickles down from above and you're lying on wet moss. Even in summer you could catch your death."

Once again I tried to raise myself and cried out with pain.

"I've got to help you. I'll try not to hurt too much."

He eased his left hand beneath my left shoulder and gently moved it until he had brought it across to my other. His right hand slid beneath my waist on my right side.

"Put your arms around my neck," he said. "Do it slowly so you won't hurt so much."

I did as he said, pressing my lips tightly so I wouldn't cry out from the pain. Every muscle felt violated.

He eased me very slowly and gently to a sitting position and told me to rest, but to keep my arms around his neck and place my head on his shoulder. I felt no embarrassment, for it was not a time for shyness. Even though he was on one knee, I judged him to be about six feet tall. He was wearing a maroon pullover sweater and corduroy trousers. He had a narrow face with high cheekbones, and thick, unruly blond hair. His eyes were deep-set and such a beautiful blue. What a waste on a man, I thought. A woman could set the world on fire with such eyes. Yet he was far from handsome.

He insisted I rest for about five minutes. It was a good time to ask his name and how he happened to be in such a place at a perfect time for me. I moved my head back slightly so I could observe him.

When he smiled at my question, I noticed he had dimples. Once again, I thought, what a woman could do with those.

"My name is David Lathrop," he replied. "I always take a walk along here sometime during the day. Usually in the afternoon. Today, for no reason I can fathom, I found myself strolling down along the pathway this morning. I was on my way back when I heard the rockslide, followed by your screams."

"How lucky for me you came," I said.

"The worst of it was over by the time I reached you," he said.

"You were struck also. I heard the thud of a rock as it hit you. If you hadn't pulled me to safety, then protected me with your body, I'd be dead."

He didn't dispute my statement, but made light of the part he played.

Then he said, "Let me know when you feel able to move."

"I'm sure I can now. I'm bruised here and there, but I was more frightened than anything else."

I started to move my arms from around his neck, but he ordered me to keep them there. "I'm going to lift you."

"I'm much too heavy," I protested. "Besides, you couldn't possibly carry me on this path. It's too narrow."

"I can by stepping sideways and that's exactly what I intend to do." He lifted me as he spoke, then leaned back against the cliffside. "Are you comfortable?"

"Yes. I'm also quite capable of walking."

He smiled down at me. "And I'm quite capable of carrying you. We'll do no more talking until we get up on your aunt's property."

I didn't argue. I liked his commanding way. He started to sidestep, moving cautiously, his hold on me firm. Yet he was careful not to use pressure, knowing I had taken a battering from the rocks and that the bruises were already painful.

It seemed a long time before we reached the stairway. I again requested him to let me down and he again refused. He was in fine physical condition, for he carried me up the stairs and wasn't even breathing heavily when we reached the top.

"Don't ask me again to let you down," he said. "I'm carrying you to the house."

"That's ridiculous," I said. "I'm really not injured."

"You're badly bruised and what you went through was quite a shock. I would certainly like to know who would cause such a rockslide."

"So would I," I replied. "Though I can't imagine it was done to injure me."

"Have you lived here long?"

"I arrived only yesterday. Scarcely long enough to have made an enemy."

Mr. Lathrop agreed. "It could have been a youngster up to mischief, meaning only to frighten you, not realizing he could injure you mortally."

I said, "That makes the most sense. I think it's the only logical explanation since I'm a complete stranger in these parts."

"The important thing is," Mr. Lathrop said, "that you survived the avalanche. We'll go along on the theory that no one meant you harm."

We had traversed the lawn and he was about to move around to the front when one of the screen doors leading into the breakfast room opened and Kate stepped out.

Her look of concern vanished when I called to her that I was all right.

"Come in, sir." She held the door wide so Mr. Lathrop might enter.

Once inside, I introduced them.

Mr. Lathrop said, "The young lady was caught in an avalanche. Please lead me to her bedroom. She was struck by both rocks and boulders and I'm sure she is severely bruised. If not worse."

She looked over her shoulder as she moved quickly ahead of us. "Why did you ever take that walk, Miss Celeste? It's very dangerous."

"It wouldn't have been ordinarily," I protested. "It just happened there was an avalanche of rocks and boulders."

"Just happened," she mocked. "There are always rock-slides there. I wouldn't set foot on that path for any amount of money. I'll send Zeffrey for the doctor."

"Really, Kate, there's no need for that," I protested.

"Let me be the judge," she scolded.

"She's right, Celeste," Mr. Lathrop said. "I apologize for using your given name, but you didn't identify yourself."

"Well, now you know my first name. My last is Abbott."

We'd made the ascent of the stairs and had reached my room. Kate again held the door wide, then moved swiftly ahead of us to draw down the bedclothes. Mr. Lathrop laid me gently on the bed and stepped back.

"I believe you should have a doctor examine you. You may be injured more seriously than you think."

A knock sounded on the door. It was followed by heavy footsteps that paused at the archway. It was Calvin.

"It's Miss Celeste, sir," Kate said. "She was almost killed on the pathway by the river."

He moved up to the side of the bed. "Why did you go there?"

I sighed, already tired of explanation. "My aunt suggested it."

He looked incredulous. "Are you sure?"

"I'm very sure," I said impatiently, "and I'm tired of all this attention."

"I'll go for the doctor," Calvin said. "I'll make it in one-third the time Zeffrey would."

"You would indeed, sir," Kate said firmly. "He's too independent for me. Why the mistress lets him get away with such misbehavior, I don't know. Besides, he isn't even in the house."

Calvin couldn't have heard her. He had moved swiftly from the room. Less than two minutes later, the pounding of a horse's hoofs drifted through the open window.

Mr. Lathrop said, "With your permission, I would like to stop by and see how you are."

"It's very kind of you, Mr. Lathrop," I said. "Thanks, also, for saving my life."

His dimples were evident as he replied, "I'd say you saved your own life when you spun back against the cliff-side. However, I'm glad I heard you cry out."

"So am I," I said, returning the smile. "Thank you again, Mr. Lathrop."

"You're welcome, Celeste." His eyes held a hint of deviltry, but his final words and his tone were serious. "I don't think I need to ask you not to go exploring on that pathway again."

"I shan't go near it for the time being," I replied.

"I'm certain of that. I'm sure the doctor will suggest you rest for a few days."

"I hope not," I protested.

Kate's eyes never left me during my conversation with

Mr. Lathrop. But suddenly her glance switched to him. "I think you had better go, sir. I'll see you out. Then I'll come back and help Miss Celeste."

"Stay with her," he urged. "I'll find my way."

Kate nodded and flashed him a look of gratitude. She didn't move though until he left the room. Once we heard the sound of the door closing quietly, she went to the dressing room closet and got my nightgown and negligee, which she laid at the foot of the bed.

"I'll help you, child."

"I can manage, Kate." I thought I could, but when I started to raise myself, I cried out with pain.

"You can't manage," she replied sternly. "Now be quiet. I have to get you ready before the doctor arrives. His name is Seth Carney. He's about fifty or thereabouts. A very good physician—and a surgeon when need be. People in these parts put a lot of faith in him. They'd better. He's all they have. He's kind to your aunt and looks after her welfare."

As Kate talked, she gently removed my garments and exclaimed aloud at the swellings and bruises on my body. "You'll be sore for a month. Your aunt will feel real bad. Perhaps take to her bed again."

"Take to her bed because of my bruises?" The idea seemed preposterous.

"Yes," Kate spoke firmly. "She'll blame herself. No matter what happens here, she blames herself. She's so filled with guilt because of the three deaths. I wasn't here when the first happened. The second, as you know, was your mother. The third—Nora Martin. A lovely girl. So young, so filled with a love for life. It hit Mr. Calvin real hard. He seemed quite smitten with her. Not that she ever knew. He knows his place."

"Kate, you sound like a snob," I chided.

"Maybe I am," she replied. She took the pins from my hair, gently coaxed it down with her fingers and spread it on the pillow. "Now don't you move until the doctor comes. I'll wash your face. Your brow got skinned and there's blood on it. Also, you have a black-and-blue mark on your jaw. Besides a hundred and one all over your body. You must have been terribly frightened."

"I was while it lasted. Thank goodness Mr. Lathrop heard my cries and arrived in time to pull me out of the path of the second rockfall."

"What possessed you to do such a thing?"

"Is it really considered that dangerous?"

"No one in this house would walk along it. Except, possibly, Mr. Calvin. And he wears rubber-soled shoes. Didn't you notice Mr. Lathrop was wearing them?"

"No." I tried to smile, but quickly gave up. My face must have received a worse battering than I thought. Probably when I spun around and slammed against the bank.

"I don't blame you for smiling," Kate said. "I shouldn't have asked such a question. How could you notice anything at such a time?"

A timid tap sounded on the door. Kate whispered, "That's your aunt," and went to answer.

I heard soft voices, followed by my aunt's short footsteps. Kate followed in the rear.

My aunt stopped at the foot of the bed and gripped one of the four posters. "Why did you go there, my dear?"

I was so stupefied by her question, I couldn't answer.

"Answer me, child. Why?" Though her statement was a command, her voice was gentle.

"You suggested it, Auntie."

Her features took on a pained look and I was certain I saw fear in her eyes. She bowed her head. "I'm sorry. I don't know what could have got into me to have suggested you do such a thing."

There was another tap on the door, followed by brisk footsteps. It was Wanda. She stood beside my aunt and regarded me with concern.

She said, "I was taking a stroll in the yard when Calvin came running out. He told me what happened. Why did you go there?"

My aunt covered her eyes with her hand as she replied. "I told her to go, Wanda. At least, that's what she said."

"You did, Auntie," I said quietly.

She dropped her hand to her side. "I believe you. Please forgive me. My mind sometimes plays tricks on me." She sighed wearily, then added, "Dr. Seth Carney will come shortly and attend to your injuries. I hope they're not serious."

"They're not, Auntie."

Kate said, "We won't know for sure until the doctor comes, Miss Emma. She's got some terrible bruises on her body. And a good-sized lump on her head."

I wished Kate had kept quiet. My aunt started to sob. I

tried to get up and go to her, but my body protested so violently, I cried out and fell back on the pillow. The sight of that further unnerved her and her sobs grew louder. Kate and Wanda got on either side of her and walked her from the room. Between her sobs my aunt said something about how wrong it was of her to invite me here.

It was all I could do to hold back my own tears. Not for myself, but for my aunt who was filled with guilt because of what had happened to me. Yet why had she suggested I go there if it was dangerous? Certainly I hadn't dreamed it. I was sure she would take to her bed again, as Kate had stated. Whereas before I hadn't wanted Dr. Carney to come, I now was impatient for his arrival. I wanted to question him about my aunt. I recalled Calvin and Wanda telling me they never questioned her orders. Could it be they were being discreet? Had they meant my aunt was confused at times, due to a mental abberation of some sort? Perhaps the result of the three tragic deaths that had taken place in this house.

I could see why Wanda had tried to get her away from here. I knew that, regardless of what Dr. Carney said, I would be up and about tomorrow. My common sense told me that that would lift my aunt's spirits more than anything. I thought of Zeffrey and wondered why he hadn't put in an appearance. Everyone else concerned with the household had. Then I recalled Kate saying he wasn't in the house. Could it have been *his* face I'd seen? If so, had he caused that rockslide merely to be mischievous? Or had he done it with lethal intent? If so, what could have been his motive? Why should he wish me ill? Was his mind so warped that he resented my presence here? Did he feel it was his niece who should have been here instead of me? I made myself stop thinking that way. I hadn't a shred of evidence to back me up.

◆ Four ◆

The hoofbeats of a horse pounded the earth as it approached the house. That would be Calvin returning from the village. If he found Dr. Carney in his office, he would be along shortly. He was. Despite my pain, I couldn't help but be amused by the sound of the creaking wheels, badly in need of grease.

Apparently the door to my room was open, for the sound of the downstairs door being opened and closed was clearly audible. It was followed by voices speaking in an undertone—Kate and Dr. Carney, I suspected. Moments later, Kate entered the room with him. The talking ceased immediately, confirming my suspicion that I had been the topic of their conversation.

Dr. Carney was of medium height, a bit corpulent, but pleasant-faced. His hair was iron gray and already thinning at the temples. His hands were his most impressive feature. They were small, yet they gave the impression of great strength. He examined my head first, his fingers moving gently, but with practiced skill, over my skull. After that, he held my head and regarded the lump at the hairline.

He touched it gently, also the area surrounding it. "Do you have a headache?"

"No, Doctor. Only the area near the lump is sore."

He nodded. Kate remained in the room until he completed his examination. His manner was professional, and though I cried out twice when he moved my arms and legs, he assured me he wouldn't hurt me any more than necessary. Once he completed his examination, he went into the bathroom and washed his hands. Kate took the opportunity to smooth the bedclothes, fluff my pillow, and ease me back onto it.

I was exhausted, but impatient to learn his diagnosis.

When he returned, he picked up a straight-backed chair that sat against the opposite wall and brought it over to my bedside. He set it down, eased himself onto it, and stifled a yawn.

"Apparently you had little sleep last night, Doctor," I said.

His features softened as he spoke. "At two this morning I delivered twins. A boy and girl to a couple who had been childless for twelve years. The new papa and I did a little celebrating with a bottle of brandy. I'm afraid it was too much for me. Ordinarily, I don't touch the stuff." He gave me a knowing glance. "Not that I'm against it. I just don't have the time. And I can't afford to overindulge, never knowing when I'll be called out in the middle of the night. Or the day."

"I'm sorry you had to be disturbed. I really didn't want them to send for you."

"It's best to make certain," he said. "I'm glad to tell you nothing's broken. Though it was foolhardy of you to go on that pathway."

"Everyone has told me that," I admitted.

His brows raised questioningly. "What made you do it?"

"My aunt suggested it this morning while we breakfasted."

He frowned. "I'm sorry to hear it."

"How do you mean that, Doctor?"

"I was fearful these spells she has had over the years might eventually tax her brain. Kate tells me Emma has taken to her bed."

I nodded. "She broke down and sobbed when she came in here after I was brought back."

"Brought back?"

"Mr. David Lathrop pulled me out of range of the second rockslide. By doing so, I believe he saved my life. Several large boulders landed on the pathway where I'd been standing when the rockslide occurred."

"David Lathrop?" Dr. Carney squeezed the flesh beneath his lower lip as he pondered the name. "It's a new one around here."

"I can't help you, Doctor. Except for the occupants of this house and yourself, everyone in these parts is a stranger to me. Anyway, he said he believed the rockslide was man-made."

Dr. Carney looked skeptical. "Who would want to do such a thing? No one could have a grudge against you."

"That's exactly what I thought. Mr. Lathrop suggested it might be a mischievous boy who didn't realize he might kill someone by his actions."

"That's possible."

"Is the pathway avoided by people around here?"

"Perhaps not by everyone. But certainly by women."

"I'm glad you pronounced me uninjured. I don't want to remain in bed."

"I did not say you were uninjured," he replied sternly. "You are badly bruised. There's an ugly lump on your brow that goes right into the hairline."

"That can be easily covered by my hair. You see, Doctor, if I get up and move about, my aunt will be assured I am quite all right."

"I advise you to remain in bed at least one more day."

"And if I don't follow that advice?"

"You'll survive. You're young." He arose and picked up his black bag, which rested on the table. "I'm going to see your aunt now."

"Please reassure her, Doctor."

His dark eyes regarded me appraisingly. "I will—on one condition."

"Name it."

"That you let Kate give you a sleeping draught now and you stay in bed until tomorrow morning."

"I'll obey you. And please tell my aunt I feel better already and I'll be in to visit her tomorrow."

He smiled down at me and gently touched the top of my head. "Very well, Celeste Abbott. Oh—one more order. Stay off that pathway."

"You may be assured of that. Doctor, I won't rest until you answer a few questions that have been troubling me."

"Make it brief, young lady. You need rest. So do I and I want to see your aunt before I leave."

"That's why I wish to speak with you. When you spoke of mental aberration, did you mean senility?"

"No. Your aunt is a very shy and sensitive lady. She never fully recovered from the shock of her husband's sudden death from a heart attack. She dwells too much on the past. Then there were those three tragic and fatal accidents. Her mind is burdened with them. I have been fearing she might have a mental breakdown."

"I want to help bring her out of that world of yesterday she is so obessed with. I believe I can."

Dr. Carney regarded me thoughtfully before he replied. "In the few moments I've spoken with you, Celeste, I can tell you have a cheerful personality. That's what your aunt needs more than anything. Wanda and Kate do all they can, but someone young around would do more for her than any medicine I could prescribe."

"Did you know Nora Martin?"

Dr. Carney resumed his seat. "I know I'll not get out of here until your mind is at ease, so I'll answer your questions. I saw her around the village. The family has a home here, though they haven't visited in several years. She was here only a short time before her death. Your aunt took an instant liking to her. The girl did her a lot of good, too. Took her for rides in the country, took her into town and walked her around the green, even accompanied her to church. The von Linden pew hadn't been used in years. I think the villagers would have forgotten their hostility toward her if Nora hadn't met the same fate as Libby and your mother."

"Did you know my mother and Libby?"

"I knew Libby well. I was just getting to know your mother when she fell down those stairs."

"Was there any evidence of foul play?"

My question astonished him. "Such a thought never occurred to me nor to the constable, I'm sure. I'd suggest you not ask such a question of your aunt. Not if you want to help her."

"I won't, Doctor. I'll take up where Nora Martin left off. My aunt must not remain cooped up in this house."

"I agree. There was tremendous ill-feeling in the village toward your aunt when your mother came. She did a lot to dispel it. She just about had the villagers won over when she was killed in the same manner as Libby and, most recently, Nora Martin."

Dr. Carney stood up, but before he took a step, I asked another question.

"Was Libby liked in the village?"

His smile was reminiscent. "One would think the women would hate her because she was so beautiful. Yet everyone was drawn to her because of that. That's why the town turned against your aunt."

"Do you think they would have if she had adopted Libby?"

"That was planned while her husband was alive."

"Didn't my aunt want her?"

"I never queried her about it. It was none of my business, Celeste."

"I'm sorry, Doctor. I know I overstepped myself in asking you those questions. But my concern now is for my aunt."

"My concern is for both of you. I know you'll get up tomorrow. Use a cane. Two, if you need them—and you may. I'll tell Kate. I'm sure there are some about."

"May I ask one more question?"

"No." Without even a farewell, he left the room.

Kate came in shortly after with the sleeping draught and sat by my bedside while it took effect. I did ask her how my aunt was. She replied Miss Emma had taken to her bed, but relaxed a little when Dr. Carney told her I had suffered no severe injuries and would be up and about tomorrow. She looked disapproving as she related what the doctor had said, then added she knew I'd put him up to it. The draught had already relaxed me and I managed a half-smile. She chided me with a glance and that was the last I remembered until the following morning.

I'm sure it must have taken me fifteen minutes to raise myself and sit on the side of the bed. However, my spirits brightened when I saw two sturdy canes of thick, gnarled wood. Just the thing to help me get about. I wasn't the least bit sensitive about using them. They would be a help.

However, before I got as far as the dressing room, Kate entered. She said, "I have a hot tub drawn for you. It will ease your muscle pain, though you'll need help getting in and out."

I didn't argue. She was a wise lady and I knew she enjoyed mothering me. I must confess I liked it too. It had been four years since a woman had given me attention, other than at the school, and there it was a duty.

However, I cried out as Kate helped me into the tub. My muscles felt as if they were being torn from my flesh. But as she had predicted, the water eased the stabbing pains I felt all through my body. Once Kate was assured I could manage, she went into the bedroom, stating she was stripping the beds to change the linen. After I was bathed, she helped me out and assisted me in drying myself. I returned to the bedroom, insisting on dressing myself, though I let her put up my hair. She did it most attractively, drawing it to the top and letting the ends fall in loose curls to my shoulders. I told her I felt as if I were going to a ball.

Only then did she reveal she had a little surprise for me. "Mr. Lathrop is downstairs. He stopped by to inquire about you. I couldn't tell then how you were since you weren't awake when I looked in on you earlier. I don't know whether he'll be pleased or displeased when he learns you refuse to spend the day in bed."

"He's probably gone by now," I said.

"Indeed he hasn't," she replied briskly. "He said he'd wait until I came down. I told him it might be a while, but he said he had the whole day."

I regarded my reflection in the mirror. My simple eyelet cotton dress was pretty, but I wasn't. The lump on my brow was visible and there was an abrasion on my left cheek that had caused it to swell, but my skin had a healthy glow. Kate, standing behind me, smiled and nodded.

"One would scarcely know you were almost killed yesterday."

"Kate, do they think my aunt would mind if I invited Mr. Lathrop to breakfast?"

"I'm sure she would not," Kate said. "She's still sleeping. Wanda and I took turns staying with her through the night. I was glad you had a sleeping draught. Her sobs could be heard all through the house."

"I wish she hadn't taken it so hard."

Kate shook her head. "She doesn't remember telling you to take that walk. But she says strange things now and then. It's been like that for years. Sometimes months go by and she's herself. Then . . ." Kate shrugged and her voice trailed off.

Kate used a buttonhook on my white shoes and helped me to my feet. I used both canes to gain the hallway. Once she was certain I had no difficulty maintaining my balance, she moved ahead of me. At the head of the stairs, she paused and made a motioning gesture. I knew she was inviting Mr. Lathrop to come upstairs and assist me. I didn't mind. The stairway had a bad reputation.

He reached the landing before I did and nodded approval at my progress. "I don't know if you are doing the right thing, Celeste, but it's a joy to see you up and about. I'll carry the canes down. Slip your left arm around mine and grip it with your hand. Place your right hand on the railing and use it as a support. No talking while we're making the descent."

"Before we start, I would like to extend to you an invitation to breakfast."

"I accept. Thank you. And thank you, Kate."

She laughed and said, "I'll have it on the table by the time you get there."

She did too. However, the descent was slow and torturous. I was elated to have Mr. Lathrop as a breakfast companion. I needed a friend my age. I judged him to be about twenty-six. I learned later he was twenty-eight. In the brief time I had spent with him, I knew he was a mature man and had a great deal of common sense. That was what I needed, for I had to talk to someone. I was puzzled by my aunt's behavior. Puzzled and worried. I wondered what his reaction would be when I told him my aunt had no recollection of having told me to enjoy a walk on a path that was recognized by all as very dangerous, and was, for the most part, a place to avoid.

I directed Mr. Lathrop to the breakfast room, which was as inviting as the day before. This morning the centerpiece was a bouquet of pink roses. Mr. Lathrop placed the canes on the chaise longue as we passed it and guided me to the table. I found that so long as I had his arm to help support me, I could walk without difficulty, though very slowly. He helped me into the chair, eased it closer to the table, then took the chair opposite.

Kate entered with a large silver tray. On it were the silver dishes. She set the tray on a side table and brought the covered dishes over to the table, along with a large pot of coffee. She removed the lids, revealing fried eggs, bacon, sausage, and potatoes. There were also hot rolls covered with a napkin. In small, glass compote dishes were butter, marmalade, and honey. The aroma of the food filled the room, making me ravenously hungry. Kate warned us, in mock severity, that she expected us to eat all of it. Both Mr. Lathrop and I agreed it would be an impossible task, though I must say, we did justice to it. He was quite at ease as he served me, then himself.

Once we settled down to our meal, he asked me what the doctor's diagnosis had been.

"Nothing serious, you may be sure, or I wouldn't be sitting opposite you. Anyway, I'm sure Kate gave you all the details."

"She did," he admitted. "But I wanted further assurance from you."

"Except for stiffness and soreness, I'll be as good as new in a few days."

"I hope you won't try to do too much today," he replied.

"I shan't, other than to pay my aunt a visit to reassure her. She collapsed when she learned what happened to me."

He paused in the act of putting a generous portion of marmalade on a roll and regarded me with puzzlement. "I can understand her grave concern, but why would she collapse?"

"It is puzzling," I admitted, "for someone who doesn't know her. I questioned Dr. Carney about it. He told me she lives too much in the past. First, the sudden death of her husband from a fatal heart attack. Then the three tragic deaths that occurred in this house have made her emotionally unstable."

"Perhaps mentally also," he suggested.

It was my turn to express surprise. "Why would you say that? Or have you heard anything about my aunt?"

"I haven't lived here long enough to hear anything about anyone. I've been to the village only a few times and I found that strangers or newcomers, of which I am one, are regarded with suspicion. Especially an artist."

"How exciting," I exclaimed, completely forgetting the subject of my aunt. "Is that why you're here?"

He nodded. "I've rented the house about a mile up the road from this one."

"Lucky for me you did," I said. "Otherwise . . ."

He interrupted me with, "It was meant for me to be where I was and to hear you crying out."

"More coffee, Mr. Lathrop?" I extended my arm to pick up the silver pot, but he was faster.

"Let me pour you more." He did so, then refilled his cup.

"Mr. Lathrop, may I talk with you as a friend? I mean—I have friends here, but no one close to my age."

He smiled. "Thank you for the compliment. I already consider myself your friend, Celeste. I'm pleased you regard me highly enough to suggest it. Just one thing seems to be in the way."

"And that?" I queried.

"You're too formal. My first name is David. I think I told you."

"You did. And you wish me to call you David?"

"Good thinking, Miss Abbott," he teased.

I played the game. "Thank you, Mr. Lathrop. I shall call you David from now on. It seems only fitting since I am going to confide in you—at the risk of seeming disloyal to my aunt."

He became serious. "I'm sure you would never be that. What you feel toward your aunt is concern."

"I'm gravely worried. You see, it was she who suggested I take a walk along that narrow and dangerous path yesterday. The reason she collapsed is that she had no recollection of telling me to do so. She is aware of how dangerous it is, just as Kate and Wanda and Calvin are. I haven't talked with him or Wanda since the accident. Dr. Carney ordered a sleeping draught after he examined me."

"It was the best thing for you. You act quite normal, except for your walk, but I expect by tomorrow you will have walked most of the stiffness out of your muscles."

"I hope so, since I am going to New York City on Monday." I hadn't meant to make such a revelation and I ended the sentence abruptly.

"Surely you're not serious," he replied, disapproval edging his voice.

"Indeed I am," I assured him.

"Is that where you live?"

"Yes."

"Since you've just come from there, why are you so eager to return? Or have you decided to leave Linden Gardens?"

"Indeed not. I want to help my aunt. I understand the young lady—Nora Martin—who was killed when she fell down the stairs, was doing a great deal to restore my aunt's confidence. Also, because of her efforts, the antagonism of the villagers toward my aunt seemed to be lessening."

"And you intend to take Nora Martin's place," David reasoned. "I'm not so sure I approve."

"Do you think the house is cursed?"

"I'm not superstitious, Celeste," he said. "Still, so much that is bad has happened here. It makes one wonder."

"Then you are superstitious."

"Possibly. Also, worried."

"About me?"

"Have you forgotten the face you and I saw at the top of the cliff yesterday?"

I had, completely. I nodded.

David said, "I thought a great deal about it last night. So much so. I couldn't sleep. This morning I investigated the area where the rockslide occurred. Unfortunately, I found nothing that could be presented as evidence that someone wished you ill. Was everyone in this house accounted for?"

"Everyone except Zeffrey. He's the coachman. Also, he oversees the gardeners. So that could explain his absence. Or he could have been in the barn."

"The grounds are evidence of his competence."

A sudden thought occurred to me. "The day I came here, I visited my uncle's mausoleum. Zeffrey was there. Have you ever seen it?"

"I've visited it, though it could be called trespassing. My interest in it was as a painter. A lover of beauty. It is a work of art."

"Did you know Libby Innis was buried there?"

"I saw her name. Who is she?"

"Zeffrey's niece. She was a maid in the household and was the first victim of the stairs."

"Why would she be buried there?"

"I can think of only one reason. My aunt's generosity. Also, my aunt and uncle were going to adopt her. My uncle died before the adoption proceedings were started. I asked my aunt if she still would have done so. She said she would have, once the period of mourning had ended for her husband."

"But she didn't."

"Libby suffered a fatal fall down the stairs before my aunt could do so."

"You mean before the period of mourning ended?"

I nodded. "Zeffrey told me that day I encountered him in the tomb that the stairway would claim me as the fourth victim."

"What a nasty thing to say."

"I don't know if he meant to be nasty. Or if it is something he believes. I was surprised to enter the tomb and find him there. I almost had the feeling he had seen me head for it, took a shortcut, and reached the place before me. Anyway, he pointed out the niche where his niece's remains are interred."

"I think we should keep an eye on Zeffrey. Especially if he was not in the house yesterday when that rockslide occurred. He may resent your presence here, feeling it was his niece's place to inherit all this."

I stiffened. "That isn't why I'm here."

"I know it isn't, Celeste," he said. "But I'm sure your aunt sees you as the rightful heir. She has brought you here so she may become acquainted with you—to see if you are competent and deserving of such a rich legacy."

"I think you're impertinent."

He smiled at my irritation. "Don't get angry. I don't mean to be. I'm an extremely honest person. It has gotten me into trouble often. People somehow don't like honesty."

I relented and returned the smile. "You're right, of course. Even my aunt told me she doesn't love me, adding, quite sensibly, how could she since she scarcely knew me?"

"That must have been a blow."

"It was. Particularly since she had clothed and educated me since Mama's death. She shattered my childhood dreams of how I thought she regarded me."

"And your father?" Almost as an afterthought, he added. "Is he alive?"

"He raised me. At least I lived with him during the summertime."

"When you wanted to be here playing the role of fairy princess."

"I should be angry with you, but I can't be since you speak the truth. It was my father who made me aware of the fact that I had become a snob."

"A quite charming one," David said. "Though I think you have grown up a little since coming here."

I sobered. "I wish you could convince me of it."

"First of all, you realize that the person who loves you the most is your father."

I quickly corrected him. "Papa is the *only* one who loves me. He didn't want me to come here."

David looked surprised. "Why not?"

"Because of what happened to Mama. I know he is terribly worried something might happen to me. Just as it happened to Mama."

"So you're going back to talk with him Monday."

"No. I'm going on an errand for my aunt. It's a private matter. I feel it would be a breach of confidence for me to tell you about it. I've really talked too much as it is."

"You said you needed a friend. Please trust me. Now I must be leaving. Not that I want to, but I wish to be invited back. This time I invited myself. Your accident served as an excuse. I'm sorry about it, but we might never have met otherwise." He contradicted himself. "Of course, we would have—somewhere. May I help you upstairs?"

"Yes please," I said. "My aunt must have awakened by now. I want her to see me up and about."

"I suggest you lie down this afternoon, however. Especially since you are journeying to New York City the day after tomorrow. Though your aunt may have second thoughts about that since your accident."

"Even if she has, I'm going to insist on making the journey. I want her to be assured my injuries were only minor."

"They weren't, though. Dr. Carney told me you received some severe and extensive bruises. He said you should remain in bed a few days, but you were a stubborn and very brave young lady."

I smiled. "I mentioned you to him, but he didn't know you."

"I went to his office and I introduced myself. I felt since I was the one who brought you back to the house, it would not be improper."

"It was very kind and thoughtful of you."

"I think you had better start walking again before you become too stiff."

He walked around the table, bent down, and told me to put my arms around his neck so he could raise me. I obeyed and his hands gently gripped my waist. He had moved the chair out first to make my movements as easy as possible, but I gasped for breath as he raised me to my feet. He insisted I rest my head against his chest for a few minutes. I did and was able to hear the steady beat of his heart beneath the thin sweater he was wearing.

He loosened his hold on me and I stood there while he

went to get the canes. He handed me one and, as before, I slipped my arm around his and gripped his forearm, using it as a support. We made slow progress from the room to the stairway. There I paused to rest before we made the ascent. I nodded when I was ready. He relieved me of the cane and we went upstairs, one step at a time.

Kate met us at the landing. I was breathing hard and trembling from my exertions. but I refused to let David carry me to my suite. Once again, he insisted I rest my head against his chest until my breathing returned to normal. He told Kate I should lie down for a while. She said she would see to it. I protested, stating I wanted to see my aunt so she would know I was up and about. When Kate revealed she was still sleeping, I was relieved, knowing I needed rest. David stated wisely that she'd not be reassured seeing me now, for I was pale and my eyes revealed my exhaustion. Kate promised to let me know when my aunt had wakened.

I told David I now felt quite capable of resuming the walk to my suite. I stepped back, refusing to take the canes he extended to me. I lost my balance and grabbed onto his sweater for support. It was his pocket I'd grasped and my weight tore lose one side of it. I'd have fallen if he'd not caught me. I apologized, but David made light of it. He offered his arm again, cautioning me to use one of the canes. I did so and we walked the length of the hall to my room. There, I bade him farewell, granting a quick consent to his request for a visit on the following day. He thanked me and handed me the second cane.

Kate had gone on ahead and had the door open. I used my canes to reach the privacy of my bedroom. Kate unbuttoned my shoes and helped me out of my dress. I eased myself gratefully between the bedclothes and let her cover me. She lowered the window shades and in seconds I was asleep.

True to her promise, Kate wakened me and informed me my aunt was propped up on pillows and ready to have me visit her. She warned me that my aunt was listless, part of it caused by the sleeping draught and part of it by the depression that followed an emotional upset. Nonetheless, Kate added, she was pleased I'd been able to breakfast downstairs.

"Here's a notebook I found in the hall. I think Mr.

Lathrop must have dropped it. It wasn't there when you left your room because I went back with fresh linen. Calvin went to the village early this morning and Wanda has only just got up. No one else was in the hall while Mr. Lathrop was here."

She extended a small leather notebook, held closed by a small, narrow elastic band. It was new, for it bore the smell of fresh leather. I opened the drawer of my night table and dropped it in. I told Kate I would give it to David when he came to call tomorrow.

My progress was still slow, but I could navigate with only one cane. Another good sign was that the soreness of my muscles was not as severe. I bathed my face and wrung out a washcloth in cold water to press against my brow. I had suddenly acquired a slight headache. It was to be expected. I did have a severe lump on my brow. I said nothing about it to Kate and returned to the bedroom. She took down my hair, brushed it, and put it up with the same skill as she had this morning. I also needed her help to slip into my dress and shoes.

I reached for my cane and started for the door, Kate in the lead. "Don't stay too long," she cautioned. "Your aunt tires easily. But she should have a quick recovery seeing you looking as well as you do. The sleep did you good."

She held open the door for me and stood in the hallway until I crossed it to my aunt's room. I knocked softly on the door and heard her faint command to enter.

Kate and I exchanged glances and she nodded reassuringly. I opened the door and went into the room.

"You poor child." My aunt's tone was one of deep sympathy. "It must be terribly painful for you to walk."

"It really isn't, Aunt Emma." There was a chair by her bedside, no doubt occupied by either Kate or Wanda through the night. "May I sit down, Auntie? Or are you too tired?"

She managed a smile. "Do sit down, child. I love to look at you because you are the image of your mama. Ruth was so kind to me. Always. She was younger than I, but so much more mature. I'm lucky I met your uncle. I never could have coped with poverty. I guess God looks after us more than we realize."

I nodded, trying desperately to think of a way to get the conversation on a brighter note. David came to mind.

"I felt so well, Auntie, that I invited a guest to breakfast this morning. Kate assured me you wouldn't mind."

She regarded me curiously. "Whom do you know in these parts?"

"His name is David Lathrop. He carried me back yesterday. He rented the house just above here. He's an artist."

"The Martin residence," my aunt said dolefully. "Where poor Nora lived."

I'd certainly picked the wrong subject.

"Anyway," my aunt went on, "thank God he was here and close enough to hear you cry out."

"He's an artist, Auntie," I said.

"What does he paint?" my aunt asked.

"I'm ashamed to say I never even thought to ask." It wasn't quite the truth. I was more concerned with confiding in him about my aunt. She made an enchanting picture in her lavender negligee with frothy lace collar that hugged her neck and an old-fashioned lace cap that covered most of her hair. At this moment, there was no visible sign of her constant depression. The doleful expression had left her features and her eyes took on a pixy look as she eyed me mischievously.

"You sound as if you are quite intrigued with the gentleman. What did you say his name was?"

"David Lathrop."

She thought a moment before her head moved in slow, negative fashion. "I knew the Martins who occupied that house. They were a charming couple. They had two children. A boy and a girl. The girl, of course, was Nora."

"Then you knew Nora as a child."

"No. I didn't socialize, my dear. Your mother knew them. Mr. Martin was also an artist. He painted the portrait I sent your papa. She sat for him in their home."

"Then she wasn't with you constantly?"

"Almost constantly. Though Wanda insisted she leave the house for brief periods. I was in a deep state of melancholy because of Libby Innis. I didn't even want to live, so neither your mother nor Wanda nor Kate would ever leave me alone."

"Didn't it unnerve you to have someone always with you?"

"Oh no. It's loneliness I fear. That's when I start to think about what happened here."

"Did Mr. Martin paint anything other than portraits? I mean—do you have any of his work hanging in this house?"

"I don't know. Mostly we have paintings only by big-name artists. I mean foreign ones. Mr. Martin was an American, of course, and he did achieve great fame in later years. He wasn't a very big hit with society women because he would paint them only as he saw them, not as they saw themselves. But for anyone who wanted a true likeness, he was the man."

"That should be of interest to David."

"I'm sure it will be. Why don't you look at the paintings in your suite. There might be something signed by David Martin."

"*David* Martin?"

"It is coincidental, isn't it? Same first names." my aunt replied. "Anyway, I'm sure your David Lathrop has heard of David Martin. That is, if your young man is interested in studying others in his field."

"Is David Martin alive?"

"No. Both he and his wife were stricken with pneumonia while on a visit to California, of all places. Their children were grown when that happened."

"How would you know that, Auntie?"

She smiled. "I have the New York City papers mailed to me. And though I am a recluse—through choice—it does help me to keep up on world affairs and do an enormous amount of reading."

"I'm glad you do," I said. "I enjoy reading."

"Then you shall read to me," she said. She sighed and settled deeper into her pillows. "You know, your visit has served to cheer me."

"Does that mean you will get up and dress?"

"Not today, my dear. But if I am awake when your young man returns, please bring him up to meet me."

"He won't be back until tomorrow."

She glanced at the ornate gold clock that sat on her night table. "Oh my, it's almost five o'clock. I slept the day away. I hope you didn't."

I had, but I gave a negative shake of my head and smiled.

"Good," she said, stifling a yawn. "I think I shall have a nap before my tray is brought up. Celeste. I'm a wee bit tired."

"I'm sorry, Auntie. Kate warned me not to stay here so long I would weary you."

"You haven't. I'm so glad you are here. Promise you won't leave."

"I promise, Auntie. I was hoping Zeffrey might take you and me for a ride tomorrow."

"You are free to go if you wish. Zeffrey will take you or you may use the buggy yourself. Oh no," she quickly corrected herself, "you couldn't just now. I don't think you should consider riding for a few days. Dr. Carney told me that while you suffered no broken bones, your body was almost entirely covered with bruises."

"With each minute I am becoming less and less aware of them," I said.

"Wanda and Kate are right. You do have a cheerful disposition. As your mama did. You should be good for me."

I stood up. "May I come in and see you tomorrow?"

"You may. And the day after. And soon, hopefully, I will go for a ride with you. I'm beginning to find the very thought of it intriguing."

"Good," I exclaimed. "Rest now, Auntie. I'm going to examine the paintings in my room to see if one might have been done by David Martin. If so, I'll bring it downstairs tomorrow and show it to David Lathrop."

◆ Five ◆

I didn't though. Not right away. Kate was awaiting me outside my aunt's room and told me Wanda would like me to dine with her in her suite.

"Does that mean Calvin will have to eat alone?" I asked.

"Calvin hasn't returned from the village," Kate informed me. "He may even have gone into the city. It's lonely here for him, Miss."

I nodded. "I wonder how such a handsome gentleman can stand it here. It's so isolated and my aunt never entertains."

"That's true," Kate admitted. "But I'm sure your aunt pays him and Wanda as well as she does me. He has no expenses here, no more than Wanda and I have, and one day—when your aunt no longer needs us—you know what I mean, Miss. Well, we'll have our little nest egg and no worries."

And so I found myself in Wanda's suite, which was quite ornate and flamboyant. Heavily fringed Spanish shawls were thrown over a chaise and two settees that were in the sitting room. Smaller shawls were thrown over the myriad chairs in the room. A table was set before the fireplace, which was burning and sent a welcome warmth into the room. Somehow, the house seemed to have a coldness that penetrated one's clothes.

However, in the very center of the room was a small round table covered with a green velvet cloth. That was also fringed, and its bottom edge touched the floor. There was nothing on the table except a glass ball on a round base. It wasn't very large, but it was crystal clear and almost seemed to glow with light. I wondered if this was the room Kate had warned me to stay out of. It couldn't be since she'd seemed pleased that I would dine with Wanda.

When I asked if Kate didn't dislike having to carry trays of dishes upstairs, Wanda informed me that there was a dumbwaiter that was concealed in an arched alcove in the hall.

Wanda was wearing a black sequined gown with enormous sleeves, which were also sequined. A turban covered her head. It was caught up in the front with a large, blue-faceted pin that caught both the glow of the fire and the lamplight and sent prisms of colored light about the room. She thanked me graciously when I complimented her on her appearance.

"I feel I should have dressed," I said. "You look stunning."

"Nonsense, my dear," she replied. "You did a very brave thing getting up today. There'll be time enough for dressing."

"It wasn't brave. The muscle pain seems to be lessening with each passing minute."

"Nonetheless, I feel you should not go into New York City as you had planned."

"I must go. I want my aunt to be completely reassured about the state of my health."

"She would never consent to your going," Wanda argued.

"Then she'll know nothing about it until I return. Unless, of course, it couldn't be managed without her knowing."

Wanda said, "I'm sure Calvin has the envelope ready. He usually does that a few days prior to whenever he or I deliver it."

"You don't really mean deliver it, do you?"

"Yes. Because that is what we do."

"And you've never seen the gentleman retrieve it?"

"Our orders are not to linger. Those are your orders too, my dear."

"I know."

A knock on the door prevented further conversation. Wanda opened it and Kate wheeled in a serving table. Once again, the aroma of good food teased my appetite as she uncovered the dishes.

There was roast chicken, giblet stuffing, mashed potatoes, gravy, rolls, vanilla cream pie, and coffee. She placed the food on the table, told us she hoped we would enjoy it, and departed. I knew I would. Wanda held my chair for me until I was seated. She hooked the cane on the back of a chair nearby, then sat down opposite me.

We wasted no time on conversation. I realized suddenly that I hadn't eaten since breakfast. When I told her, she replied she had had nothing but coffee since our dinner the evening before.

However, once we had a few mouthfuls, we did start to talk. I began it, once again with David as the topic of conversation. I asked Wanda if she had met him in the village.

"I never even heard of the gentleman until he rescued you from the rockslide. I'm grateful he was nearby."

"I'm sure everyone is."

"Calvin asked me to give you his best wishes for a rapid recovery. He had to perform a few errands in the village."

I said, "I can't help but wonder how Calvin can live here."

Wanda looked surprised by my statement. "What do you mean?"

"He's comparatively young. And very handsome."

She laughed. "So you noticed."

"One would have to be blind not to. I should think that for someone like him, this would be the end of the world."

"Not quite," Wanda said. "Calvin likes beauty and luxury. He has all that here and few responsibilities."

"Doesn't the running of this household entail great responsibility? That is, if he does it."

"He does," Wanda assured me. "And most competently."

"Another thing I wonder about is Kate. How can she do all she does? I mean, keeping up this house."

"She doesn't really. Calvin and I make our own beds. She makes yours and your aunt's. Every Monday a corps of workers comes here from a town a few miles away. I already told you why. Calvin has the duties of each one listed. They've been coming for years and each one knows his or her chores."

"I won't be here Monday," I said regretfully.

"You should be glad. They don't waste a moment. I usually stay with your aunt until they are ready to clean her room. At which time we adjourn to the suite you are now using."

"So that's why it's so spotless."

"Nothing is left untouched by either feather duster,

scrub brush, or polishing cloth. The closets are also cleaned. Once a month the clothes, boxes, shoes, and whatever else is in them are brought out and the room aired. Even the closed rooms are cleaned."

"I know one closet it hasn't been done to," I said.

Wanda looked puzzled a moment, then smiled and nodded. "Your mama's. Your aunt won't allow that to be touched."

"Didn't she know the room would acquire a musty odor? Even the clothes?"

"One thing you have to learn, my dear, is that I am an employee here. Just as Calvin and Kate are. We can't disobey. However, I will tell you that whenever I could I would go in there and open the window and closet door."

"I mean no offense, Wanda, but it couldn't have been very often."

"It wasn't. Your aunt dislikes being alone."

"She told me. It just seems a shame that those clothes were left in there to rot."

"I know what you mean. Your aunt ordered the wardrobe for your mama just as she did for you before you came here."

"Mama's should be thrown out."

"I agree. I thought, at first, your aunt wanted to keep them as a memento. But with the passage of years, I believe she kept them because they added to her feeling of guilt."

"Why is she so bent on torturing herself this way?"

"I have asked myself that question many times through the years. The only answer I come up with is that she feels each of those individuals would be alive today if it hadn't been that they were in this house at her request."

"Even Libby Innis?"

Wanda nodded. "She wanted to get to know her before adopting her."

I smiled and Wanda asked, "What do you find so amusing?"

"My aunt has the same thought regarding me."

Wanda dismissed that with an airy wave of her hand. "Nonsense, Celeste. You're her niece. She loves you."

"She does not love me." I felt no disloyalty making such a statement because I am sure my aunt would have said the same thing had Wanda been present.

Wanda appeared shocked by my statement. "Why do you say that?"

It was my turn to smile. "She told me she didn't, and couldn't because she scarcely knew me. She brought me here in the hope that she could grow to love me."

"I would say that her reaction to your accident is proof she already feels a deep fondness for you."

"Did she love Libby Innis?"

"Of course not. Libby was a servant."

"Since my aunt and uncle were going to adopt her, that shouldn't be important."

"I'm sure it wasn't, yet I don't believe your aunt regarded her with affection. In time, no doubt, she would have, but she was mourning the loss of her husband. I think she completely forgot about the adoption."

"It sounds logical. I think that has increased my aunt's guilt regarding Libby. This overwhelming culpability she feels regarding the three deaths doesn't make sense. Each one was accidental." I paused as a sudden question came to mind. "Or were any of the deaths suspicious?"

"Oh no," Wanda said fervently. "The only question asked, and that was by Calvin and me, was what caused each one to want to go downstairs."

"It is strange," I agreed. "Certainly, it has had a devastating effect on my aunt."

"It has ruined her life. I fear if it hadn't been that she still had you to look after, her mind would have cracked when Nora Martin met with her accident."

"She really didn't have to look after me." I spoke in loyalty to Papa, whom I know now felt cheated when my aunt took over the responsibility and expense of clothing and educating me.

"I know what you mean. But please don't resent what she did. You must understand she was trying desperately to make up for the loss of your mother. If she thought you felt a trace of resentment toward her, I dare not think what she might do."

"What do you mean?"

Wanda pushed her chair back and stood up. "I will tell you something in the strictest confidence. First, you must promise you will never divulge this to anyone."

"I promise."

"Your aunt tried to take her own life after Nora's death."

I was too shocked to reply.

"I caught her in the act of mixing a large quantity of a sleeping draught. She ran into the bathroom and locked the door before I could reach her, but fortunately. in her haste, she dropped the glass. It fell on a small rug and didn't break, but the liquid spilled out."

"Does Dr. Carney know?"

"Only two people knew. Your aunt and me. She begged me not to tell anyone, even Dr. Carney. I told her I would not if she gave her word she would never do it again. She swore she would not. I trust her. I am hoping your presence here will eventually raise her spirits. Just stay away from that walk along the cliff."

"Be assured I will," I said. "I can see now why she is so mixed up in her thinking. Because she *is* mixed up, Wanda."

"Yes. And I don't know of anyone who can help her but you."

Wanda walked over to the crystal ball and stared down at it. I said, "Do you think that sort of thing helps my aunt?"

"What sort of thing?"

"The crystal ball."

"I think if I had used it more often, I might have prevented those accidents."

"Doesn't my aunt care about the crystal ball?"

"Oh yes. But she likes astrology better. Sometimes tarot."

"Why?"

"Because I see mostly good things for her in those fields. Though I don't hold them in the same esteem as the crystal ball." She walked back to the table and looked down at me. "Have you forgotten what I saw in the crystal ball regarding you?"

"Yes," I replied honestly. "I've completely forgotten."

"Then I'll refresh your memory. I saw you lying down, your features filled with fear. There was a figure towering over you who seemed to be menacing you."

"The rockslide," I exclaimed. "The figure towering over me must have been David. Yet he wasn't menacing me."

"No," Wanda mused. "He brought you back here."

"I did see a figure at the top of the cliff," I told her. "So did David. At least I thought I did. Could that have been the one who was menacing me? Was the rockslide man-made? David seemed to think so."

"A pity he couldn't have got up there."

"He did later, but could find nothing to support his be-lief."

"It sounds incredible."

"You said you believe in the crystal ball."

"I do. And though I'm shocked to learn the rockslide might not have been accidental, I'm relieved to know Mr. Lathrop wasn't the villain."

"Why should you be?"

"Kate says he's a very likable young man."

"He is," I agreed.

"She also said you seemed to regard him as someone more than just a gentleman who came to your rescue."

I gave a negative shake of my head. "Kate must be a romanticist. I like David. But that's it."

"What you're saying is you would have to get to know him better."

"Not exactly, Wanda. Just now I would like to help my aunt. She is uppermost in my mind. She needs help. I want to see if I can't be the one to bring her out of this depression she's been in for so many years."

Wanda's hand rested lightly on my shoulder. "I'm pleased to hear you say that. Calvin and Kate will be also. But remember one thing, Celeste. You're young. If you do not succeed, you must leave this house or it will destroy you as it has your aunt. There are times when I think it is the house."

"Why do you stay then?"

"I've already told you. Besides. I've grown fond of your aunt through the years. I couldn't leave now. Nor would your aunt leave this house. I think you already know that."

"Yes. Not only the house, but the mausoleum."

"Very true." Wanda walked back to the table where the crystal ball sat. "It's a magnificent tomb. You'll agree once you've seen it."

"I've already seen it."

She was surprised by my revelation. "When?"

"The day I came here. Zeffrey was there. It was from him that I learned my aunt and uncle were going to adopt his niece."

"That man seems to be everywhere." Irritation tinged Wanda's voice.

"Where was he when that rockslide occurred?"

My question startled her. "I have no idea."

"He wasn't in the house. Kate told me that in my bedroom."

"Zeffrey and his wife worshiped Libby. I was surprised they would let her do domestic work. Not only because she was so beautiful, but she was also delicate. She seemed almost like a sprite. Ethereal."

"Didn't she want to work here as a maid?"

"Oh yes. Your uncle used to bring her into his study and have her read to him. He was preparing her for the life of a lady. She read all the classics. One night a week she dined with us. She performed beautifully because she had been tutored beforehand by him as to which fork or spoon to use for a particular dish. Your uncle was very proud of his student. That is how he referred to her. He was teaching her all the social graces. There is a portrait of him in the large library—the room he favored—above the fireplace. Mr. Martin, the artist who lived above here, painted it."

"David Lathrop has rented the place."

"I'm glad it's being occupied. Perhaps he will purchase it. This is a scenic area. Perfect for an artist. It would help people forget that Nora Martin lived there."

"I wish the townspeople didn't bear my aunt such enmity."

"So do I. It's bad enough for her to blame herself, but to have the villagers against her makes her plight more desperate."

I shifted myself sideways in the chair and reached for my cane. "Thanks for inviting me to dine with you, Wanda. I can't believe it's after six o'clock."

"I suggest you exercise a little in the hallway, then retire. I'm going to visit your aunt. Kate is there now. I'll send her to help you undress."

"I'm improving so rapidly I believe I won't need any help. Or if I do, I'll not need it after tomorrow."

"I believe you, though I know Calvin won't permit you to make the journey to New York City alone. Either he or I will accompany you. He will make the decision since you're bent on going."

With the flat of both hands on the table, I pushed myself to a standing position and reached for my cane. Wanda nodded encouragement and walked with me to the door. Her sequined gown sent slender shafts of light all over the room, serving to brighten my spirits. It seemed almost prophetic, as if things would now take a turn for the better. I expressed my thought to Wanda.

She smiled and said, "Let us hope you are right, my dear."

She moved briskly down the corridor to my aunt's room, tapped lightly on the door and entered, closing it soundlessly behind her. It took me almost five minutes to cover the same distance and enter my room. I couldn't believe the exhaustion that overcame me. Much as I wanted to examine the oils that hung on the walls, I had to ease myself into a chair by the window and rest for a half hour. There was little daylight left, but what there was let me feast my eyes on the beautiful grounds and gardens, which were a riot of color.

Finally I got to my feet again. still tired, but determined to check every oil in the room. I found none in the sitting room bearing the name Martin, and I moved on into the bedroom. Kate had already lit the lamps and I had no difficulty viewing the paintings. so I continued my search. I finally came upon one that wasn't very large, but which featured a girl and boy seated side by side on a swing that hung from a large branch of a tree.

The girl was pretty and she seemed to be giggling. The boy was also smiling. I started to smile back when I noticed something that made me catch my breath. The little boy had dimples. The painting was signed in the right-hand corner. The signature was D. Martin. David Martin. Was Lathrop really David's last name? If not, why would he lie? Could it be his father who died first and his mother had remarried a gentleman who adopted the children? Yet the young lady who had been the third victim of the stairs was named Nora Martin.

My thoughts were confused. I couldn't make sense out of it and I had no idea of how I could find out. Why would David tell me his last was Lathrop when it was Martin? If he deceived me, there had to be a reason. But first of all, I had to find out if he had lied about his identity. I hadn't the faintest notion of how to go about it, but I was determined to do so the first thing tomorrow.

Suddenly I was filled with fatigue and I felt a great

sense of relief when I recognized Kate's tap on the door. I called to her to come in.

She regarded me carefully, then motioned me to the side of the bed. She helped me out of my dress, unbuttoned my shoes, and slipped them off. I sat there until she returned with my nightdress and negligee, which she laid across the foot of the bed.

"I know you're exhausted, so I won't waste time talking. But I just want to say I found your aunt much better after your visit."

"It was pleasant being with her, though I hope I didn't tire her."

"You didn't. Mr. Calvin just returned. He asked about you and hopes you will allow him to take you for a drive tomorrow if you feel up to it."

"I'm certain I will and I'm rather excited at the thought of it."

"Don't let him keep you out too long. The roads are bumpy and full of holes, though he's a good driver and will be most considerate."

I asked Kate to put out the lamps except for the one by my bed. I wanted to do a little thinking before I settled down to sleep. She wished me a good night's rest and carried out her duties.

I lay there quietly, still puzzled by the resemblance of David Lathrop to the little boy in the painting. I wouldn't have thought so much of it except for the dimples. I still carried a vivid picture of David's in my mind.

Kate returned to the arched doorway and asked if I was certain there was nothing I wanted. I assured her there wasn't. Almost as an afterthought she said, "I just had an idea of a ride you might take."

"Where?" I asked.

"To return Mr. Lathrop's notebook. It has to be his. It might be important to him."

"Of course, Kate," I exclaimed. "Good night."

"Good night, Miss."

I don't know if she noticed the sudden elation in my voice at her mention of the notebook, which I'd completely forgotten about. I couldn't wait to hear the door close so that I could examine it. I let a few moments pass, then shifted my position carefully, in deference to the aches that still plagued me, so that I could open the drawer in the night table. It moved smoothly and I reached in and took out the notebook. Without a thought as to the propriety of what I was doing, I slipped the elastic off and opened the cover. Inside was the inscription *David Martin.*

So he *had* lied to me. Why? Should I examine the contents of the pages? I felt I had a right since he had been dishonest with me. Right or wrong, I was going to examine it. The first few pages contained notes regarding oils and canvases he wished to purchase, plus comments concerning areas that were picturesque and ideal to paint. Needless to say, I was disappointed at what I found, and I riffled through the remainder of the pages. Halfway through the book I saw more writing. Not very hopeful, I went back to those pages. Though I was shocked at what I read, I was rewarded for my efforts.

The page was headed *Linden Gardens.* Beneath was a list of each occupant. It began with my aunt, identifying her as the owner. Next was Wanda, a few words outlining her duties. Calvin was third. Once again, a brief resume of his duties as secretary and organizer of the household. Kate followed. Zeffrey and his wife were listed near the bottom of the page. Her name was Hester. Though Zeffrey's place in the household was described, the only thing following her name was a question mark. On the next page I found Dr. Carney's name, which was followed only by the notation "family physician." The final name was mine, identifying me as Emma von Linden's niece.

There were several questions written below my name, each one listed numerically. I read them aloud, though I kept my voice low.

1. Why is she here?
2. Could the rockslide have been meant for me?
3. Was she used as a lure?
4. What motive could aunt have had for such wanton murders of three young ladies—one her sister?
5. Is Emma von Linden mentally ill? (If so, she should be put away before she does more harm.)

There was no further question in my mind. David Lathrop was really David Martin, the brother of Nora Martin. He did not believe her death to be accidental. He did not believe any of the deaths were accidental. Why would he doubt? There was just one reason. My aunt! He believed her to be mentally ill. He also believed her to be the most logical suspect in the murder of the three victims.

I could not believe it. I would not believe it. The more I thought about the situation, the more I believed his suspicions to be preposterous. He had deliberately sought to gain entry to this house. and I had presented him with an opportunity. Since he believed the rockslide might have been meant for him, I could not suspect he had set that up as a way to make my acquaintance and pretend he had saved my life. He had. There was no doubt of it. He was also guilty of deception. He was a devious person and I didn't want to have anything further to do with him. I certainly would take advantage of Calvin's invitation to go for a drive. I would use the opportunity to return David's notebook along with a note, informing him I had taken the liberty of reading its contents and I did not wish him to call on me again.

Tired as I was, I rose from my bed and went to the writing table, where I had already placed my correspondence paper and envelopes. I gave careful thought to what I would put on paper. I decided to make it formal, for the short-lived friendship would now come to an abrupt end.

Dear Mr. Lathrop:

Fortunately for me, this notebook dropped out of your sweater pocket when you escorted me to my suite this morning after breakfast. I am sorry I tore the pocket of your sweater, though had I not done so, I might never have known of your deceit.

I was shocked to read the contents of this small book. It is bad enough for you to suspect my aunt of murder. It was equally deceitful of you to use me to gain entry into my aunt's residence. Be assured I wish to have nothing further to do with you.

Make no attempt to see me or to come to Linden Gardens. You would be wasting your time now that I have discovered your little game of playing detective. Believe me, sir, there is no cause for you to do so. I hope you will take leave of these parts as soon as possible. Should you attempt to gain the good graces of any other member of this household, I shall expose you for the fraud you are.

This is the first time I have ever read any confidential matter belonging to another. However, because of your guilt, I feel there is no need for an apology.

Sincerely,

I signed my name in full and slipped the letter into an envelope. I removed the stationery from the box and placed the notebook and my letter in it. I slipped the elastic that had held the notebook closed around the box. I would not reveal Mr. Martin's deceit to Calvin. I caught myself up sharply on that. I would have to continue to think of him as Mr. Lathrop. I doubted very much he would remain in these parts once he knew I was aware of what he was up to. He hadn't rented the house at all, he owned it, since he was now the sole survivor of his family. He would not have to leave, but I was sure his pride would force him to.

Certainly, I had given him short shrift in the letter. Had he suspected anyone else of murder but my aunt—timid, gentle, and guilt-laden because of the dreadful deaths those three women had suffered—I might not have been so outraged. And one of those women had been my mother. If anyone had a right to be suspicious. it was I—or Papa. I was certain he had never believed that Mama's death had been anything other than accidental. His resentment toward my aunt was based solely on the fact that he felt Mama's first loyalty should have been to me. He believed that had she refused my aunt's request to come. she would be alive today. But at the thought that Mama could have been murdered in this house—and by her own sister—I gave a rapid shake of my head. I wished I hadn't, for it started throbbing again. I left the box on the writing table and returned to my bed. I was so exhausted, my muscles were beginning to protest. Despite the pain, I fell into a deep sleep.

◆ Six ◆

Calvin lifted me gently into the carriage, moved around the horses, and raised himself with the grace of an athlete into the seat. He picked up the reins, urged the animals into motion, and we proceeded down the drive.

He had mentioned two or three different drives we might take, but I asked him to take me to the Martin residence.

To my surprise, Calvin said. "Mr. Lathrop introduced himself at the Inn yesterday. I thanked him for all he did for you."

"I'm grateful too," I said.

Calvin turned the horses out onto the road, then gave me an amused side-glance. "Kate tells me he made quite an impression on you. I would imagine it was the other way around. You're a comely miss, you know."

"Mr. Lathrop was only doing his duty. Kate read too much into it."

I suppose I sounded rather prim because Calvin's tone became mocking as he said, "Oh, come now, Celeste, you must admit you found David had a certain appeal."

"Are you on a first-name basis with him?" I asked, still keeping my tone formal.

"Do you disapprove?" he asked, his tone still mocking.

"I have no feeling at all on the matter," I said. "I am merely returning an article that belongs to him. It dropped out of his pocket yesterday when he visited me."

"Don't tell me you were able to bend down and pick it up," Calvin said.

"No. Kate did. Since it had his name on it, there is no doubting the identity of the owner."

"You're quite right. Do you suppose he's missed it?"

"Quite possibly. It contains a list of paints and brushes

he had to purchase. Also, places he considers ideal to paint. He must prefer doing landscapes."

"I like street scenes of cities. Paris is my preference, with the rain-soaked streets reflecting the buildings and pedestrians."

"You are really a cosmopolite at heart."

He nodded. "You could say that. I would love to travel around the world."

"Why did you never persuade my aunt to do so?"

"That would be in bad taste."

"I disagree. My aunt is lonely. The house is beautiful, but it has such unhappy memories for her. I'm amazed she has retained her sanity living there."

"I agree with you, Celeste. Also, I must say that Wanda tried to get her to travel, but was unsuccessful. She will not leave that house."

"Is she deliberately punishing herself?"

"If she isn't, the villagers are doing a pretty good job of punishing her. She is completely unacceptable to them."

"Do you suppose I will be?"

"The only way to find out is to attempt to get acquainted. Your mother overcame their animosity. Unfortunately, before she could bring your aunt back into the fold, so to speak, she was killed by a fall down the stairs."

"As was Nora Martin."

"She also had made progress in the brief time she was here."

"You mean with the villagers."

"Yes."

"Just how?"

"First of all, by making the church bazaar a very big thing this year. She persuaded your aunt to have a small circus brought to the village. It was quite spectacular and everyone loved it."

"They didn't mind that my aunt bore the expense?"

"No. Nora was such a dear, lovable young woman, she just made them like it. It lasted an entire week. The final night she persuaded your aunt to attend. Many of the villagers came up to her and thanked her. Both Wanda and I thought it would be a new beginning for her. We were as elated as Nora."

"If Nora lived, would my aunt have invited me here?"

"I can't answer that. I'm not certain your aunt could either."

The horses were moving at a lazy pace, but my question so startled Calvin that he jerked the reins and the horses broke into a rapid trot. He gave his attention to them until he had quieted them, then he turned to me.

"I'm sorry about that. I hope you didn't get bounced around too much."

"I didn't. I'm just about well, you know. I ache only here and there."

"Nonetheless, I will accompany you tomorrow. That is, if you still insist on going. There's no need for it, you know. Either Wanda or I can do it. Your aunt certainly would not object under the circumstances."

"I wouldn't mind company, but it doesn't seem right for me to travel with a gentleman."

"I would say it is quite all right, so long as he is a gentleman. Also, should you trip or lose your balance, I could catch you. I don't have much faith in Wanda's capabilities in that respect."

"I wouldn't want her to," I said. "I do want to go."

"Then you have no choice but to accept me as your escort. We'll be back the same day—long before dark."

"Very well, Calvin. I am truly appreciative. I'm also appreciative you're taking me to Mr. Lathrop so I may return his notebook."

"We're about there. It's a pretty drive."

"It's enchanting." And it was. The road was narrow though not as rutted as I had feared. There were both shrubbery and trees on either side. The trees were so high they formed an arch, giving welcome shade, for the day was hot and the sun high. But I was quite comfortable and Calvin appeared to be so in his white linen suit with flowing black tie.

"Aren't you lonely here, Calvin?"

His laughter was deep and hearty. "Not at the moment, fair lady."

"I wasn't trying to flirt with you," I said, feeling color flood my face.

"I'm only teasing, Celeste. You look enchanting when you blush."

"I was serious. You just don't seem the type to live in such isolation."

"When you get to know me better, you'll realize I'm quite happy here. It's true I go to the city from time to time and enjoy the pleasures one finds there, but I always love the feeling of serenity that envelopes me when I return to Linden Gardens. I should say about you what you've just said about me. You're so young and vital, I can't imagine why you would want to spend a summer here."

"I suppose because I like the luxury of it also. I never had it before."

"Your mother appreciated it, but I recall her saying that the little flat she shared with you papa and you was her heaven on earth."

"I probably wouldn't have understood that before I came here, but I do now."

"You mean you're not remaining with us?"

"Only until I can bring my aunt out of that valley of depression she is lost in."

"I wish you luck. I believe you can do it." He guided the horses into a drive that was quite overgrown with weeds. "This is the Martin residence. It's quaint, but architecturally beautiful."

Calvin was right. It was both, and resembled a church more than it did a house. It was constructed of vertical strips of upright boards with external insulation strips. Each side was gabled, as were the windows that projected beyond the low roof. Probably the servants' quarters. Or had been when Mr. and Mrs. Martin resided there. What made the edifice stand out was the decorative woodwork, which had been cut in the form of grape leaves. It was appended to each of the gables. Above the rectangular windows and doors was more of the wooden tracery in the form of a hood, making the tall windows and entrance door look arched. The entrance projected in the form of a vestibule and the protective roof had a grape-leaf frieze, giving it a further air of refinement.

"Attractive, isn't it?" Calvin was already urging the horses up the drive. They didn't seem too pleased by the weeds and shrubbery in the drive, which were so high they scratched their underbellies.

I nodded assent, still too impressed by the uniqueness of the architecture to speak. The door opened and David, or rather, Mr. Lathrop, as I would now address him, stepped onto the miniature entranceway. He shaded his eyes against the sun to make identification of his visitors easier. When he recognized us, he gave a whoop of joy and bounded off it, onto the ground, ignoring the two narrow steps. He was wearing white trousers and a blazer over a silk turtleneck sweater. He wasn't handsome, but with those dimples, his smile was irresistible.

Calvin called out a greeting, using the familiar term of David. David returned the greeting. Calvin stopped the horses and David turned his attention to me.

"How nice of you and Calvin to call, Celeste." His arms extended and his outstretched palms awaited mine.

"We didn't come to call, Mr. Lathrop," I said quietly. "Are you aware you are missing a notebook?"

"Yes," he replied. "Did you find it?"

"Kate did. I suppose you recall escorting me to my suite yesterday after breakfast."

"So I did," he exclaimed. "Good of you to bring it to me, though I'd have picked it up later. I was going to stop by this afternoon to inquire about your health."

"My health is quite all right," I said. "The aches and pains are fast abating."

"Good," he exclaimed heartily. "Won't you at least come in and have some lemonade? It's freshly made."

I'd have loved some and Calvin had already blurted acceptance, but I expressed regret, saying we had other plans for the day. I felt a malicious pleasure as David's eyes flicked momentarily to Calvin, then back to me.

I extended the box. "This is yours, Mr. Lathrop. You'd not have lost it had I not grabbed your sweater when I lost my balance. I apologize for tearing the pocket of your sweater. I'll gladly replace it."

My manner was so formal, David sobered. "I'm glad it wasn't lost either, Miss Abbott. I set great store by what is in that book. As for the sweater, I already sewed the pocket."

"It seemed like a lot of balderdash to me," I said coolly. "I'm referring to what was in the book. Please, Calvin, we must be getting on or we'll be late."

"Late for what, Miss Abbott?" David folded his hands across his chest and eyed me cynically. "Or do you know, Calvin?"

Calvin's glance switched from David to me. "Frankly, no. But if I'm included in Celeste's plans for today, I'm delighted."

"I should think you would be." David's coldness now matched mine. "I gather I'm not welcome at Linden Gardens, Celeste."

"It's not my home," I said. "I'm a guest of my aunt. You should ask her."

"I will wait until I receive an invitation from you," he said.

I said, "My aunt is the only one who issues invitations, Mr. Lathrop—or Calvin does, when she requests it."

"Which she never does, from what I gather in town," he replied.

"You are insolent, Mr. Lathrop. Please, Calvin, let's go."

Calvin gave David a salute with his hand, which David returned. I realized Calvin thought it amusing. David did not. I warned myself to stop thinking of him as David Lathrop. He had made an utter fool of me. I had played right into his hands.

I sat stiffly erect until we regained the road, retracing the course we took. Calvin maintained a discreet silence until we were well beyond Mr. Lathrop's property.

"I hope you won't be angry with me, Celeste," he said, a note of apology in his voice, "but may I ask what David did to offend you?"

"He did absolutely nothing," I replied icily.

I didn't cast a glance Calvin's way, but I could well imagine the puzzlement expressed on his features. I was assured of it with his next question.

"Then why did you treat him so rudely?"

"I wasn't rude."

"You weren't?" He still sounded nonplussed. "Cold, then."

"I wasn't cold either. I'm afraid you are just like Kate. Reading something into my feelings for Mr. Lathrop that doesn't exist."

"Kate told me you were calling him David."

"Kate talks too much. I would be pleased if you would stop asking questions. Or at least stop asking them about David. Or Mr. Lathrop. I do not expect to see him ever again."

"I gathered that from your terse comments. I believe you convinced him."

"I hope so. If you won't be bored, will you please take me for a ride to the village? I've not seen it yet."

"It will give me great pleasure. Just settle back in the seat because I'll let the horses have their head. It's a fairly long ride."

"Don't worry about me," I said. "It's a beautiful day, an elegant carriage, two magnificent bays, and a handsome escort."

Calvin gave me a side-glance.

"I mean every word of it," I said.

"My God," he exclaimed. "You're smiling."

"I do smile," I said. "I just haven't felt much like indulging in light-heartedness these past few days. I had a rather unpleasant experience, in case you forgot."

"I haven't forgotten," he said. "You weathered it beautifully. I am curious, though, as to how David incurred your displeasure when you've seen him only once since your accident."

"The very fact that I did see him only once since the rockslide should be proof that it doesn't make sense to think he did anything to incur my displeasure."

Calvin gave in with, "Very well. I'll not mention him again."

"Thank you." I settled back and thoroughly enjoyed the ride to the village. It was exactly as Wanda had described it. The green was well-shaded and there were green benches for the strollers on the various flower-bordered paths. Some were already occupying them. All were decked out in their Sunday best. There was a bandstand in the very center of the green, with benches encircling it. I could imagine it was well patronized during the summer months.

Calvin assured me of it, saying, "You'll notice some of the seats are already taken. They come from miles around to hear these concerts. Your aunt is instrumental in getting some of the best bands in the East to come to Wilmot. She pays all their expenses."

"Certainly the villagers must be aware of it."

"I'm sure they are."

"Then how can they possibly treat her as they do?"

"I don't know, Celeste." Calvin's tone was almost sad. "You know what happened at Linden Gardens. Then there's Hester Innis."

"Zeffrey's wife?"

Calvin nodded. "She's been confined to a wheelchair since their niece fell down the stairs."

"Why?"

"No one knows. Doc Carney says it's beyond him.

Shock, I guess. They worshiped their niece. Of course, they expected your aunt and uncle to adopt her."

"I know. Wanda told me. I also discussed it with my aunt. What prompted my aunt and uncle to want to adopt her?"

He gave me a curious glance.

"Oh, please, Calvin. I'm not thinking that she would have cheated me out of my inheritance. I don't associate an inheritance with my aunt. You don't know me well, but as you get to know me better you will understand that."

"You are the most outspoken young lady I have ever known."

I couldn't help but smile. "Have you known many?"

"To be as frank as you—yes. A great many. Just because I live the life of a monk here, doesn't mean I do so when I go to New York."

"I will expect you to behave in a decorous fashion when you accompany me to New York tomorrow."

"You may be assured of that. It's business."

"Let's get back to Hester. I'd like to know more about her."

"There's little to know. She used to be the housekeeper at Linden Gardens until Libby was killed there. Since that night, Hester has been confined to a wheelchair."

"Where does she live?"

"In the village."

"Couldn't we pay a call on her?"

"I suppose we could, but it's highly unusual."

"I don't see why."

"It's not customary for the niece of the owner of Linden Gardens to pay a call on the wife of the coachman-gardener."

"Calvin Rosby, you sound like a snob."

"If I do, it's because I'm thinking of you."

"Zeffrey is employed by my aunt. I see nothing wrong with my paying his invalid wife a visit. My aunt is a compassionate woman. It is my opinion she would be pleased at the gesture."

"I hope so. I'm an employee of your aunt, you know."

"Does she make you account for every moment of your time away from Linden Gardens?"

"Certainly not. She isn't that type of lady."

"Then why tell her?"

He gave a resigned sigh. "Zeffrey might tell her. He

divides his time between his home and Linden Gardens. Since the death of his niece, he goes home each night to look after Hester."

"You mean in case she should become ill?"

"Yes."

"That's kind of him. With an invalid wife, I should think he would want to be close to her, should she need a doctor."

"I believe Hester's illness is more mental than physical. I wish you would reconsider it. You won't find the visit very pleasurable."

"I'll risk it. I'd like to meet her."

"Why?"

I thought of the question mark after Hester's name in David's notebook. I'd not give that as the reason. I didn't believe it was.

"Well?" Calvin prodded. "You must have one."

"I'm intrigued." I said the first thing that came to mind.

It seemed to satisfy Calvin. "I guess I have no alternative other than to take you," he said.

His tone was mildly scolding, but he softened it with a smile. We had traversed one side of the green. He rounded the end, and halfway down, turned into a side street that was most attractive, with white fences surrounding each of the yards. The houses all seemed to be freshly painted and the yards were a riot of color, as if each occupant tried to outdo the other in gardening. Calvin drove to the very end.

The house he stopped in front of was a little larger than the others. The curtains were lace and seemed quite expensive.

"The interior will be a surprise. It is expensively furnished—done by your aunt almost as a gesture of penance for Libby's tragedy."

"I asked you a question you didn't answer."

"I've forgotten what it was. Please ask it again."

"Why were my aunt and uncle interested in adopting Libby?"

"I thought you might have known."

"I have no idea. I didn't even know of Libby's existence until I came here."

"I don't know if your aunt would want you to know this, so I must ask that you not mention it to her. If she should confide in you, please pretend ignorance. It is, understandably, a very sensitive issue with her."

"In heaven's name, Calvin, tell me," I exclaimed impatiently.

"I wish we hadn't taken this drive. I'm getting far too involved."

"You were going to reveal the reason my aunt and uncle wished to adopt Libby."

"I'm not at all certain your aunt was in favor of it."

"The reason for the adoption, Calvin. Please!"

"Your aunt was incapable of having a child," Calvin spoke under his breath. His guilt at disclosing the information was evident in both his voice and his eyes, which bore a look of resentment as they regarded me. "And now, Celeste, I swear I will not answer another question."

"I shan't ask any more. There's no time, anyway."

"Just time enough to prepare yourself for Hester Innis."

"I'm eager to meet her. And I'm very sorry she is confined to a wheelchair."

"I wouldn't mention that to her if I were you."

"I'm not stupid."

"No," he replied, "you're not stupid. Just burdened with an overactive curiosity."

"I'm sorry to learn that about my aunt."

Calvin didn't reply until he'd jumped down from the carriage, moved around it with ease, and lifted me down.

I thought he hadn't heard my statement, but with his hands still lightly holding my waist, he looked down into my eyes and said. "I'm sorry I had to tell you."

"Was it only my uncle's idea to adopt . . . ?"

He broke in with, "No more questions, Celeste. We're going in now to visit Hester—uninvited. I hope she will overlook our breach of etiquette."

"Being shut in as she is, I imagine she must welcome visitors. Even unexpected ones."

"We'll see." Calvin didn't sound too confident, but I wasn't the least bit fearful. I felt a great deal of sympathy for Hester because of the loss of her niece and what it had done to her. I was also curious to meet the wife of Zeffrey, who was a strange and rather unappealing individual.

◆ Seven ◆

Calvin knocked firmly on the front door and, without the slightest hesitation, opened it. At my look of surprise, he gave an explanation under his breath. "I come here from time to time, and since she's in a wheelchair, I let myself in."

We walked along a carpeted hall that was spotlessly clean. The rooms were all on one floor, which made sense, since Hester was confined to a wheelchair. At the far end, I caught a view of the kitchen. Calvin caught my elbow lightly and guided me through a doorway on our right.

It was a parlor, beautifully furnished with green velvet upholstered furniture. The room was fairly large, with four windows. Two facing the front and two on the side, where a flower garden was in full bloom. One could tell at a glance that the lace curtains framing the windows were expensive. There was a great deal of bric-a-brac covering the tables. And attractive pictures covered the walls.

I had no idea Hester was in the room observing me as carefully as I was looking over the room. Not until she let out a scream.

"It's all right, Hester," Calvin said. "This is Celeste Abbott, your mistress's niece."

"She's not my mistress no more," Hester retorted. The harsh tone of her voice made it evident she had no use for my aunt.

"Come now, Hester," Calvin's tone was placating, "you know all that Miss Emma has done for you."

"She could never do enough," came the ungrateful reply. "And she knows it."

Calvin flashed me a look of "I told you." Regardless of the woman's physical disability, I felt I should speak a few words in defense of Aunt Emma.

"My aunt is a very compassionate lady," I said.

"You could well say that since you're going to inherit everything."

"Such a thought was not on my mind."

"Wasn't it now?" Her tone was malicious.

"No. I can understand your bitterness since you lost your niece. I am told she was a very beautiful girl."

"She was. You couldn't touch her for looks. I have a painting of her. One done by a gentleman who lived close to Linden Gardens."

"May I see it?" I asked.

"It's above my head." Her tone softened when she spoke of her niece.

I had to step farther into the room to view it. I couldn't help but exclaim aloud at the portrait. Libby Innis was the most beautiful young lady I had ever seen. Her hair was golden, her eyes blue and deep-set, making them seem even larger than they were. Her oval features were perfect, with high cheekbones and a beautifully shaped mouth. There was a half smile on her face that gave a strangely mature look to her girlish features. As if she had a secret or shared a secret with someone.

Her hair fell on her slender shoulders, which were bare, her peasant blouse having been pulled down on her arms.

"Did Mr. Martin paint her?"

"He did. Your uncle paid well for it. Your aunt gave it to me after she died, as well she should."

"Hasn't my aunt been kind to you and your husband?"

"She gave us this house and every stick of furniture in it."

"And you show her absolutely no gratitude?"

"Why should I when she killed our little girl. We raised her from a baby. We thought of her as ours. I couldn't have children anymore than your aunt could. I think she hated any woman who could. That's why she killed Libby."

"She did no such thing," I exclaimed indignantly.

"She did." Hester's voice rose shrilly. She wheeled her chair closer to me, extended her arm full length and pointed a bony finger at me. "Your mama came to see me. I told her she'd be next. And she was. Murdered by her own sister."

I was shocked and angered by her words.

"What horrible talk. You are a very bitter woman. And a most ungrateful one."

"Because your aunt gave me all this? What else could she do? She'd committed the greatest sin on earth. Murder."

"If you believe my aunt murdered your niece, why didn't you summon the constable and insist he arrest her?"

"Who would believe me?"

"Did you see her kill your niece? Did you see her kill my mama?"

"I wasn't in that house when your mama died. I was when my Libby died."

"Did you see my aunt push her down the stairs?" I exclaimed, my anger almost as great as Hester's.

"No. But I saw her standing at the head of the stairs—and my niece's lifeless body lying at the foot of the stairs." She looked up at me, nodding her head vindictively. "Your aunt knew what she did. It near killed me, seeing our baby dead. And your uncle responsible. It was done deliberate."

"First you say my aunt is responsible for the death of your niece. Then you say my uncle is. Which one committed the murder?"

"Both."

"My uncle was dead when your niece fell down the stairs."

"Only two months."

I turned to Calvin, who was eyeing Hester with open disgust. "Is that true?"

"Yes," he replied. "Hester, you're as bad as Miss Emma in keeping alive these sorrowful memories of Libby. She's dead. You must stop mourning her. You can't bring her back."

"You're right, Mr. Calvin. But I'll never let that woman forget."

"Suppose she stopped being so generous to you. There's no need for her to be, you know."

A smile spread across Hester's bony features. She gathered the silk robe she was wearing closer to her. I knew it was a gift from my aunt. Or was Hester free to purchase what she chose? Certainly she had no fear of my aunt. It was almost as if she had a hold over her and my aunt gave in to her every whim to keep her content. Only in that way would she keep her quiet.

"Come, Celeste, this is no place for you."

"I'm glad you came." Hester shrilled. "I screamed because I thought it was your mother. She came several times trying to win me over. I laughed at her as I am laughing at you. I told her what I told you. And I told her she would be the next to die. I knew it because she had a child. Now you will die because you are a healthy young woman and can bear a child. Your aunt never could. No more than I. But I didn't hate because of it. She did and sought vengeance. She got it. You'll be next. Mark my words. You'll be next."

Calvin's arm enclosed my shoulders and he urged me gently toward the door. "Good-bye, Hester. I'm going to tell Miss Emma about this. She may have second thoughts about continuing to spoil you."

"Tell her," she mocked. "Tell her. She'll do nothing. She wouldn't dare. I know Emma von Linden. Just as I knew her husband Eric von Linden. He died sudden too. They said a heart attack. I don't believe it. He wanted an heir and Emma couldn't give him one. My niece could have."

I slipped free of Calvin's arm and turned to face her. "What are you saying?"

"I said it. And you heard it. Have you ever heard the word divorce?"

I was too shocked and sickened by all I'd heard to reply. Calvin didn't need to urge me to go. I couldn't escape this house fast enough. I left it to her shrieks of, *"You'll be next. You'll be next. You'll be next."*

We were silent as we returned to the carriage. Not until we got under way did Calvin break the silence.

"I'm sorry you were subjected to that, Celeste. She's been a harridan ever since Libby's death."

"It was my fault. I insisted you take me there."

"Why not let me take you to dine at the Inn? The food there is quite good and members of the band are already in the grandstand. The music will drift through the open windows of the dining room. Since your aunt pays for the band, you ought to enjoy it."

"I couldn't eat, Calvin. I know it's late and you must be starved, but I couldn't eat. And the music would get on my nerves. I'm too upset."

"I understand. I'll get us back as soon as possible. Are you going to tell your aunt about Hester?"

"I'd like to, but I know it would only add to her misery."

"It would," Calvin admitted. "Hester has been a thorn in your aunt's side for years now."

"Is that why Zeffrey continues in her employ?"

"Yes. Although I admit he is extremely competent. The gardeners obey him because they respect his judgment and knowledge."

"Do you believe my aunt or uncle was responsible for Libby's death?"

"Of course I don't. Nor does anyone else except Hester."

"What about Zeffrey? He also told me I would be next."

"When did he tell you that?"

"The day of my arrival. He seemed to be awaiting me at the mausoleum. You told me about it and I decided to investigate. It is beautiful. I did think it strange that Libby was buried there. But I didn't give it further thought since I too have been the recipient of my aunt's generosity."

"As have Hester and Zeffrey. They had a modest place in the village. Your aunt had the house they now occupy built and furnished it completely. She also pays for a woman to come in and clean and cook for Hester."

"My aunt is really a prisoner in her castle."

"That's an excellent way of expressing it. The only way she could escape it is to move away. Why don't you try to persuade her to do it?"

"You know I could no more do that than you. She lives in the past. She still loves her husband, though after Hester's tirade, I don't understand why she allowed Libby to be buried there."

"I can give no reason other than that it is just another example of your aunt's generosity."

I nodded and suppressed a yawn. Calvin noticed.

"The ride was too long for you, Celeste. You look exhausted."

"I am tired. I'm also troubled by much of what Hester said."

"I didn't want you to go in there."

"I know. I wish you had been more firm."

"Had I known you longer, I would have been. You're a most appealing young lady. Also, stubborn and spirited. I must confess if I were younger—or you were older—I would do my best to engage your attentions. I would also be bold about making you forget about Hester and concentrate on me."

"At the moment, your words hold great appeal, even though I know you are merely being kind."

"I'm being honest. But I must remember I am an employee of your aunt. And you are a potential heiress."

"I wish people would stop talking like that. I'm beginning to hate the word."

"Whether you do or not, you cannot dispute the fact that it's true."

"I would like to think of you as a friend, but when you talk that way, you make it very difficult."

I was so weary I'd closed my eyes when we started back, but now I opened them. Calvin was regarding me with open admiration. I couldn't help but smile, for he made me forget for a few moments the ugly vilification Hester had subjected me to.

I reached over and rested my hand on his arm. "Will you be my friend?"

"I'm honored, Celeste. You must know how I regard you. Also, I trusted you enough to confide in you today."

"I'm grateful you did. It helped me to better understand my aunt's misery."

"I hope you don't believe what Hester said—about your aunt hating any young woman who could bear a child."

"Of course not. Hester is a very bitter person. She is well on the way to destroying herself. So is my aunt, though for a different reason, and I must do something to stop it."

"The quicker, the better."

I was relieved when we turned into the drive of Linden Gardens, for I felt burdened with fatigue. Zeffrey relieved Calvin of the surrey and Kate opened the door for us.

Her welcoming smile faded at the sight of me. "You overdid it, Miss."

"Perhaps," I admitted. "I'm going to lie down."

"It's after four. Wouldn't you like me to bring up a tray?"

"No, thank you, Kate. Not until I awaken."

"Very well, Miss."

She headed for the stairs, but I stopped her.

"No need for you to come up, Kate. I can manage quite well." I turned to Calvin who was also regarding me with concern. I gave him a reassuring smile and said, "I know you're famished. Forgive me for not accepting your invitation to dine in the village."

"It would not have been wise, Celeste. You're very pale."

"Sleep is all I need. I will journey to New York City with you tomorrow."

"Rest first. Then we'll decide."

I was too fatigued to bandy words, but I knew no argument would deter me from making the journey. It didn't take me long to undress, take down my hair, don my nightgown, and get into bed. Once there, I thought I would review the vitriolic words Hester had spoken in hatred of my aunt, but my exhaustion was so complete, sleep claimed me in a matter of minutes.

It was almost nine o'clock when I wakened. There was dim lamplight in the sitting room, but the bedroom was dark. I stretched lazily and when a few still-sore muscles protested, I let out a little cry.

"Ah, you finally woke up."

It was Kate's voice. She came to the door, a lighted lamp in her hand. She said no more until she had lit the two on the bureau and the one on my night table.

"You overdid it, Miss Celeste," she said. "I worried when you were away so long. I even thought you had met with an accident. Mr. Calvin is a fast driver."

"He was most considerate, Kate. We went visiting."

She cocked her head to one side and regarded me with puzzlement. "You went visiting?" she repeated.

I nodded. "Hester Innis."

She gave an indignant shake of her head. "I should think Mr. Calvin would have more sense than to take you there. She's a harridan, that one."

"You know her?"

"I've been there a few times. Only when your aunt ordered me to do so. When the holidays come around, I do extra cooking for the less fortunate ones in the village. I wouldn't consider Hester one of those, but she gets the same as the others. And never a thank-you."

"I think she gets much more than the others. At least, judging from her home and the expensive negligee she was wearing."

"I know what you mean, Miss. Your aunt spoils her. And gets nothing but abuse for thanks."

"Why does my aunt put up with her?"

"Because Hester has her convinced she is responsible for the death of Libby Innis."

"She told me my aunt murdered Libby." I made my tone disbelieving so Kate wouldn't think I'd been taken in by Hester.

"She tells everyone that."

"Why?"

"Because Hester found your aunt at the head of the stairway the night Libby fell down the stairs."

"Is there anyone who believes Hester?"

"The whole village believes her," Kate exclaimed indignantly. "It's a crying shame your aunt has had to put up with her."

"Why doesn't my aunt sell Linden Gardens and move away?"

"I guess she feels she deserves the hatred of the town. Also, there's her late husband. I understand she worshiped him."

"Who told you?"

"Both Miss Wanda and Mr. Calvin. Also, Dr. Carney. He doesn't believe your aunt guilty. Nor does the preacher—Reverend Gates."

"Does he come here to offer my aunt spiritual solace?"

"She won't let him. There would be trouble with the congregation."

"Yet she contributes to the church and to the town's social activities."

"Other than the Reverend, you're the only one who appreciates it. I hope you can bring her out of this malaise she's been in. But I don't know. It's been going on for too many years."

"I'll do my best," I said quietly. "And now I must tell you, Kate, I'm starved. I've not eaten since breakfast."

She let out a cry of dismay. "Forgive me, child. I'm bringing you up an omelet with some creamed chicken. And I made a chocolate mousse. Mr. Calvin was so hungry I thought he'd never stop eating. I was lucky to save a serving of mousse for you."

I smiled my appreciation and she went off to prepare my supper. I got out of bed and slipped into a negligee. For some reason, my thoughts turned to David and the notebook I had returned. I was still resentful concerning what I had read in his book about my aunt. He didn't know her or he would never have written such an observation. Yet I reminded myself that he had lost a sister who was in the prime of life. Hers had ended as abruptly as Libby's and Mama's. Were they accidents? For the first time, I questioned it.

Was Hester speaking the truth? Could my aunt have been so jealous and resentful that she murdered three young women because they could have children and she couldn't. Yet how could anyone know Libby was capable of procreation? Or Nora Martin? Mama, yes. But the other two were young maidens. Especially Libby. I didn't know Nora's age, but I was certain she was not married.

In a way, I wished I had not been so hasty in my condemnation of David, but the damage was done. Had I had my encounter with Hester before I read the contents of the notebook, I wondered if I would have been so harsh or bitter with him. Yet, I still could not entertain the idea that my aunt was capable of murder. I'd never consider that. But I could and should consider the fact that it was very coincidental that three young women, one scarcely out of her girlhood, could have suffered fatal falls down the same staircase.

Kate returned with a tray of food, told me to leave it outside the door when I finished, and left me to enjoy it. I had only half completed my meal when a soft tap sounded on the door. It opened and Wanda asked if she might come in.

"Please do, Wanda," I said.

She looked quite elegant in a flowing gown of green silk with gold threads woven through it. It trailed at least a foot behind her. The sleeves were so deep, they seemed to come out of the waistline of the gown. Her slippers were gold with rhinestone rosettes and they sparkled brilliantly. Truly, she was a stunning dresser. A turban of the same fabric as the dress covered her head. She never changed her earrings and so I associated her with the tiny tinkle of bells. They seemed appropriate, almost as if they were worn to announce her coming.

She picked up a small straight-backed chair that was just inside the door, carried it over to the table, and placed it opposite me. She studied me as she sat down.

"You look rested, but I imagine you won't have difficulty going back to sleep, will you?"

"No." I replied without the slightest hesitation, for I was still tired.

"Calvin told me you visited Hester. I wish he had refused to take you."

"When we came out of there, I wished he had, but now I'm glad he didn't. She's a very bitter woman."

"Also a vindictive one."

I nodded. "I wish my aunt would assert herself. Issue an ultimatum, so to speak."

"What do you mean?"

"Either Hester stops accusing my aunt of the death of Libby Innis immediately, or my aunt will cease contributing to her support."

Wanda thought a moment before she spoke. "I know how you feel, Celeste. However, I must say I feel it would be unwise."

"You are referring to the villagers and the animosity they already bear my aunt."

She nodded.

"Why should they?"

"Calvin should never have taken you there," she exclaimed.

"I disagree. But even if you are right, why do you say such a thing?"

"I shouldn't talk about this and I wouldn't if it weren't for Hester."

"About what?"

"Your uncle. You never met him."

"I never met my aunt until she came to my graduation."

"Which I persuaded her to do. I told her it was in the cards that she should make a short journey to meet one who held her in high regard."

"Meaning me, of course."

"Meaning you. I was clutching at straws. But I feared for her sanity after Nora Martin's death. You were all she had left."

"You know, of course, what Hester said about my aunt."

"The whole town knows."

"What a vicious person she is."

"My dear," Wanda spoke slowly, almost reluctantly, "you can't blame her completely. Nor can you blame the town completely. You see, Libby was with child when she fell down the stairs."

I had just taken a spoonful of mousse and had it halfway to my mouth when she revealed the shocking news.

Not that I thought any the less of Libby because of the revelation, but it was so unexpected. I set the spoonful of mousse down untouched and looked across the table at her, my eyes mirroring my disbelief.

"It's true," she said.

"Are you saying Libby was carrying on a romance with a young man in town?"

"She lived here. Your uncle tutored her. They spent hours together. The door to the library closed." She looked away, as if embarrassed by what she had told me.

"I can't believe it."

"It came as a shock," Wanda said. "No one would have known if Hester had kept quiet."

"Did she accuse my uncle of fathering her niece's unborn child?"

Wanda gave an affirmative nod. "Of course, your uncle was already dead when your aunt learned about Libby's condition. You may be assured it was Hester who told her. Your aunt refused to believe it until she confronted Libby, who stated it was true."

Wanda sighed and looked away. The only sound in the room was the ticking of the clock. I knew she was reluctant to complete the story, yet I had to know and so I broke the silence with a request for her to continue. A full minute must have passed before she turned to face me. Even then, she didn't speak.

"You *must* tell me, Wanda. How else can I help my aunt?"

"That revelation," she began and continued to speak very slowly, as if wanting to detail the past with complete accuracy, "following so quickly on the death of your uncle, was too much for Emma. She had a stroke. A mild one, but she never regained her zest for living. Up until then, she was active in social and church activities. She and your uncle were highly respected. Of course, the news of Libby's pregnancy did not get out until after her death. It was Hester who told about it, even though she swore she would keep quiet about it if your aunt buried Libby in the mausoleum and provided them with a home, plus all the comforts they deserved. Your aunt did so. The fact is, Hester doesn't have to do a thing."

"She can't in a wheelchair," I said remindfully. "Except spread malicious gossip."

"True," Wanda said flatly. "I mustn't be unfair. Whatever happened to her, she lost the use of her legs after Libby's death. I suppose it was the terrible shock she endured."

"Libby's pregnancy explains why she was buried in the mausoleum."

"Yes. Your aunt felt it only fair, although, as I already told you, Hester insisted on it, swearing she and Zeffrey would never tell anyone their niece had been seduced by Eric von Linden. I don't believe Zeffrey did."

"She's a vindictive woman."

"Calvin informed me he told you some of the story. I have told you the rest. You must not let your aunt know you have any knowledge of the situation that caused her depression. I believe that eventually she will speak of it to you. When she does, please pretend you had no prior knowledge of it. I am referring, of course, to the liaison between your uncle and Libby."

"Why did my aunt want Mama to come here?"

"She was frightened when Libby fell down the stairs and was killed. Frightened and filled with guilt. She felt God's punishment was directed at her. I tried to convince her she had done no wrong. That it was your uncle's sin. He had seduced a young, innocent girl."

"How did my aunt respond to that argument?"

"She said I was trying to make excuses for her. That she should have started adoption proceedings the day she learned of Libby's pregnancy. She didn't because she was both shocked and hurt that her husband would commit such a deed under this roof. Also, she still fears Libby threw herself down those stairs to end her shame. Unfortunately, there is no one to dispute it."

"Hester spoke of divorce."

"Your aunt told me your uncle mentioned it shortly before his death. She was stunned because he gave no specific reason for it. He did, of course, want an heir. One bearing his name, if not one of his bloodline. With Libby pregnant, he had what he desired. There was only your aunt standing in the way."

I couldn't finish my food after what I had just heard.

I said, "Did Mama know this?"

"If so, she didn't learn it from me. You are the only one I have ever told this to."

"Did Nora Martin know?"

"Not unless your aunt told her. Nora was a very easy-going young lady. Also, bright and cheerful. Your aunt liked having her around. I thought Emma had, at last, forgot her grief."

"In view of what happened to Nora, I can understand why my aunt is once again filled with guilt."

"It was an accident, but to happen to one so young . . ." Her voice trailed off.

"Did Nora visit Hester?"

"Yes. Though she went alone."

"Do you know what prompted her to go?"

"I suppose her motive was the same as yours. Curiosity."

"Was Hester rude to her?"

"Nora received the same treatment as you. She was quite shaken, just as you were."

"How would you know that?"

"Calvin told me she confided in him. They were together a lot."

"Oh yes."

"I was angry with him for taking you there."

"Don't be. If he'd refused to accompany me, I'd have gone alone."

She gave me a look of quiet resignation, though she softened it with a smile.

Another question occurred to me. "Did Nora ever make the trip to New York City for my aunt?"

"No. Her place in the household wasn't the same as yours."

"What do you mean?"

"She never really lived here."

"I recall you telling me she did stay here."

"Yes. So that I might have a little vacation."

"I should think Kate could manage quite well, even with you away."

"She could," Wanda admitted. "I often told your aunt that. Yet I knew if I was away for any length of time, she would take to her bed."

"I don't believe it's good for one human being to be so dependent on another."

"I agree. And if it weren't for what your aunt went through, I doubt I would be able to live in such splendid isolation. Granted, I love the magnificence of the surroundings, but it's almost like being buried alive."

I reached across the table and rested my hand over

Wanda's. "Thanks for showing such kindness to my aunt. I know living in such isolation has made her strange in many ways. She says things she doesn't remember, and when there is a minor crisis for which she blames herself, she takes to her bed. I know that's mental. She has reached the point where she can't control her emotions."

"What happened three times in this house was not a minor crisis," Wanda said remindfully.

"Yes. And each one who died was a young lady. Did Calvin tell you Hester said I would be the fourth to fall down the stairs? Of course, Zeffrey also said it and seemed to derive satisfaction from it."

Wanda's eyes hardened.

"I thought Hester was mad to speak the way she did," I went on. "Now I have a better understanding of her anger, which was directed at me. I'm sorry for what happened to Libby. Yet it had to be an accident. Mama fell down the stairs So did Nora."

"I'm sure they were accidents," Wanda replied. "Tragic ones."

I continued my train of thought. "I understand Hester believes my aunt murdered Libby because she was made pregnant by my uncle. And she believes my aunt murdered Mama and Nora because they could bear children and she could not."

"That's what she rants about. And the villagers believe her."

"Why are they so unforgiving? Especially when my aunt has given so generously to the church and the village?"

"They feel she is trying to buy forgiveness."

"My aunt should stop donating money for charitable and civic causes," I said indignantly.

"She never will. Your aunt is a good woman. A saintly woman."

"Have you said that to her?"

"I've tried to reason with her."

"I shall try also and I'll not stop until I've convinced her she is completely innocent." There was one final question I had to ask, though I hated to. "Do you believe my uncle seduced Libby?"

"I have no proof. No one has. His will never mentioned Libby."

"That's strange. Since he asked my aunt for a divorce.

Or could he have known about her condition at the time of his death?"

"He died two months before she did. Hester said Libby would have had the baby in three months."

"Was Dr. Carney the medical examiner?"

"He was."

"Was there an inquest?"

"No. Her death was declared accidental."

"Was there any reference in the newspaper accounts regarding her condition?"

"None. It would only have cast a shadow on the girl's reputation."

"But everyone in town knows."

"Hester didn't reveal the news until your mother arrived here. Your mother also visited Hester, more than once, in an effort to win her over."

"Hester told me," I said flatly. "I imagine her tongue was as vitriolic toward Mama as it was toward me."

Wanda covered her mouth with her hand to stifle a yawn.

I smiled an apology. "I'm sorry, Wanda. I've wearied you with my questions."

"No, you haven't. I'm just worried you will bother your aunt with more questions."

"I shan't. That's why I had to learn everything I could from you. It will help me now. And I'm grateful you told me. I understand now why my aunt has lived in such misery all these years. I must do my utmost to bring her out of this depression and I'm going to."

"Just now I think you had better get to bed. That is, if you're still determined to travel to New York City tomorrow."

"I am. Calvin doesn't need to accompany me."

"He insists. It will be good for him to get away for the day And your aunt will be relieved to know you will be chaperoned. Kate will call you at five."

"I'll be up with the birds. I'm ready for more sleep, but with what I've already had, I'll probably not need her to waken me."

"I told Calvin to watch over you. There will be time for you to have your midday meal at the hotel."

"You mean we'll dine at the same hotel where I leave the envelope of money?"

"Of course. You will enter the lobby first. Calvin will

follow. It will be as if you had a rendezvous there. You'll meet in the dining room."

I couldn't help but laugh. "It does sound conspiratorial."

"You look as if you're going to enjoy it."

"I daresay I will."

After Wanda left, I stacked my dishes on the tray, placed them on a table in the hall, and returned to my room. I drew water for a leisurely bath, relaxed in the warm water, and felt the tenseness leave my muscles. I was still a little stiff in my movements, but the intense pain was gone, and so, amazingly, was my headache. I marveled at that, especially after what I'd been through today.

I felt I finally had a clear picture of what had happened here at Linden Gardens. What I'd learned would help me to better understand my aunt. I knew I must help her. How to go about it was a challenge I must meet. Certainly I'd exhaust every means at my command to change her mental attitude. I could do it in a way that Wanda could not. As she and Calvin both pointed out, they were employees.

I thought of Papa. I'd not even written him a note telling him of my safe arrival. After I dried myself and slipped into my nightdress, I went to the writing table and did so. It was only a brief note, for I wouldn't alarm him by informing him of the rockslide, nor of the third death that had occurred here only six months ago. I was still puzzled as to why he hadn't told me about Libby's death, but I suppose he was so heartbroken when Mama suffered a similar fate, he never gave a thought to Libby Innis.

I sealed the envelope and placed a stamp on it. I would put it on the tray in the downstairs hall in the morning. I'd seen letters there. I imagined Zeffrey took them to the post office once a day. I couldn't mail it in New York City. If Papa ever knew I went there without even walking through the store so we could exchange a brief greeting, he would never forgive me.

That done, I went to bed. I didn't drift off to sleep immediately. My mind was too filled with the events of the day and thoughts of David, Hester Innis, Calvin, Wanda, and my aunt. Gradually, though, they slipped out of my mind and sleep took over.

◆ Eight ◆

I was awake at a quarter to five and I left my room at five-thirty. I wore the same outfit I had worn the day I arrived. It was both attractive and serviceable. Calvin met me at the landing and we descended to the breakfast room together.

After exchanging greetings, he said, "I really didn't expect you."

I said, "Kate was to wake me at five. She didn't."

"I wouldn't let her," he said. "I could have gone alone. I'm still not certain you should go."

"I'm going." I spoke with quiet firmness. "I only hope Kate made breakfast for two. I'm famished."

I needn't have worried. She was in the breakfast room and had already placed a half melon at each place. I knew the silver-covered dishes contained more food than we could eat. I also knew it would be delicious.

"Did you sleep well?" Calvin asked.

"Yes. I usually do."

"I was concerned that your visit with Hester yesterday had upset you to the point where you wouldn't."

"I learned a lot more from Wanda last night," I said.

"I wish she hadn't told you." He sounded irate.

"After what I learned from Hester, there was little else she could do. Don't forget, you also gave me some information."

He nodded. "I suppose it was inevitable you would find out sooner or later. It just seems that what your aunt had hoped would be a restful vacation for you has turned out to be the opposite."

"I didn't know my aunt's predicament when I came here. I don't believe I will enjoy myself until I find a way to help her, which I'm determined to do."

"I'm not sure she would be happy if she knew what was in your mind."

"Then we mustn't tell her."

Calvin expressed agreement. We ate quickly, both anxious to be on our way. I wasn't surprised to see Zeffrey already in the carriage. Calvin and I rode in the back seat in silence. Zeffrey gave no indicaiton he knew I had visited Hester. Somehow, it didn't even surprise me.

The train ride was uneventful except that Calvin handed me the envelope and once again gave me instructions. I put it in my handbag and sat back to enjoy the scenery. Fortunately, since it was early morning, there was no need for the windows to be open, so I wasn't blown, nor did I get cinders in my eyes.

At Grand Central Station we took a hack to the hotel at the foot of Fifth Avenue. As planned, I entered alone. It was very elegant, and though I'd never been inside it, I'd passed it many times on walks with Papa.

Calvin had instructed me as to the exact location of the chair where I was to conceal the envelope. It was in an alcove that was almost entirely shut off from view by large potted palms. The lobby was large and I noticed several alcoves, but this one was the only one just beyond the desk where the guests signed in. It was isolated and at a dead end, so that unless one was familiar with the man-sized niche, one wouldn't even be aware of it.

I had no difficulty finding it and I sat down in the chair, which was large and luxurious. I waited a few minutes to make certain no one would intrude on my privacy. Calvin had already gone to the dining room to wait for me. How I wished it was situated so that I might have a view of this alcove and could observe the gentleman who came to retrieve the envelope.

When I felt quite secure, I opened my handbag and took out the envelope. Its thickness was sufficient indication that there was a large amount of money inside. Knowing my aunt's generosity, I was certain the bills were also of a large denomination.

I was told to slip it down the right side. I did so, taking care that none of it protruded. In fact, I pushed it down so far, I feared the gentleman would have difficulty retrieving it. It was held securely between the springs and the side of the chair.

I sat there a few minutes longer, then went to the desk

and asked for directions to the dining room. The young clerk was gracious and told me to proceed down the corridor to the very end. The room was on the left and dinner was already being served. I thanked him and found it without difficulty. Needless to say, I had no view of the alcove.

I gave Calvin's name to the headwaiter and he escorted me to a window table. Calvin saw me coming and stood up until I was seated. My heart was pounding with the excitement of what I had just done. It seemed foolish, but at the same time I was pleased that it had turned out so well.

Calvin smiled at me across the table. "Your face is flushed, and from the way your eyes sparkle, I know you accomplished your mission without mishap."

"No problem at all," I said.

"I hope you have an appetite. I've ordered a full course dinner."

"I think I can do it justice," I said, basking in his open admiration. The eyes of every woman in the room were on him, yet he had eyes only for me. Any woman would have been flattered by his attention. Yet I had no foolish romantic fancies about him.

Our dinner was hearty, consisting of oysters on the half shell, roast beef with Yorkshire pudding, and three vegetables. For dessert we had Baked Alaska. I had eaten so much I could take only a few sips of coffee. I suggested we walk back up Fifth Avenue to Grand Central Station. Calvin compromised, stating we would walk five blocks, then take a hack to the station. That proved to be a good idea, especially after the first block. I was still stiff.

Before we started out, Calvin asked me to wait in the lobby for a few minutes, stating he wished to make a purchase. The moment he left, I thought of the envelope stuffed down the side of the chair and wondered if it was still there. On impulse, I walked swiftly to the spot, hoping no one was sitting there. Luck was with me. I sat down and thrust my right hand down the side, not really expecting that the envelope had already been picked up. But it had been. My fingers groped the length of the side and back again in an effort to discover it. *It was gone! Someone had already come for it.*

I returned to the lobby, expecting Calvin to be looking for me, but he was nowhere about. However, I spotted him approaching shortly, carrying a large, heart-shaped box.

"For you, Celeste," he said. "You performed so beautifully, you deserve it."

"A box of chocolates," I exclaimed. "Such a beautiful box."

It was heart-shaped, with a padded red satin fabric edged with gold. An enormous bow covered almost the entire lid.

I was flattered by his thoughtfulness. "You will have to help me eat them."

"I will. And so will Wanda. And Kate."

"What about my aunt?"

"You might try. I've brought her home a box of chocolates from time to time, but it's Wanda and Kate who devour them."

"Calvin, I have something to tell you."

He looked quizzical. "It must be something important. Your face is flushed with excitement."

My smile was triumphant as I said, "Just on impulse, I went to the chair and checked to see if the envelope was still there."

"My God, you shouldn't have done that," he exclaimed worriedly.

"What difference does it make?"

"Suppose that gentleman had shown up and gone there while you were seated, your hand exploring the side of the chair where you'd placed the envelope for him."

"Don't be upset. Nobody came."

"It's not that I think you would be in danger. It's just that your aunt would be terribly upset if the stranger wrote her about what you had done."

"He'll never know."

He took my arm. "Let's get out of here."

I held back. "There's no hurry. The envelope's gone."

"What!" His voice could be heard all over the lobby. He gave a quick look around, noticed all eyes on him, took my arm, and escorted me hastily from the hotel.

Once on the street, I protested. "Please, Calvin. I hurt too much to walk this fast."

"Forgive me." He stopped so abruptly, I was caught off balance and he had to make a grab for me. I couldn't help but cry out. He didn't mean to hurt me, but he had to get a strong grip on my arms to keep me from falling.

"I'm sorry, Celeste," he said, once more in control of himself. "I know I hurt you. Please forgive me."

"It's all right. I'm sorry you are angry with me for not being able to contain my curiosity."

"I'm not angry. I hate to say it, but the truth is I got a little frightened. You do have a habit of forgetting I am an employee of your aunt. I could be dismissed for what you did."

"No one will ever know,' I said. "I promise I will never do anything again to jeopardize your position at Linden Gardens."

His handsome features broadened in a smile. "You do have a charming way about you, Celeste. I shouldn't have got upset. After all, there's one thing we know now we didn't know before. He doesn't wait long to pick up the money. I'm almost sorry we didn't leave the dining room sooner. We might have seen him."

I made no comment. There was no need. Calvin had expressed the exact thought that had crossed my mind.

It was mid-afternoon when we returned. Wanda met us in the hall and told me my aunt would like to see me.

I expressed the hope that there was nothing wrong. Wanda assured me there wasn't. It was just that my aunt wanted to make certain the envelope had been delivered.

I went upstairs and tapped lightly on her door. Kate opened it and brightened at sight of me. I motioned her out into the hall.

"How is she?" I spoke in an undertone.

Kate kept her voice low as she said, "She doesn't want to talk—at least not to me. Perhaps you can cheer her. She's in one of her moods."

I nodded and went inside. Kate closed the door behind me.

My aunt was dressed in a Watteau gown of pale green. Her hair, almost entirely gray, was braided and hung over one shoulder reaching almost to her waist. She had dainty green satin slippers on her feet, which rested on a footstool.

"Hello, Aunt Emma. You look very pretty."

She ignored the compliment and asked, "Did you deliver the envelope?"

"Yes."

My aunt gave me a wan smile. "Thank you, my dear."

I held up the large box of candy. "May I open this and share it with you? Calvin bought it for me."

"No, thank you." She seemed totally without interest in what I was saying.

We sat there in silence a few moments. I racked my brain trying to think of something to say. Nothing came to mind. At least, I could think of nothing that would catch her interest.

The prolonged silence was beginning to unnerve me. I said, "When do you wish me to make another journey to New York City?"

She eyed me with indifference. "I will let you know at the proper time. I am tired now, Celeste. Please go. I must rest."

I couldn't believe I was being dismissed so coldly. My aunt's eyes never left my face, but there wasn't a trace of warmth in them. I was beginning to feel very uncomfortable in her presence. In fact, I couldn't think of any place I would rather be at the moment than back in the modest flat I shared with Papa.

"Please go, Celeste." My aunt repeated her request in the same listless tone of voice.

"Yes, Auntie." I replied, my tone as dull as hers. She had taken the spirit out of me. I had expected a quite different welcome. I thought she would be proud that I had carried out my mission so well. Granted, there was nothing earth-shaking about it; neither was it open and above-board. Perhaps that explained her manner. Thinking about it made me feel a sudden discontent with myself.

I left the room and met Wanda in the hall. She could tell from my features that the meeting had been less than I expected.

"Don't feel too bad, Celeste. She's been like this all day. First, she was worried you wouldn't carry out her orders. Once she knew you did, the feeling of guilt that is with her so much returned."

"Why should she feel guilty when she's performing an act of kindness and generosity?"

"Perhaps because of the way it has to be done."

"Why does she allow it to be done that way? Since it's her money she should be the one to state the manner in which it is to be delivered."

"I know. Try not to think about it. I must go to her."

"I can't help but think about it," I replied testily. "It's

all I can think of. Going in there just now and informing my aunt I did as I was told and finding her less than friendly was just too much. I'm angry, but not at my aunt."

"I hope not at me," Wanda said, regarding me with sympathy.

"No, Wanda." I spoke reassuringly. "Please forgive me for sputtering. I'm hurt and confused and so mixed up, I don't know what to think."

"You're tired," Wanda said. "I suggest you have a nap. You can have a late supper. After you've rested, you'll be able to think better."

"I couldn't lie down."

"Then take a bath. That will refresh you. Don't brood on the way your aunt treated you. You know she is in one of her moods."

I knew Wanda was doing her best to console me. I also knew she was concerned by my voice, which had risen with my irritation. She placed the forefinger of her left hand to her lips and pointed with the forefinger of her right hand to my aunt's closed door. I knew what she meant. My aunt must not be upset.

I nodded an apology and didn't move until Wanda had entered the suite and closed the door noiselessly behind her.

I wondered how my aunt had retained her sanity with what she had endured all these years. That and the knowledge her husband had wanted a divorce so he might marry a young girl whom he had seduced. I wondered if she had been aware while he was alive that he no longer loved her. I could well imagine her hurt and humiliation. He had lived with her in what she thought, until the very end, was marital bliss, when all the time he wanted to be rid of her so he could marry a young girl.

It was a relief to regain the privacy of my suite. I removed my hat and gloves, undressed, and slipped into a negligee. At least, here I could think. I started for the chaise longue, which sat before the fireplace, when I heard the patter of rain. I hadn't noticed the day darkening. I went to the windows and closed them, then returned to the chaise. I stretched out, relishing the softness of the goose-down pillows I lay on. The feeling of luxury was so wonderful, I couldn't help but relax. And relax I did, wakening to the aroma of chicken broth. Kate, thoughtful as always, had brought me a tray.

She had removed the covers from the dishes so that the odor of freshly cooked food would waken me. She laughed softly as I blinked my eyes against the soft lamplight.

"You looked so young and helpless and beautiful lying there," she said, "I hated to waken you. But you must have something to eat before you go to bed."

"What time is it?"

"After ten."

"Goodness. I slept over four hours."

"You needed it. Making a trip to the city after that accident that nearly killed you. And would have if Mr. David hadn't rescued you. Come to the table and get some nourishment."

Her tone was mildly scolding, but her eyes showed a fondness for me. I got to my feet slowly, almost reluctantly, for I was still filled with sleep. I went to the bathroom, washed my hands and splashed my face with cold water. It served to make me come fully awake and alert.

Kate was still in the room when I returned. She said, "Did you get the letter from Mr. David? I left it propped up against the lamp on your night table."

Her news startled me. "I didn't even see it, Kate. I was so exhausted when I came back, I lay down and promptly fell asleep."

"I'll get it." She was in the bedroom before I could protest. I didn't like her waiting on me when she had so many other household chores to perform. I told her so when she returned.

"I have less than you think. The kitchen mostly and your aunt when Wanda has other duties. But the help came today and the place is spotless."

"I noticed that."

"Even the rooms that are closed up—and most of them are—are gone over each week."

She handed me a long white envelope with my name on the front. "Mr. David brought it this morning. He inquired after your health and couldn't believe it when I told him you had left for New York City. He looked very concerned and said he hoped the journey wouldn't be too much for you. I told him Mr. Calvin would see that you didn't overdo."

"Calvin was most kind," I said.

"He is perfection itself. For one so handsome, he leads a very quiet life."

"I agree, Kate. Though he tells me he enjoys himself when he goes to the city."

She gave me a knowing smile and a rapid nod of her head. "Well, child, when you've finished, put the dishes out as before. I made an omelet because it's light. And custard. I hope you like it."

"I like everything. You're a superb cook."

"Thank you, Miss Celeste. I'll go now. I'm a wee bit tired, having had all the help to supervise today. But that will be the end of it till next week."

I was going to save David's letter until I had eaten, intending to read it in bed, but on second thought, I went over to the table, picked up the letter, and eased myself into a chair. I wondered if I would ever be free of aches again.

I had difficulty getting the flap of the envelope open. It was as if David had used extra glue on it to make certain it wouldn't open. It was of no consequence. What the letter contained was. My anger toward him had abated as my knowledge of what had transpired here increased. I hadn't taken into account that he had lost a sister. Or if I had, I hadn't given it serious thought. I did now. Along with the fact that I had lost a mother. Papa never got over that, though he couldn't afford the luxury of spending his life mourning over the tragedy of losing Mama. He had sense enough to know that, though he, too, held bitter feelings toward Aunt Emma.

I finally reached over, picked up my knife, and slid it beneath the top of the flap, cutting the envelope open.

I took out the letter, expecting it to be a brief letter of apology for deceiving me about his real identity. I doubted I deserved one after the way I had behaved when I returned his notebook. I wasn't exactly certain why I felt so happy, knowing he had written me. Probably because he had come to my rescue during those perilous moments on the side of the cliff. Anyway, holding his letter in my hands gave me a nice, warm feeling. I cautioned myself to stop being foolish and turned my attention to the letter, which was longer than I anticipated.

Dear Miss Abbott:

First of all, an apology for using a fictitious name when I introduced myself. That was the name I used when I rented the house, which I own. However, I hadn't been here since the age of seven, so I doubted anyone would recognize me. No one did. Had it not been that you tore my pocket, you would still not know who I am. That is of no importance now. The fact is, you discovered my true identity.

The reason I resorted to trickery of a sort is that I suspect my beloved sister, Nora Martin, was murdered at Linden Gardens. I cannot believe her death was an accident. It isn't just a hunch which makes me say that. It's a letter I received from my sister shortly before her death. A letter in which she stated that Emma von Linden, whom she admired, was mentally ill. She said her reason for thinking so was that Mrs. von Linden's emotions ranged from periods when she seemed quite happy and content, to those when she seemed scarcely aware of her surroundings.

My sister also commented on the abuse your aunt had taken from the villagers, particularly Hester Innis. She mentioned the fact that no one in the village would set foot in the house. Also, that the house seemed to hold your aunt a prisoner. She told how she had met your aunt; of how her compassion had been aroused and she had returned at your aunt's invitation.

She wrote a second letter that stated she was going to be a guest in the house for a period of two weeks. It would be to allow Wanda Vargas to take a vacation. Nora stated that she was eager to live there briefly, so she might get to know your aunt better. And to understand her moods better. Or discover a reason for them—other than her melancholy.

It is difficult to put what little I know on paper because it doesn't make too much sense.

I am going to ask you a great favor. I would like to call on you. Since you read the contents of the notebook, you know I hold your aunt a suspect in the murder of my sister. I do so because of my sister's puzzlement at her behavior.

If you don't wish to, I will understand. However, I feel you will, since your mother was also killed in that house. A death deemed an accident. Three accidental deaths (there is also Libby Innis), happening in the same way, seem too coincidental to me.

I will add one final statement. With each passing day, my concern for your safety in that house grows. Though I could find no evidence to the contrary, I do not believe the rockslide, which could well have killed you, was accidental.

I hope I will hear favorably from you. The quicker, the better.

> Your loyal friend,
> David (Martin)

Though there was nothing in the letter to bring a smile to my lips. his last name, in parentheses, did. I liked the letter, though it did give me further pause for thought. I liked David and knew, even if he hadn't written, I would have written a letter of apology to him for my behavior. I knew a great deal more than I had when I returned his notebook.

I replaced the letter in the envelope, slipped it into my handbag, stacked the dishes on the tray, and brought it into the hall. I was just turning back to my room when an acrid odor assailed my nostrils. I automatically walked over to my aunt's room, my first thought being of fire. I couldn't detect any trace of it there. I returned to my side of the hall, moving slowly. Once there, the odor became more apparent.

I closed my door, picked up the lamp that Kate had left lit until I set out my dishes, and moved along the hall, keeping to the side where the odor was detectable. I reached the stairway and paused. The thought suddenly occurred to me that I had no idea where Calvin's rooms were located. I turned down the corridor leading to Wanda's suite and paused outside her door. I put my nose as close as possible to the side of the door that opened, yet could not detect the odor. It didn't seem that it was coming from there.

I continued on. Suddenly the scent became stronger and

I recognized it as incense. Who would be burning it—in this house and at this hour? Curious, I continued on. I hoped I had passed Calvin's door, because where the fragrance was strongest was at the very end of the hall. I paused, but only momentarily. I'd come this far and I'd not turn back. I turned the knob and the door opened noiselessly.

I held the lamp aloft as I entered the room, though it wasn't necessary, for it wasn't in complete darkness. Directly opposite and set against the wall was a long table. On it, at either end, were two five-pronged candelabra. All ten candles were lit. In the center of the table was an exotic figure. In its lap was a plate on which the incense burned. The room was filled with the aroma. It was almost overwhelming, but my inquisitive nature served me in good stead, enabling me to ignore my aversion to the pungent odor.

The walls had drawings of the twelve signs of the zodiac. Each one was draped in filmy black material that even in the stillness of the room moved gently. In the very center of the room was a small round table, covered with a black velvet cloth. I had approached it now and could see a deck of tarot cards to one side. In the exact center was a brass stand with a large oval ring attached. Hanging from the center of the ring was a small, round, double-faced mirror, about the size of an eyepiece. Two chairs on either side of the table faced each other. I pulled one out and sat down.

I studied the brass stand and noticed a delicate wire along the inner side of the metal circle. I set down the lamp and with the forefinger of each hand, I traced the wire to the top. I could see it was a part of the wire to which the suspended mirror was attached. I retraced the wire and at the very base of the stand I found a slight appendage. I gripped it lightly between my thumb and forefinger and turned it gently. I was fascinated to see the mirror turn also. It caught both the candlelight and the lamplight, sending shafts of light through the room. It was so bright it made me blink. I wondered what its purpose was. More mumbo jumbo, I supposed. At any rate, I had found the so-called secret room. I quickly corrected myself. It was called the Zodiac Room.

I turned the mirror in the opposite direction and was rewarded with a horrifying cry that startled me. Someone was standing in the doorway. The mirror shot such a blinding glare of light into my eyes, I couldn't see who it was. I thought of my aunt and hoped I hadn't startled her.

I covered my eyes to shut out the momentary glare and got to my feet. I moved forward a few steps to put me out of range of the mirror.

When I uncovered them, Kate was standing only inches away from me. "What are you doing in this room" she demanded.

I couldn't believe this was the Kate I knew. There wasn't a trace of friendliness in her tone.

"I smelled smoke. At first I didn't recognize it as incense, and fearing fire, I went to investigate. I traced the source to this room."

She walked over to the long table, picked up a candle snuffer and smothered the flames. She returned to the round table and picked up the lamp.

"I'll show you back to your room. I told you when you came, never to set foot in this room." Her tone was still belligerent.

"I don't like your issuing orders to me, Kate."

"If you don't want the same thing to happen to you that happened to your mother and the other two, get back to your room."

"Are you threatening me"

"Call it anything you want. I'm ordering you to get out of this room."

"And if I disobey?"

"You won't. Not if you love your aunt."

Our eyes sparred for a few moments. I was shocked by her manner and felt a quiet anger, believing she had spied on me. Nonetheless, she was right. I had to consider Aunt Emma's feelings. I walked to the door, paused, and turned to observe Kate. She hadn't moved. The belligerent look on her face had changed to a smile of malicious triumph. Up until now I had thought of her as a gentle, compassionate woman. My opinion suddenly changed. At the moment I felt she held me in the same regard as Hester. I returned to my room and closed the door softly. For the first time, I turned the key in the lock. No individual had ever inspired fear in me before. Hester had made me angry and I'd been revolted by her ugly accusations, but Kate frightened me.

I couldn't figure out why she had done it. Her manner

had been deliberately hostile. I thought at first she was warning me. But then I got the feeling her attitude was a threatening one.

She was the one who had warned me against the room. She had told me to stay out of it, saying something about its being evil. And tonight she had actually ordered me out of it. I got the feeling she felt quite at home in it and I had violated it by my presence.

I was still standing by my door when I heard her set the lamp on the table. I heard the dishes move slightly on the tray as she picked it up. I knew she would place them on the dumbwaiter and return to put the lamp out. I waited until she did so. Just as I had thought she would, she tried my doorknob very quietly. I actually saw it turn. I pressed my hand against my mouth to quiet my fear. Was she involved in some way with the three deaths that had occurred in this house? How could she be when she had told me she didn't come here until after the first, which was Libby's. I wondered what she'd have done had my door been unlocked.

I moved slowly and silently about the room, lowering the lamp wicks and cupping my hand over the globe as I blew out the flame. I did the same in my bedroom, leaving only the one on my night table lit, though turned low. If anyone gained entry to this suite, I wanted to make certain I could identify that individual.

I doubted I would sleep much tonight. I was glad I had had some rest, for it would be a long time until morning. I couldn't wait for daylight. I'd be up and dressed, waiting for a respectable hour to set out in the buggy to pay my respects to David. I prayed he would be home. I suddenly realized I was trembling. I was frightened. Just as frightened as I'd been when the rocks and boulders had come tumbling down on me. And all because of a woman I had thought was goodness itself.

For the first time, I understood Papa's concern about my coming here. Even David was worried about me. I wondered if Hester and the villagers were right. Could my aunt be guilty of the murder of three young women? Had she enlisted the help of Kate as an accomplice? Had I deliberately been brought here to be the fourth victim? Kate had asked if I wanted the same thing to happen to me that happened to the others? Had she deliberately frightened me?

As the night wore on, my impatience to see David grew greater. First to apologize, then to confide in him and enlist his help in trying to find out what was wrong at Linden Gardens. I no longer questioned that something was terribly wrong. I also realized I needed someone I could talk to, someone who was as concerned as I and who had as great a reason as I for learning the truth about Linden Gardens. David didn't believe the three deaths were accidental. Now I was beginning to doubt they were, especially when I thought back to Zeffrey and Hester, both of whom predicted I would be the fourth victim to fall down the stairway. Yet how could they be so sure? Did they know something I didn't? And Kate. She had said practically the same thing less than an hour ago.

I slept fitfully, wakened from time to time by the heavy rainfall that was blown against the closed windows by the wind. It seemed to make the menace greater. But who was the menace? Was it my aunt—or the house?

◆ Nine ◆

It took only the first gray light of dawn to bring me from my bed. I bathed and dressed quietly, and while I waited for a proper hour to go downstairs, I penned Papa another letter. This one wasn't so cheerful—perhaps because I hadn't completely shaken off my fear of the night before when Kate confronted me.

I told Papa that I was disturbed by my aunt's behavior. I also asked him if Mama had ever mentioned it in her letters to him. I had no idea how many she had written. Perhaps a great many. I didn't even know if he had kept them.

I omitted my journey to New York City, but did mention I had met a charming gentleman named David Martin whose father had painted the portrait of Mama. I didn't mention Nora Martin's untimely demise, nor Libby's. I ended the letter by telling him I missed him and hoped to be back with him soon. I could see his brows raise in surprise as he read that. I also told him that I had acquired a new sense of values since living here. I reminded him of what he had said about my having more growing up to do. I ended the letter by stating I believed I had accomplished it, and so it was good that I had come here. I would appreciate our humble flat all the more when I returned.

I visualized his quiet smile as he completed the letter, replaced it in its envelope, and sat back to ruminate on what it was that had enabled or forced me to reach a greater maturity. I'd not been explicit and that might disturb him. But I hoped the ending would be sufficiently reassuring so that he'd not worry.

I went downstairs promptly at eight. I wondered how Kate could know the exact time when the various members of the household would come to the breakfast room.

Yet she seemed to. There was only one place set and Kate stood beside the chair, waiting to hold it for me. My walking was completely normal now, for the aches and stiffness had almost completely disappeared. I had always been one to heal quickly and I was grateful I'd been blessed with a healthy body.

My greeting to Kate was subdued and so was hers to me. There was no trace of the former camaraderie I had enjoyed with her. Up until my encounter with her in that strange room last night, I felt she had developed a fondness for me. And perhaps a feeling of sympathy because of my aunt's strange behavior toward me.

The dish of freshly sliced peaches looked very attractive. I told Kate that as I poured cream on them. She thanked me and turned to leave the room. Before she could do so, I asked her if Zeffrey was on the premises.

"He's here at six o'clock, Miss," she said. "If you glance out at the grounds, you will see the gardeners already at work. Zeffrey supervises them. And well too."

"I know that, Kate. However, I would like the buggy harnessed immediately. I'm taking a ride as soon as I finish breakfast."

She looked startled and her mouth opened to make a reply. More likely to ask a question, but since my manner was as cool as hers had been when I entered the room, she knew better.

She said, "Yes, Miss."

I didn't dally, though the fried eggs and ham were enough to make me want to. I would have enjoyed a second cup of coffee, but decided against it.

There was no need for me to return to my suite, for I had brought my hat, gloves, and handbag down, along with my letter to Papa, which I had placed on the tray. I was pleased to see the letter was still there. I put on my hat before a wall mirror, using two hatpins to secure it. The road had had potholes when I'd ridden over it two days ago. After the storm, I imagined it would have a few more. I didn't want my hat knocked askew should I be thrown off balance by one.

The hat was of natural straw devoid of trimming except for a green ribbon band that matched the color of my tailor-made dress. The only trimming on the dress was on the bodice, which was decorated with diagonal pipings of green silk.

I opened the door and, on a hunch, turned back briefly. Kate, half concealed by the stairway, was observing me. I had no doubt but that she was consumed by curiosity as to where I was going.

Had she asked, I'd have told her. After all, she did deliver David's letter to me. I gave her no further thought and went out to the buggy that awaited me. Zeffrey was already seated in the buggy holding the reins.

When I approached, he slid over to the passenger's side and lowered both hands. I gripped them and he lifted me easily.

He slid back over on the driver's side, picked up the reins, and said, "Where to, Miss?"

I smiled and held out my hands for the reins. "I'm going alone, Zeffrey."

"You know how to handle an animal?" he demanded.

"I do," I replied firmly. I had been taught horseback riding in school, but that was the extent of my knowledge of guiding a horse.

He made no move to surrender the reins. "We had heavy rains last night. I don't think your aunt would like me to let you take the buggy alone, Miss."

"Would you care to go upstairs and ask her if I might?"

"That's for you to do, Miss."

I'd had enough impudence from both Hester and Zeffrey. I said, "My aunt made no mention of the fact that I was to take orders from you. Nor will I. I told you I was going alone. I intend to do exactly that. Now please get down so I may be on my way."

He started to protest, but I reached over and relieved him of the reins. His mouth compressed tightly and he regarded me with open anger, but I paid no heed.

"Get out of the buggy, Zeffrey," I said quietly.

He could do nothing but obey, yet he had to have the last word. "You won't be so high and mighty for long. I told you what was going to happen to you. And it will. Sooner than you think, Miss Biggety."

I slapped the reins lightly against the horse's flanks and he started a leisurely pace down the drive. I had no trouble guiding him out onto the road, and since he was so docile, I felt that if the carriage did hit a pothole, he'd not be startled by it.

Nor was he. Though the sky was still a threatening

gray, the ride was thoroughly enjoyable and I liked being by myself. I realized it was the first time I had been alone since coming here—except for the brief walk along the cliff.

I turned into the drive leading to David's home and hoped the animal would not get skittish because of the high growth that almost hid the road and that would scratch his underside. I had no idea if this was one of the two animals that had been hitched to the surrey. If so, I was lucky. This one preferred moving slowly and didn't seem to mind the wild bushes.

Once again, I was fascinated by the appearance of David's house. It really seemed more like a church, because of the lobated leaf cutouts that formed hoods over the windows and doors.

As before, the door opened and David stepped out. Of course he'd not expected visitors and he was wearing corduroy trousers and a shirt open at the neck. Even so, he looked very appealing, especially when his smile, hesitant at first, widened when I called out a greeting.

He stepped down, ignoring the two steps at the entranceway, and his arms extended to help me down. I placed my hands on his shoulders and his hands enclosed my waist.

"I guess the fact that you came here is proof you've forgiven me for the deception."

"I owe you an apology for my behavior of last Sunday when I returned your notebook."

"No. I should have told you the truth. After all, your mother was killed in that house, just as my sister was."

"I'm the one who was selfish," I said. "I didn't think about your sister. I was too concerned with the fact that you had practiced deceit and you believed my aunt guilty of three murders. Just as that terrible Hester does. And Zeffrey, I suppose."

"Will you come inside and talk about it, please? It's wet and damp out here. I'll apologize beforehand for the appearance of the house. I was in Europe when my sister was killed. I sent a telegram requesting that her body be sent to Virginia. When my mother's father died, we moved there. My grandmother was an invalid and Mother wished to be close to her. That is where my parents are buried. And my sister."

The house had a small circular entrance that could best

be termed a vestibule. From it we entered a larger room that had an enormous fireplace. It must have been where the family had spent their time because there were several divans and tables with chairs on either side. One wall held bookshelves from floor to ceiling, but they were empty. The furniture was shrouded with dust covers, as were the wall decorations. There was a slightly musty air to the place, giving evidence it had not been lived in for many years.

David took the cover off one of the divans facing the fireplace, his movements slow and cautious.

"I flipped the covers off some of the furniture upstairs and couldn't stop sneezing from the dust that filled the room. I learned my lesson."

"Let me help." Together we folded it and he placed it on a covered table.

David said, "I just made a pot of chocolate. It's my favorite morning beverage. Will you join me?"

"Gladly," I said. "I didn't realize the damp chill had penetrated my bones."

"You sit right there." He grasped my shoulders and eased me onto the divan. "The fire will warm you. I'll be right back."

The flames sent light and cheer into the room and I settled back, feeling quite relaxed and happy to be here. Certainly it wasn't the room that gave me such a feeling. It had to be David. I had a friend in him. I was certain of it. I couldn't wait for him to return.

It seemed ages before he did, though no more than ten minutes had elapsed. Besides the pot of chocolate, he had coffee cake, which he told me he had purchased from a bakery in the village. There was a table to one side of the divan. When he placed the tray on the table, I took over and told him to be seated. He obeyed and I served us both. However, he did get up to bring over a low table on which we placed our cups and saucers. It eliminated the precarious business of having to balance them in our laps, along with the dishes that held our coffee cake. I tasted it and told him it was delicious.

We wasted no time on small talk. Our conversation began with the subject uppermost on our minds. Yes, I was also beginning to question the theory that the three deaths had been accidental.

David said, "I was in Europe when Nora was killed.

Reverend Lawrence Gates cabled me. He is unmarried and was quite taken with Nora. I would like to think that, in time, she would have fallen in love with him. He's a splendid gentleman."

"I imagine your sister was a warm, loving person. She must have been to spend so much time with my aunt, who certainly is not a cheerful lady to be around."

"Reverend Gates said she is much maligned. Naturally, I didn't agree. At least, not at first. Now I'm wondering."

"I'm wondering if Hester is telling the truth."

He almost choked on his coffee cake. At his look of amazement, I repeated my statement.

"What makes you say that?" he asked.

"My aunt's behavior. She's so strange."

"I had no idea you thought that about her the day you were injured in the rockslide."

"I didn't. Though I was taken aback when she told me she didn't love me. That she had invited me there in the hope that she could learn to."

David couldn't help but smile. "She's frank, anyway."

"I already told you that she said she had no recollection of having suggested I take a walk along the cliff."

"Please go on."

"This is the strangest thing of all. Yesterday I performed an errand for her. I went to New York City."

David said, "I remember your telling me you were going. Kate also told me when I delivered the letter."

"I'm also having second thoughts about her."

"That's surprising. First, though, tell me why your suspicions have been aroused about your aunt."

"It's shameful to discuss her in this fashion, especially when I'm a guest in her home."

"You must have good reason to do so."

"The truth is, I haven't. It's just that her behavior is so puzzling, I wonder if she is in her right mind."

"Have you talked with Dr. Carney?"

"Only briefly. He said anyone's mind would be affected by having gone through as much as she has."

"Which means he doesn't hold her suspect," David reasoned.

I nodded. "Would you like to hear about my journey to New York? Rather, the reason for it?"

"I would indeed."

I related everything that had transpired from the moment we boarded the train, to our return when I made a report to my aunt, who not only didn't praise my success in carrying out the clandestine errand but didn't even seem interested in me.

"That is odd," David agreed. "I know she was a quite different person when her husband was alive."

I eyed him with new interest. "How would you know that?"

"Before I tell you, I would like to hear the remainder of your story. Or is that the end?"

"Not quite. I learned a little more from Calvin regarding Libby's death after he took me to visit Hester—at my request. I learned still more from Wanda, who visited me the night before last while I was having a light meal in my suite." I smiled, self-consciously. "It seems as if I'm there a great deal. I seem to tire so easily."

"Of course. You still haven't completely recovered from your injuries."

"When I wakened, Kate had brought a tray of food to my room. She told me about the letter you delivered to the house and asked her to give to me. She said she had placed it on the night table. I didn't see it, but I was so filled with hurt because of my aunt's behavior, it isn't surprising. Your letter was exactly what I needed to lighten my spirits."

David smiled. "After the dressing down you gave me, I was afraid you might tear up the envelope without even opening it."

"Speaking of opening it, I had quite a time. I finally used a knife. You must have put extra glue on it to hold it closed."

"I didn't," he said. "It should have opened quite easily. I wonder if it wasn't in the room when you returned. Someone else may have been curious as to its contents."

"Kate?"

"Why do you say that?"

"Because of something that happened last night when I placed my tray of dishes in the hall."

I related the incident in detail. He interrupted a few times, asking questions he considered pertinent. He wasn't surprised about the room, having learned about it from Nora. He informed me she was fascinated by the occult and anything pertaining to the supernatural. She had written him about it. He even knew it was called the Zodiac Room.

"I can see why she was interested in Linden Gardens. Did you know Wanda Vargas is a gypsy?"

"Yes. Nora told me in one of her letters. She also told me Wanda read her past in the crystal ball, and looked into her future. She told Nora she would fall in love with a handsome gentleman who had a deeply passionate nature."

"That sounds like Calvin," I said.

"Yes," David agreed. "And yet, I can't see Nora falling in love with him. She was a deeply religious person, even though she did have a weakness for the supernatural."

"Do you consider Calvin too worldly?"

"Not *too* worldly," David stated quietly. "But worldly."

"I've wondered why he is so content here. Though it shouldn't really surprise me. Wanda told me he has a love for beauty and certainly Linden Gardens has all of that, plus luxury."

"Yes. And Calvin does make trips to New York City where he can make up for his boredom."

"How did you know that?"

He smiled. "I think I had better start at the beginning. At least, it's the beginning for me."

"You mean the death of your sister?"

"I didn't mean that exactly, but you're right. That is really the beginning."

"I had no suspicions regarding her death when the telegram arrived from Reverend Gates. I was in Paris, but returned immediately. I came here with the idea of selling the house. You can see that Nora never took the time to have the house cleaned and aired."

"Why did she come here?" I asked.

"She found a diary belonging to our mother. I guess there were nostalgic references to our home in Wilmot. Nora decided to visit the place. At least that is what she wrote me. I was in Europe at the time. In fact I'd been there for over a year, studying the French artists. Their style, techniques, and so forth. Nora had gone with me, but she became restless and returned home. Up until the time she came here, she was a social butterfly. She seemed to love the life. Then suddenly she grew tired of it. I think Reverend Gates helped her a great deal. They met at an affair at the town hall. Nora was a confirmed letter writer and she wrote in detail about it. And about him. He was kind, thoughtful, a forceful speaker in the pulpit—she even joined his church. I believe she found herself here. She became very involved in church activities. That is how she met your aunt."

I nodded. "Wanda told me."

David set down his empty cup and stared into the fire. "Sad that when she finally found her niche in life and it became purposeful, it came to such an abrupt end."

"If Nora was murdered," I said quietly, "the culprit must be exposed. Regardless of the identity of the person."

"Yes," David agreed. "And it must be done as quickly as possible before there is a fourth victim."

"Meaning me?" I asked flatly.

"Yes," he replied. "I'm gravely concerned for your safety."

"At Linden Gardens?"

He nodded. "Hester's argument doesn't ring true."

"I can't believe my aunt would resent any woman, regardless of her age, who could bear children."

"Nor I," David replied. "Though it seems the most logical motive, doesn't it?"

I gave David a sharp look. "When did you first suspect your sister's death was not accidental?"

"When I learned two others had died before her in the same way."

"That was after you arrived here. And discussed the matter with Reverend Gates."

"He had no suspicion that my sister's death was other than accidental. He thinks highly of your aunt."

"Would he think evil of anyone—in his calling?"

David smiled. "I suppose not. As I told you, I came here to put the house up for sale. Before that, I wanted to check through it to make certain there was nothing of value left here. By that I mean personal things."

"Of course."

"I found something of my mother's that intrigued me greatly. It was in a hope chest that seemed to be empty, yet had a secret drawer. I must have known about it as a child, because when I knelt on one knee and lifted the lid, there was what appeared to be a shelf that ran the length of the chest, but was only half the width. Without pausing, my right hand went to the very end of the shelf and found a small knob. I pulled it forward and out came a small drawer. In it was my mother's diary. At least, one of them. She was an inveterate keeper of diaries."

"David," I exclaimed hopefully, "was there anything in it that could shed light on these deaths?"

"I'm not sure. As I said, it was my mother's diary and so it is extremely personal. I almost didn't read it. It seemed indecent. If it hadn't been for Nora, I'm certain I'd have tossed it into the fireplace. But I read it, then put it back in the drawer. I think it's the safest place for it."

"Can you tell me what you learned?"

"I'll tell you everything. You're entitled to know. Just how valuable it is, I don't know. It concerns Libby."

He paused, as if reluctant to continue.

"Please, David."

"My mother had observed Libby with a young gentleman—that is the only way she identified him. She was walking through the forest one day and heard girlish laughter. It was followed by a man's laughter. She didn't think too much of it until she happened to catch a glimpse of Libby through the trees. The man was chasing her. He caught up with her, drew her to him, and smothered her with kisses. That day Mother wrote that she quickly retraced her steps and returned to the house. The mention of Libby and the gentleman comes up again on a later page. This time Mother came upon them in a compromising position on the ground making passionate love. She spoke to Father about it and asked if it would be wise to tell Emma. Apparently, my parents knew about the adoption because Mama was concerned Libby might get herself in a mess and that would end the adoption plans. Father's advice was that she should keep out of it."

"Didn't your mother identify the man in any way?"

"No. Just that he was young."

"I doubt Eric von Linden was that young."

"It seems incredible he would seduce Libby in his home, especially considering what Mama wrote about the von Lindens—that they were very happy and so proud of their new home. However, there was a reference to the fact that your aunt was most unhappy because she had despaired of ever giving Eric an heir. She told my mother that, despite the embarrassment, she had forced herself to go to the best doctors available, but none seemed able to give her any encouragement."

"That seems to bear out what Hester said. At least, partly."

"Hester puzzles me. Particularly the wheelchair that she has been wedded to since the death of her niece."

"Is she mentioned in your mother's diary?"

"No. It is mostly concerned with our own family. I was surprised when I came across a reference to your aunt. It gave me hope that I might find a clue somewhere in those pages. There was nothing more."

"Did Nora keep a diary?"

"Yes. Mother encouraged her to. I searched her room for it, but apparently she was too busy once she came here."

"Do you suppose Hester and Zeffrey used my aunt for their own purposes? Pretending it was Eric who made their niece pregnant so that they might blackmail her? I can think of no other word for what they forced her to do. Purchase them a pleasant home and furnish it."

"And have their niece buried in the von Linden mausoleum."

"That in itself would back up the ugly statements Hester made about Aunt Emma."

"And her husband," David said. "I have something else I must tell you."

"I hope it's not more bad news."

"I'm hoping it will be a help. I've engaged the services of a private detective firm. I was going to anyway in the hope I might learn the identity of the young man who, I believe, fathered the child Libby would have had, had she lived. I want them to learn what they can regarding that. But I also want them to keep an eye on you. I don't want anything to happen to you. I have contact with just one man."

"Where is he staying?"

"At the Inn. Posing as a traveling man. I'll tell you no more. It's better that you don't know who he is. You might give the show away."

"If I see a gentleman trailing me, I might give it away, not knowing who he is," I admitted. "I might also think he is going to murder me."

"You'll have to risk that and so will I. I think it's wiser for you not to know."

"How can he observe me when I'm not at home?"

"I have given the firm *carte blanche*. If it wishes to put

another detective or five more on the case, it is free to do so. The important thing is, I want to know you are safe. I'll do my best to see you each day, but should you not be able to see me, I'm hoping the one detective I have contact with will make a point of learning that you are safe. How he does it is none of my business."

I smiled. "I take it being a private detective is not exactly an honorable profession."

"So long as they accomplish their mission, I'll not ask how they do it. So many years have passed since the first two deaths, I'm not certain just what they can learn."

"What made you do it?"

"The three deaths. The animosity the village bore your aunt. I sent a telegram to my attorney in Virginia, asking that he contact a reputable agency in New York City and have them send up a man. He came here under cover of darkness. That is the only time he visits me. I'll tell you no more."

The logs were mere embers now. We'd finished our chocolate and cake and we'd had an engrossing conversation. Both of us had learned a great deal about the tragic past associated with Linden Gardens. But we were no closer to solving the mystery of the three deaths. Were they accidents or murders? Could my aunt have committed such a heinous crime as murder? The thought made me shudder.

David grasped my shoulders, his eyes filled with concern. "What is it, Celeste?"

"My aunt. I am filled with guilt for the thoughts I've been having about her now. She was so kind and generous to me all through my growing years. Papa couldn't have given me the education she provided. She sent me to the best schools and bought me expensive clothes."

"Did you ever discuss the past events with him?" David asked.

"He didn't want me to come. He said he feared what had happened to Mama might happen to me. I laughed at his fear. I wanted desperately to come—to see Linden Gardens. To live in luxury. Now I almost wish I'd never come."

"You didn't answer my question." David's tone was persistent.

"I did. I told you Papa didn't want me to come. He never mentioned either Libby's death or Nora's. I'm sure he couldn't have known of them or he would never have allowed me to come."

"I'm equally certain," David agreed. "I hate to think we might never have met."

He was seated very close to me, his breath warm on my cheek. My heart was beating madly and I knew why. I loved him. He was almost a stranger, yet I felt as if we'd always known each other.

"What are you thinking?" he asked.

I felt color flood my face. His smile was not one of mockery but of tenderness. He bent forward and kissed my cheek.

"I know you didn't come here to declare your love for me, but I'm going to tell you I love you. I thought I'd lost you. I couldn't bear it. I walked the floor thinking of a way I could see you. When I couldn't find an answer, I wrote you. Thank God that Kate gave you the letter."

"I wonder if it was steamed open," I said.

I took it from my purse and handed it to him. He examined the envelope.

"It looks as if it was opened and resealed. If so, there's nothing we can do about it. Besides, I have more on my mind at the moment than a letter. I want to kiss you. Do you mind?"

"I would mind if you didn't," I said.

I gave my lips willingly. Outside, a songbird started to trill a melody. It was beautiful, but no more so than the wild throb of my heart beating in unison with David's as he held me close in a prolonged embrace. We were both breathless when he released me. His brows raised questioningly. I knew he wanted to hear me say I loved him. And I did. Over and over. I wished that time could stand still for both of us. I'd never known such exquisite happiness. Yet I knew I had no business here unchaperoned. David tried to draw me close again, but I eluded his embrace and stood up.

I managed to speak, but my voice was shaky. "I must go, David. Please visit me."

"I'm sorry it won't be today. I have an appointment with the gentleman I told you about."

"It's just as well. I have an errand in the village." My voice was still tremulous with emotion, but I felt no embarrassment.

"May I call on you tomorrow?" He gathered me close.

"No, that's too long a time. Let me come with you to the village. The other can wait."

"No. I think it would be wise not to let the villagers know we regard each other as more than friends. For the present, at least."

"Perhaps you're right. I'll call on you tomorrow."

I was disappointed he hadn't said this afternoon, but I hid it with a smile. He escorted me out to the buggy where we embraced again, but this time in a more decorous fashion.

"I love you," he whispered. "Take care, my darling."

I nodded, too overcome to speak. He hoisted me into the carriage and handed me the reins. Once again I slapped the horse's flanks and he started off at an easy gait. I looked back and saw David still standing there, watching me. I blew him a kiss, then turned my attention to my driving. At least I tried to, but my heart was pounding so and I could think of nothing but that rapturous moment when our lips first met.

I'd not intended to ride to the village when I left for David's. The thought suddenly occurred to me while we were discussing the tragic events that had occurred at Linden Gardens that a visit to Dr. Carney might shed more light on Libby Innis. And so here I was, seated in the good doctor's office, awaiting my turn. There were two patients ahead of me, but there were several magazines stacked on a table to help pass the time.

I selected a copy of *Woman's Home Companion*. An article titled *"The Rebellion of the Female Sex"* caught my interest. I hadn't known there was a rebellion going on, but as I got deeper into the article, I became quite aware that there was. It discussed women seeking employment in all fields of work. It presented a valid argument for the right of women's suffrage. I agreed with every word. I was pleased that I had been able to complete it before Dr. Carney spoke my name.

I placed the magazine back on the stack and returned the greeting. To my surprise, the office was empty. I'd not even been aware that the two patients—an elderly gentleman and a woman of middle years—had already seen him and departed.

Since the waiting room was empty, he didn't bother to close the door to his consultation room. He looked quite professional in his long white coat. He was wearing spectacles, which he removed and set on his desk. Moving to the swivel chair behind his desk, he motioned me to the chair alongside it.

"You look well, Celeste," he said. "I hope you've had no further misadventures."

I was surprised by his statement. "Why would you think that, Doctor?"

He chuckled. "I'm just making idle chitchat."

He gently rubbed his eyes, sighed quietly, and rested his head against the leather back of his chair. I sensed his weariness, which he was now in the process of shaking off by letting himself relax.

"I am just about recovered from my misadventure," I told him. "I'm here not to talk about myself, but about the young lady who was the first to meet her death at Linden Gardens."

His gray eyes, which had been regarding me kindly, became stern.

"Libby Innis," he said. "Why should you wish to discuss her? She's been dead almost seventeen years. Let her soul rest in peace."

"I don't mean to do her memory any harm," I said quickly. "It's really my uncle I'm thinking about."

"Eric von Linden died of a heart attack. Libby Innis died from a fall down the stairs at his home."

"I understand she was going to have a baby." I kept my tone conversational, though I already sensed hostility or at least a growing coolness in Dr. Carney's manner.

"Was she?" he asked.

"That is what I was told," I replied. "I was also told Eric von Linden seduced her."

"I know nothing about a seduction or the so-called pregnancy of Libby Innis."

"You're not being honest with me, Doctor." The sternness in my voice matched his.

He leaned forward, rested his arm on the desk, and looked me directly in the eyes. "If you weren't an adult young lady—and I question the adult—I would take you across my knees and spank you. Don't you realize what you are doing by coming here and asking me such a question?"

"Yes." I refused to be intimidated by his sternness. "Trying to find out what happened at Linden Gardens."

"Everyone knows what happened there."

"Including the seduction of Libby Innis by my uncle?"

"I know nothing about that. I don't listen to idle gossip. Nor do I allow this office to be a place where a person's reputation is maligned. Particularly a young girl who has been long dead and has no one to come to her defense."

"I'm not trying to malign Libby," I exclaimed desperately. "I'm only trying to find out the truth."

"Keep your voice down, young lady." His voice held a warning tone. "Now you listen. I know only the facts. Which are that three young women met tragic deaths at Linden Gardens. Deaths that were accidental."

"I know that. And I've been told I will be the fourth victim of that staircase."

He snorted in disbelief and eyed me scornfully.

"It's true," I insisted. "Both Hester and Zeffrey told me I would be the fourth."

"Hester is a sick old lady who is almost bereft of her senses because of grief at the loss of her niece."

"She hates my aunt and she hates me," I retorted.

"Yes," he admitted, his manner softening. "In her warped mind, she believed your aunt was jealous of Libby's youth. She probably thinks in the same fashion regarding you."

"What about my mother?" I asked. "She and my aunt were sisters."

"What about your mother?"

"She was killed from a fall down those stairs."

"And so was Nora Martin," he said. "The only answer is that the stairway is treacherous. Or the three women were reckless—descending them in the dark without even a candle to light their way."

"What was their reason for going downstairs in darkness?"

"I have no idea," Dr. Carney said. "Nor did anyone else."

"Don't you think three deaths in the same fashion too coincidental to have been accidents?"

"Did you think about that when you learned of them?" he countered.

"I didn't know about them until I came here."

"All right. My question still stands."

"I believed them to be accidental. May I remind you about the rockslide?" My words came faster as the thought occurred to me. "I believe I saw someone at the top of the cliff. So did David Lathrop."

"Is that what he said?"

"Yes. You know he rescued me."

"I know. He paid me a visit to inquire after your health. He said nothing about having seen anyone."

"I suppose it's useless taking up more of your time."

"It is," he replied.

"Were you the medical examiner at the time of Libby's fall?"

"I was," he replied. "Each death was the result of a skull fracture that occurred when the victim's head struck the marble stairway."

"And Libby Innis was not with child?" My question was daring, but I had to ask. "As the medical examiner, you must have had to put that in the record—if there is a record of her death."

"There is," he replied. "There is no record of the pregnancy—if there was one. It had no bearing on her death."

"Don't you think it strange Libby was buried in the von Linden mausoleum?"

"Not at all. Your aunt had intended to adopt her."

"You don't think she would have if she had known Libby was carring Eric von Linden's child, do you?"

Dr. Carney leaned back, folded his arms across his chest, and regarded me sternly as he spoke.

"Celeste, I am a doctor. I have taken an oath not to violate the ethics of my profession. You are the first person who has attempted to make me do so. You're an intelligent young lady, so listen carefully. Had I known your reason for coming here, you would not have gotten into this room. I am not asking you to leave, I am ordering you to. If you do not, I shall be forced to evict you forcibly. I wouldn't like to have to do that."

"There will be no need for it, Doctor. Just remember, my concern is not for me as much as for my aunt."

"I doubt that very much."

"Now you are making me angry, Doctor. Certainly, you don't believe my aunt's behavior is normal."

"It is far from normal. She still grieves for her husband. Hester grieves for her niece. In that respect they are much alike, except that Hester's mind has become so obsessed with the fact that your aunt was the cause of her niece's death, her reasoning has become distorted."

"Not so much that she hasn't spread dreadful rumors about her niece and my uncle."

"I don't listen to rumors. And I won't sit here and discuss them with you. I have already ordered you to leave. Now I insist that you do so."

"I shall, Doctor. And be assured, I'll not bother you again. I hope my aunt will have no need of your services while I am a guest at Linden Gardens."

"How long will you be a guest there?" His question astonished me.

"That, Doctor, is none of your business."

I smiled as I stood up. Not a friendly smile, but a triumphant one.

"You're quite right, Celeste," he said, nodding agreement. "Good-bye."

As I walked to the open doorway, he called out, "Please don't think too harshly of me. I'm certain when you think it over, you will realize you were in error in coming here."

Without turning back, I said, "You made it very evident, Doctor. Good day."

To my surprise, Calvin was leaning against the white fence, apparently awaiting me. He was wearing riding togs and looked quite elegant. I wondered if he could ever look otherwise.

He came to attention quickly and opened the gate for me. "Celeste, when I saw the buggy parked in front of Dr. Carney's residence, I was fearful something might have happened to you."

"Not a thing," I said, smiling reassurance. "Or perhaps something did. I was practically thrown out of the office."

"By Dr. Carney?" He looked incredulous.

I nodded.

"What in heaven's name for?" His gloved hands rested lightly on my shoulders as he faced me. "No, don't tell me. Let's go to the Candy Striped Soda Shoppe and have some ice cream or a soda or anything you wish."

"I'd love a lemon phosphate. I am a little hungry."

"I should think so. I've already stabled the horse, since I was concerned about you. Zeffrey can pick it up tomorrow. I'll have to beg you for a ride back."

"You don't have to beg. I'll enjoy company."

"Then let's be on our way. It's only a few doors down."

It was a pretty place, decorated with red-and-white-striped wallpaper. The round tables had marble tops, and the chairs had round seats with red-and-white-striped cushions. The soda fountain had an awning with the same striped colors. The young man behind the soda fountain was dressed in a spotless white coat with red piping. Calvin gave our order and it was brought to our table. I was both thirsty and hungry and didn't object when Calvin insisted I have a strawberry sundae along with the lemon phosphate I ordered. He duplicated my order.

I didn't even attempt to engage in conversation until I had eaten a few spoonfuls. However, once my hunger was eased. I told Calvin why I had gone to Dr. Carney and the cold reception I had received.

He listened attentively until I had completed my story. Even then he maintained a thoughtful silence as he sipped his phosphate.

I waited for his opinion regarding my action as long as I could. Finally, my patience exhausted, I exclaimed, "Please tell me if you approve or disapprove of what I did."

"I approve," he replied seriously. "I can also understand Dr. Carney's position, just as I'm sure you can."

"I do," I reasoned. "Yet knowing what I know about Libby, I wonder if my aunt could have been responsible for her death."

"You're saying you don't believe Libby's death was an accident?"

"I don't know, Calvin. What is your opinion?"

"I have never thought it was anything else. Just as your mother's was. And Nora Martin's."

"Each of them died the same way. Yet none knew the other."

"What are you saying?" Calvin emptied his glass and set it down.

"That it seems too coincidental."

"It's a good point. Yet if the deaths were other than accidents, someone would have had to lure them to that stairway, then push them down."

"From Hester's viewpoint, the only one with a motive would be my aunt."

"Your aunt wouldn't kill her sister," Calvin argued. "I would never believe that and I don't see how you can."

"I wouldn't except that my aunt's behavior is so strange

at times. In fact, it's been strange most of the time I've been here."

"It was your accident that served to unnerve her."

I gave an impatient shrug. "If she hadn't suggested I go for a walk on the cliff path, I wouldn't even have known about it."

"I don't know, Celeste. I just don't know."

"Nor do I," I replied, aware that his confusion matched mine.

"I don't like the fact that you're so upset about it, though I can understand why you are."

"Why am I, Calvin?"

"I'd say because of your mother."

I nodded. I didn't add that Nora Martin was also a part of my concern. David had asked that I not reveal his true identity and I had promised though we both realized that someone else knew about it, since his envelope had undoubtedly been steamed open by someone in the house. So far as David and I knew, only Kate had any knowledge of the letter. Certainly, her behavior toward me had changed, and the change occurred after David had delivered the letter to Linden Gardens, asking her to give it to me.

Calvin said, "I think we'd better start back. It's a fairly long drive and the rain has been threatening all day."

"It will probably be a rainy summer."

"I hope not. We've had too much as it is."

The ride back was pleasant, though we were startled to meet David on his way to town. He seemed surprised to see me with Calvin and I thought I detected a trace of jealousy in his eyes. I hoped so. It would further assure me of his love. We exchanged greetings and a bit of small talk before we continued on our way.

Wanda was in a state of great agitation when we entered the house. It was evident from the wrinkled handkerchief she used to wipe the palms of her hands. Her features, tense and worried, gave further evidence of it.

"I thought you'd never get back." She addressed both of us.

"What's wrong?" Calvin asked immediately.

Wanda went to a hall table and returned with an envelope. "It's a letter from Emma's friend."

"What friend?" I asked.

"The gentleman who was to receive the sum of money you brought to New York City yesterday."

"What about him?" I asked.

"He did not receive the envelope. He does not believe your aunt had it delivered."

I said, "Is he demanding she deliver another?"

"Apparently," Wanda said. "Usually we don't see the letters. This one sent her into hysterics when it arrived. I gave her a sleeping draught."

"Shouldn't we send for Dr. Carney?" I asked.

"That's what he would prescribe," Wanda said.

"It's true, Celeste." Calvin spoke as he took the letter from the envelope. He read it aloud.

Dear Emma:

I went to the usual place for the gratuity you so graciously give me. For the first time in years, it was not there. Does it mean you will no longer furnish me with the cash I need to maintain my station in life? If so, I would like a letter from you to that effect. If it was because of the illness of your messenger, I can understand

The fact is, I need funds desperately. I will be honest. I am being blackmailed by a lady with whom I have been on most intimate terms. I did not know she was married. She has threatened to tell her husband if I do not pay her the sum of three thousand dollars immediately.

I beg of you to have your messenger bring the money in an envelope Wednesday. I do not want the one person in the entire world I hold most dear to learn of the fact that I made a fool of myself.

Calvin said, "Do you wish to read the letter, Celeste?"

"Is it signed?" I asked.

"No." Calvin held it before me so I could read it easily. "Nor is it in script. The words are printed. He's not taking a chance on his handwriting being identified."

"It's disgusting," I said angrily.

Calvin put the letter back in the envelope and addressed me. "You did say, Celeste, that you went back to that chair to see if the envelope was still there. You discovered it missing."

"That's true."

"Someone must have seen you thrust it down the side of the cushion. When you left the chair and the area, that individual retrieved it. Plus a considerable sum of money."

"What are you going to do—if anything?"

"I can't go to New York City tomorrow," Calvin said. "Attorney Luke Aarons is coming here tomorrow to go over your aunt's books. He comes once a month."

"I can't go," Wanda said. "I could never leave Emma alone in the state she is in. If she wakes up and finds me missing, she may have another case of hysterics."

"What about Kate?" I asked.

"Kate will sit up with her tonight. Someone has to be by her bedside in case she should waken. We don't want her to get up and fall."

She didn't say "down the stairs," but I knew that was what she meant.

I said, "I'll go."

"Not alone," Calvin said.

"I must," I said. "Who is there to accompany me?"

"Kate would be of no help should you be in danger," he mused.

"I don't expect my mission to be dangerous."

"We don't either," Calvin said. "But Wanda's right. There's always an outside possibility."

Wanda said, "Kate couldn't go anyway after sitting up all night. What about David Lathrop? If he isn't otherwise engaged, perhaps he would accompany you."

The very mention of his name lifted my spirits, though I tried not to let it show. "He may not be free."

Calvin said, "I'll take the buggy and drive over. If he isn't home, I'll leave a note, explaining your mission and asking if he will accompany you."

Wanda looked pensive.

Calvin said, "What's on your mind?"

"I'm wondering if Celeste and David couldn't reconnoiter sort of and see who picks up that envelope."

"You said you had strict orders not to," I reminded her.

"True," she admitted. "But this can't go on. Your aunt is so near a breakdown, another upset like this could send her over the brink."

"May I see her?" I asked.

"Of course. Kate is with her."

Calvin headed for the door. "I have a pencil and there

is a pad in the buggy. I'll go directly to David's. I hope he's there so I can discuss this with him."

"So do I," I said fervently, and headed for the stairs to see if my aunt had awakened.

She hadn't. Kate looked over her shoulder when I entered the room, but otherwise paid me no need except to put a cautioning forefinger to her lips for me to be quiet. I doubted that was necessary. From the sound of my aunt's heavy breathing, I knew she was completely under the influence of the sleeping draught. I wondered if she would waken before the following morning.

Dinner was a quiet affair. Calvin informed Wanda and me that he had left a note for David, who was not at home.

Calvin said, "I told David in the note that there was no need for him to drive over to tell us whether or not he could come."

"I don't think that was a smart thing to do," Wanda said worriedly. "How will Celeste know?"

"She won't," Calvin admitted with a smile. "I figure if he could come, he would be here. If he couldn't, he would not."

"I still don't like it," Wanda said.

I could see the humor to it, also the logic, and endeavored to explain it to Wanda. "What would be the sense of David's driving over tonight? I'm going tomorrow anyway. If he's here at the time I leave, that will be splendid. I'll have company. Otherwise, I can amuse myself with magazines."

"You forget, Wanda," Calvin said, "I already made the journey with Celeste. I know she is a most competent young lady."

"Even so," Wanda grumbled, "I don't like her going alone."

"I suggest you not worry about it," Calvin said, "until tomorrow morning when you know definitely whether she will or will not have to travel alone."

"I'm not even sure I want him to go along," Wanda said petulantly.

"In heaven's name, make up your mind!" Calvin responded, flashing her a look of irritation over the rim of his wine glass.

"We scarcely know him," Wanda argued.

Calvin joined me in laughter.

Wanda did not. She said, "What do you find so humorous?"

"I scarcely knew Calvin when he accompanied me to the city," I replied. "Please don't get all worked up about it, Wanda."

She smiled apologetically. "I'm sorry. It's just that these spells Emma gets are becoming more and more frequent and lasting longer and longer. She's scarcely been herself since you came, Celeste."

"I'm aware of that," I said, sobering. "And my concern for my aunt equals yours. I hope David can come. Two of us might have a better chance of catching a glimpse of the person who picks up that envelope. I would like to confront him."

"I wonder if he's telling the truth," Wanda mused. "Or if he is becoming more bold in his requests for gratuities."

I said, "We have no way of knowing."

"Not when we don't even know who he is," Calvin added. "At least we know it's a man from this letter."

Wanda said, "I think we always knew that."

"Perhaps," Calvin replied. "Though I've sometimes wondered."

"Is there a later train back here?" I asked.

"Yes," Calvin said. "It leaves around six o'clock. It makes quite a few stops. You'll get in around midnight."

Wanda said, "It will be a long day."

"A rewarding one," I added, "if we learn the identity of this mysterious person who makes such large monetary demands on my aunt."

Calvin said, "I don't believe you will be in any danger or I'd not consent to letting you go."

"I'm not the least bit afraid," I told him, though pleased by his concern. "In fact, I'm impatient to leave. I don't know what I will say when we confront this individual, but I shan't let him get away without informing him my aunt is going to cease contributing to his support."

"Oh, my goodness," Wanda exclaimed. "I know I suggested it, but I'm not sure you should do it. I'm fearful of what effect it will have on Emma."

"She won't know anything about it until it's been done," I said. "I'm sure David will add verbal persuasion in a manner that will assure this parasite that he can no longer depend on my aunt to support him. Particularly after the disgusting letter he wrote. He must be a man of very loose morals."

Wanda said, "I agree. I find it difficult to believe he didn't know his paramour was married. I'm not even certain I believe he is being blackmailed."

"Whether he is or not," Calvin said sensibly, "it's time it ended."

I nodded agreement. We retired early since I would be rising before dawn. I knew, just as before, I would be my own alarm clock.

Still, sleep eluded me. I threw back the covers, pushed my feet into soft-soled slippers, slipped on my negligee, and went into the sitting room. It was a sultry night and I sat before the open window. I needed no light, for I was familiar with both rooms and I moved about easily in darkness.

I had a view of the horseshoe drive and the beautiful landscaping around it. I thought of Papa and a wave of loneliness swept over me. I knew exactly what he would be doing each evening. Sitting before the fireplace where Mama's portrait hung. It took all these years for me to realize that he still derived a measure of comfort when he could look at her likeness. It must have brought back memories of the few happy years they had had together.

I thought back to the good times Papa and I had had together and of the happiness that little flat had known when boarding school was out. I compared it with the complete lack of happiness in this mansion, which could easily be termed a castle. There was an aching emptiness that pervaded it. It was evident in every room, even this one.

I know it was a sound that drew my attention back to the grounds. A metallic sound. My eyes searched the drive and the area where the trees and shrubs were placed so symmetrically. At first I saw nothing, but as my eyes continued to scan the area, I caught sight of a figure moving along the edge of the drive, but walking on the grass. That would lessen the chance of crunching footsteps being heard. Also, there would be less likelihood of making a misstep on the loose pebbles and turning on one's ankle.

From time to time, I lost sight of the figure, only to catch a glimpse of it again. As it neared the exit and passed beyond where the drive curved, I could no longer see the individual. I was puzzled as to who, in this household, would wish to move about so stealthily. Also, I wondered where that person was going.

I almost exclaimed aloud as I caught a glimpse of light. It was faint, but evident. A lantern! That's what made the metallic sound I heard. Someone was going somewhere, yet wanted no one else in the household to know, so delayed lighting the lantern. I had to know who was absent from the house. I decided against using a lamp or even candlelight.

I left my door ajar and went directly across the hall to my aunt's suite. I turned the knob softly, not certain if either Kate or Wanda would be there. It didn't matter. I could say I heard a sound and wondered if something might be wrong with her.

The room was in darkness, but I could hear her heavy breathing. She was still under the influence of the sleeping draught. I went directly to her bedside to make certain it was she. I could tell by touching one of her hands. I knew by now she was never without her rings except, I supposed, when she bathed. My hand moved carefully along the side of the bed. Luck was with me. I encountered her hand. I used only the tip of my forefinger to check for rings. I counted three. It was she.

I left my aunt's room and continued on to Wanda's. Using the utmost caution, I turned the knob soundlessly and opened the door a few inches. The sitting room was in darkness, but a light burned in her bedroom. I heard her humming softly as she moved about. I closed the door as cautiously as I'd opened it and continued, not certain just where Calvin's room was. I needed only to pause outside a few doors to find his. His snoring was evident through the closed door. The fact that I hadn't heard it as I approached the room was a tribute to the soundness of the mansion. Catacombs would be a more appropriate word for the edifice.

Only Kate's room was left. I'd never been on the third floor, but I was familiar enough with the second floor to know that a narrow closed door undoubtedly led to her quarters. I opened it, extended my arms, and let my hands explore the area. I found a slanted railing and my foot cautiously explored the space in front of me for a staircase. I discovered it easily enough and started my ascent.

At the top, a slender line of light was visible below a

closed door. I went directly to it and pressed my ear against the wood. I didn't hear a sound. I decided to risk exposure. Using the same caution as I had in opening Wanda's door, I turned the knob. No one screamed or demanded my identity as I moved the door slowly open.

I stepped into the room. It was spartanly furnished and spotless. The bedclothes were turned down, Kate's nightdress lay across the foot of the bed, but she was nowhere in sight.

It had to be she. She had left my aunt's bedside for a rendezvous with someone. I couldn't imagine who it could be, but I did know now she was not the innocent she pretended to be. Had she gone to see Hester? If so, why? I half thought of hitching up the buggy and going to the village. That would be childish, though, because I had no idea of her destination. I was glad I'd seen the figure flitting through the darkness and learned its identity.

I wondered what Wanda would say if she knew Kate had left my aunt's bedside to keep an appointment with someone. Could she, perchance, know the identity of the man who had been getting sums of money from my aunt all these years? A thoroughly despicable character. I couldn't wait to confront him and tell him what I thought of him. I was certain David would back me up—if he was able to accompany me.

There was nothing for me to do now but return to my room. For some reason, I stopped at the room that held such fascination for my aunt—the one known as the Zodiac Room. When I looked inside, there was no smell of incense, no candles burning, nothing but blackness. I was just about to close the door when I heard the tinkle of tiny bells. Though I knew it was Wanda, I jumped with a start when she spoke my name.

She held a lamp and she was at my side in seconds. "I thought I heard a sound of some kind and left my room to investigate."

I mentally berated myself for having abandoned caution. I said, "So did I. But I checked my aunt's room and moved along the corridor. Everything seems as it should."

"Good," Wanda said. "Is Kate with Emma?"

"Yes," I replied. The lie was out before I realized what I'd said.

"You've never been in the Zodiac Room, have you?"

Wanda asked, motioning with her free hand to the door I still held open.

"No." Once again a lie slipped off my tongue easily.

"I'll show it to you."

I wondered if she believed my lie. How would I have known the location of this room had I not been here before? There was no light in it to reveal that it was different from the few rooms that were used.

"Come along, my dear." Wanda preceded me into the room. I closed the door so that my aunt would not be disturbed.

Wanda set the lamp on the round table and went over to the long one. She lit a taper from a match she took from a box and touched the flame to the candles. Behind the table were long black curtains. She moved to one side of the table, reached behind the curtains, and pulled on a cord. The curtains separated to reveal a mirrored wall. The mirror had to be a special kind for it sent sharp flashes of light all around the room, making me blink and finally raise a hand to shade my eyes from the piercing, constantly moving light. However, it seemed to have no effect on Wanda.

"The parts of the walls that are covered with drapery have large drawings of hands. Would you like to see them?"

I really wanted to get back to my room so I could watch for Kate's return. In that way, I might gauge the distance she had gone. Nonetheless, I answered in the affirmative, knowing that that was what Wanda wished.

She moved briskly about the room, pulling cords and exposing drawings of enormous hands. Some had the various fingers encircled. Some had the palm encircled or a square drawn over a section of palm. They alternated with the zodiac signs. I was becoming used to the light and walked over to where Wanda stood.

"Hands fascinated me," she said. "Not so much for fortune-telling, but I feel one can read a great deal about a person's character in the hand."

"I've never thought of such a thing," I said, pretending an interest I didn't feel.

"Of course you haven't," she said. "But I'm a gypsy. It's in my blood. Take this hand, for instance. As you can see, the forefinger has a rectangle drawn around it to separate it from the others. The index finger is called the finger of

Jupiter. It was also called the Napoleonic finger, though that was a mistake since Napoleon had an extremely short forefinger. It is a demonstrative finger and is often called the world finger because it points at the outside world. Am I boring you?"

"No, Wanda. What I'd like to ask is, does this sort of thing interest my aunt?"

"Enormously. She is quite familiar with every chart in this room. As you can see, between the hand charts are the signs of the zodiac."

I moved to the small table in the center of the room. "What is this?"

"Aren't you familiar with tarot cards?"

"Yes. I mean this brass ornament with the oval ring and the small mirror suspended from the center."

"That is nothing. Usually my crystal ball sits in the center of the table. That's something I picked up years ago because it has a rather exotic look."

"I'd say bizarre is a more apt description. It seems as if it must have some sort of function."

"Have you seen one before?" she asked. She moved up beside me as she spoke and let her hand rest on the top of it.

"No. That's why it intrigues me."

She smiled. "I wish I could satisfy your curiosity. But it has absolutely no significance. I suppose that's why I put it in this room."

"That doesn't make sense, Wanda. Especially since everything else in this room has significance."

I moved over to another chart of a hand. The little finger had a square drawn around it. Above it was printed *The Finger of Mercury*.

Wanda joined me. "The little finger is called the ear finger. Do you know why?"

"No."

"Because it's the finger many people use to clean their ears."

"How interesting," I said, though not too convincingly, I feared.

"It's not the least bit interesting," she said. "Except to one fascinated by the study of palmistry. I have been most fortunate that your aunt shares my interest. You know about the lifeline, the heartline, the headline, on the palm of the hand."

"Please Wanda, some other time," I pleaded. "I'm tired. And you know what my day will be tomorrow."

"Of course, my dear. Forgive me. Go back to your room. I'll put these lights out. On second thought, I think I'll stay in here awile. I'm a little restless."

"I think that letter upset the three of us."

She nodded. "I wonder how much more Emma can stand."

"It's up to us to put an end to it for all time."

"Yes. I hope you won't have any difficulty tomorrow. I'd feel a lot better if I knew David was going to accompany you."

"Why don't you look in your crystal ball? That should tell you."

"I don't make jokes about that, Celeste. I wish you wouldn't."

"I'm sorry. I was only half joking. You do believe in it, don't you?"

"It foretold your accident on the cliff," she said remindfully.

"Also, that I would meet a young person with whom I should be on guard."

"If it was David," Wanda said, smiling, "I'm glad the crystal ball was wrong. Or perhaps it was I who interpreted it incorrectly."

"In any case, we won't worry about it. Everything turned out well."

"David was your savior rather than your destroyer."

I smiled agreement. "I'll go now, Wanda. I hope you rest tonight."

"I hope so. I must be with your aunt tomorrow. Kate is the night attendant."

I wondered why Wanda wanted to stay here. It was a depressing place, with the black draperies and unattractive furniture. The mirrored wall could drive one mad. I'd never come here again, even if I were invited. I wouldn't mind letting Wanda look into the crystal ball to see my future—even though I wouldn't take it seriously. But it would be in her suite.

I said, "While I'm here, I would like to ask if you and Kate would rearrange your schedules so that I might spend more time with my aunt. During her waking hours it would help me to get acquainted with her. We're still practically strangers. And it would give you and Kate a chance to do something else."

Wanda looked pleased by my suggestion. "After tomorrow, we will do it."

I said, "Thanks, Wanda," and headed for the door. She was already pulling the cords to close the draperies over the giant-size drawings of every size and shape of palm imaginable.

I opened the door and held back a gasp of startlement only with difficulty. Kate had had her ear pressed against it. She had no lamp, and though the hall was in darkness, the mirrored wall hadn't yet been covered by its draperies and a shaft of that wild light spotlighted her face, revealing her dismay at being discovered.

My features hardened at the sight of her, but I held my tongue, not wishing her to be disciplined by Wanda. Perhaps even dismissed. Certainly her behavior warranted it. I wondered why I should even want to protect her after the way she had spoken to me in the room I had just left.

Without a word, I closed the door quietly, moved around her, and headed for my room. I heard the door to the third floor stairway close quietly. It was impossible to hear her ascent. I imagined she was going up there to put away the large shawl she was wearing which covered her from her head to below her knees. I noted in the dim light that it was black, which was the reason I'd had difficulty in following her flight down the drive.

I locked the door of my sitting room, but remained standing there, listening for Kate's return. At least I expected her to return, since it was her duty to remain with my aunt during the night. I didn't imagine Wanda would think anything of it if they met in the hall now. It wouldn't be difficult for Kate to think of a reason for having gone to her room.

I wondered if I had played the fool in protecting her. Certainly she'd shown open fear at being discovered eavesdropping. I wondered where she had gone. Whom had she seen. And even more, what reason she had for leaving the house.

Once again, my thoughts turned to Hester and Zeffrey. Did they have a hold on my aunt no one knew about but them? Was Kate in collusion with them? Certainly she could keep track of everything that went on in the house. I'd also discovered she wasn't above devious behavior.

There was also the letter David wrote me and brought here. He had handed it to her. She had told me it was on the night table when I returned. It might well have been, though I'd not seen it. She could have kept it until she had an opportunity to steam it open, read the contents, reseal it, and place it in my room while I was sleeping. If so, she knew David's real identity. She also knew he did not believe his sister's death was accidental.

I hoped very much that David would be able to accompany me to the city tomorrow. I had a lot to tell him. I wondered if the private detective he had hired had learned anything that would be of help in solving the mystery of the three deaths. I also wondered if he was aware of Kate's existence, and if so, if he had been able to maintain a watch on her. Could it be that this was not the first night she had taken a surreptitious leave of absence from the house?

So many questions were running through my head, it was beginning to ache. I heard the soft closing of the door across the hall. Kate had returned. My aunt was not alone. I wondered if she wouldn't be safer alone. I didn't dare to start thinking that way. Enough had happened in this house. And tomorrow, I was to bring a sum of money to a man who was being blackmailed by a woman with whom he had had an illicit liaison. I sighed wearily and went back to bed. I wondered what David would think when he heard the story. I was certain Calvin hadn't gone into detail in the note he'd written.

In a way, I was pleased I would be away from Linden Gardens for the day. The house reminded me of a tomb. Each time I entered it, I felt as if I'd just been buried alive.

◆ Ten ◆

My joy was boundless when David made an appearance just as I was about to leave. Zeffrey was to take me to the depot, but David waved him away, bent down, and swooped me up into the seat beside him.

We were none too early, so our ride was brisk. One of my hands gripped the metal bar supporting the hood. My other held my hat. Even so, it seemed about to slip its moorings each time we hit a pothole.

David had returned to the depot the previous day after getting Calvin's note and had purchased two tickets. It proved to be a wise move because we were no sooner out of the buggy than the train, already in the station, was tooting a farewell. We ran like schoolchildren through the station. Once again he lifted me effortlessly onto the platform, then jumped up himself just as the wheels of the train started to move.

We were too out of breath to talk immediately. The train was quite a distance from the station before our breathing had calmed sufficiently so we could converse.

David started the conversation. "I gather this journey has a note of urgency to it."

"Very much so. I am delivering an envelope containing quite a sum of money to a gentleman who is being blackmailed by a woman who is—or was—his paramour."

"Is that the same gentleman to whom you delivered an envelope previously?"

"Yes. The letter he sent my aunt upset her so she had another one of her spells. Wanda had to give her a sleeping draught."

"I'd say your aunt is the one who is being blackmailed."

"I agree. So do Wanda and Calvin. Wanda suggested we try to discover who the gentleman is. I am going to do more than that. I'm going to confront him and tell him he has got the last cent out of my aunt he is going to."

David looked pensive. "What effect do you suppose that will have on your aunt?"

"None, I hope. Of course, I wouldn't be going today except that he didn't get the envelope I put down the side of the chair."

"You mean someone intercepted it." David made it a statement.

"It had to be someone who saw me place it there," I reasoned. "I thought I was careful, but I'll be the first to admit I'm an amateur at that sort of thing."

"That sort of thing is something I don't like to think of your doing. And I have a suggestion."

His protective attitude touched me. It had a greater effect on my heartbeat when he reached for my hand, slipped it around his forearm, and placed his other hand over mine.

"What kind of suggestion?" I asked.

"I'd like to know what is in that envelope."

Such a thought had never occurred to me, but my answer was, "So would I."

"Do you have the key to your flat?"

I nodded. "What you're saying is we can go there, steam open the envelope, and see if he is getting the three thousand dollars he asked for."

"Are you game to do it?"

I hesitated, but not for long. "Yes."

"Very well. That will be our first stop. Then we'll take a hack to the hotel and you will place the envelope in the chair as you did before. We will have to find a place where we can view the area, without being seen ourselves."

"I hope he comes."

"I have a feeling he knows the train schedules. He'll wait a sufficient length of time, then head directly to the hotel."

"I'll not let him get away, believe me."

"Just don't be so eager that you scare him away before he gets what he came after," David cautioned. "Otherwise, he could claim complete ignorance of what you are talking about. You didn't mention it, but I assume there was no signature on the letter."

"It wasn't even initialed. And it was printed."

"That's interesting. He must be known to someone. Tell me about everything you did yesterday after you left me."

"Nothing exciting, you may be sure. I told you I was going to the village."

"Yes. You saw Dr. Carney."

"How did you know?"

He smiled. "I told you I had a private detective working for me. He may have men working for him. He is free to spend any sum necessary to gain information that would prove my sister's death was not an accident. In so doing, I hope we can prove that neither Libby's death nor your mother's was either."

"Do you know the kind of reception I got from Dr. Carney?"

David eyed me with a trace of amusement. "If you went for information about Libby—and I have a hunch that's why you went—you were given short shrift."

"You must know him."

"I've talked with him, though more discreetly. I learned quickly enough he was a man of high ethics."

"He sent me packing."

"You don't really believe your uncle sired Libby's child, do you?"

"I'd like to believe he didn't."

"Have you seen a painting of him at Linden Gardens? I believe my father did his portrait."

"I would imagine it is in the master library. That is one of the rooms that is closed. Most are, though they are all kept up."

"I suggest you look at it when you return. You may have second thoughts about him."

"What do you mean?"

"I'll say no more. You must form your own conclusions."

"I suppose you know that when I left Dr. Carney's, Calvin was outside waiting for me."

"And quite impatiently, from the report I got."

"His attitude was the same as yours in regard to Dr. Carney's treatment of me."

"Perhaps not quite the same," David said, smiling. "Please go on."

"There's really not much to tell. When Calvin and I returned home, we learned about the letter my aunt had received. Calvin read it aloud. At dinner we discussed it and what you and I would do. Of course, Calvin would have accompanied me except that my aunt's attorney was due today and he had to go over the books with him."

"Lucky for me," David said, squeezing my hand slightly.

"Oh," I exclaimed, as I recalled the figure I'd seen moving down the drive in darkness. "There is something else. I did see someone on the grounds last night. It had to be Kate. Her manner toward me has changed completely. Until two days ago I'd been fond of her, and I thought she liked me. But I was wrong."

I related what I had observed from my window and told him how I had checked the occupied rooms. The only person missing was Kate. I continued my story of Wanda encountering me at the door of the Zodiac Room. I described the room and the few pieces of furniture in it, the black draperies, and the bronze ornament that I found intriguing. Also, the mirrored wall that sent almost blinding lights in every direction.

David said, "Some were probably angled and others curved."

"It was a weird place. Wanda wanted to give me a lecture on palmistry. The name of each finger, its purpose, the lines on the palm, and what they signified."

David looked amused. "Did you let her?"

"No. I was more concerned with getting back to my room so I could watch for Kate's return. I felt I might get an idea of where she went by the length of time she was gone."

"Was it long—or didn't you see her return?"

"Wanda wished to remain in the room and it was lucky for Kate she did, because when I opened the door she was so close to it, she had to have been eavesdropping."

"Did you report her to Wanda?"

"No. And I still don't know why I didn't."

"Perhaps you have a little of the psychic in you, too," David reasoned.

"I don't understand."

"Suppose I just say I like Kate. I also had the feeling she liked you."

"You wouldn't think so if you had heard her the night she caught me in the Zodiac Room. Wanda said my aunt loves that room."

"If so, it's probably because Wanda puts on a good

show for her. Your aunt is lonely. She can forget it in that room. She is probably transported to another world—or thinks she is."

"It's really sad," I said, "that she continues to live in that house when she is rejected by the entire village. Did you know she contributes generously to civic affairs?"

"So generously that no one else has need to," David said. "Also, she contributes to the church and the poor and the ailing."

"She is trying to make up for those three tragic deaths."

"There has to be another way. We've got to find it. By that I mean she has to get something out of life before it is over for her."

"How can we help, David? She's in bed most of the time. When she talks with me, she is completely uninterested in me or anything I have to say."

"Well, the first thing we are going to do is see if there is three thousand dollars in that envelope. It's thick enough for there to be."

"And we're almost in the city." I slipped my hand free of David's arm and started working my leather gloves over my fingers. The gloves were brown to match my linen suit. I was wearing a straw sailor with a brown band. On impulse I'd attached a veil with a design of flowers on it. The veil was coyly flirtatious rather than functional, though it did help conceal my features. I could see through it easily, but my face was partially hidden.

Fortunately, we had no difficulty in getting a hack, and we arrived at the flat fifteen minutes later. I immediately put a kettle of water on the gas stove, turned the flame high, and waited impatiently for the water to boil. I slipped my hand into my skirt pocket, where I had concealed the envelope. Wanda had suggested it, since my purse was small and would bulge with the envelope in it. She feared a purse snatcher. I retrieved the envelope and handed it to David, who had just come into the room after observing Mama's portrait.

"She's beautiful," he said. "It's my father's work. It's fascinating for me to see some of his work for the first time."

"Do you know I've never seen a thing you've done?"

"You will—if I have anything to say about it. I love you, Celeste. You know that. I haven't met your father yet, so I will wait until then to ask you to marry me. It's only fair he know a little about me first."

"I'm sure he will approve."

Our lips met in a brief but tender kiss. This was not the time for romance. We had some serious business to attend to, and David was as aware of it as I.

The steam was already hissing out of the kettle and he placed the envelope about it. It took time, for the envelope was long and David had to keep it moving so it wouldn't be burned by the steam. I think he was burned a couple of times, but the only evidence he gave of it was a momentary compression of his lips.

Finally, the last bit came unstuck. I shut off the gas and moved the kettle to a cold grate. David went to the kitchen table, slipped his fingers into the envelope, and drew out a thick sheaf. The bundle of bills was enclosed in the two pieces of plain paper—at least, that is what we thought at first. But as he placed each piece of paper, the exact size of a bill, on the table, our perplexity grew.

When he had gone through each strip of paper, he said, "What do you make of it?"

"Obviously, Calvin refused to give more money to this man. Yet I believe the man was telling the truth when he wrote the money was gone when he went to get it from the chair. I checked the chair before Calvin and I left the lobby. The envelope was not there."

"Even if Calvin decided not to send the money," David reasoned, "why didn't he tell you?"

"Do you suppose Wanda knew about it?" I asked.

"I would imagine so." David stacked the paper in a neat pile and replaced it in the envelope. I left the room momentarily to get some glue. He sealed the flap very carefully and wiped off the surplus glue with a cloth I had furnished so there was no evidence that the envelope had been tampered with.

I said, "There is going to be one very angry man when he opens the envelope."

"Yes," David said thoughtfully.

"What are you thinking?" I asked.

"That we'd better get to the hotel before the recipient of this"—he held up the envelope—"does."

Once again we used a hack to get us to our destination. As before, I entered the hotel alone and strolled casually through the lobby to the large niche where the chair was.

It hadn't been moved, nor had the palms. I sat down, made a careful observation of the lobby—the part that was visible—before I removed the envelope from my skirt and slipped it down the side of the chair. I sat there awhile longer, taking note that one of the arched niches was visible from where I sat. That meant at least one of us could sit there and observe whoever came for the envelope.

I didn't think it exciting this time. My thoughts were in a turmoil, wondering why neither Calvin nor Wanda had apprised me of what they had done. Did they fear I might give the show away? Or did they think I might refuse to go if my mission was nothing more than a sham? If so, why had they insisted that David accompany me in case I met with any danger? I couldn't answer any of the questions and it was pointless to sit here any longer, so I returned to the lobby. David was awaiting me and we greeted each other as if we had just met. I informed him of the niche where we would have a view of the one I had just left.

He nodded approval and we went there. It was a pleasant surprise to discover a settee placed there. We could both sit on it with ease. Like the other niches, it had potted palms placed so that the occupants of the niche would have privacy, yet could observe the well-dressed ladies and gentlemen who passed through the lobby.

David said, "I know you must be hungry. Why don't you go to the dining room and I will keep watch?"

"Never," I said adamantly. "I must see who this is."

"Don't forget," David said, "there is no money in that envelope. So it isn't as if he is getting away with a small fortune."

"I had forgotten," I admitted. "I am also wondering if it might have been my aunt who placed the paper in that envelope. Calvin didn't say he had done it."

"He took care of the envelope before, didn't he?" David asked.

"Yes."

"It's highly likely then that he did so this time."

"What time is it?" I asked.

"One o'clock. I'm going to get you a box of candy. You need something to nibble on."

I didn't protest because I was beginning to feel hunger pangs. He returned with a two-pound box.

"We'll be sick if we ever eat all these," I said. "Come to think of it, Calvin purchased a box for me the last time."

"Don't tell me about it," David spoke with mock sternness. "I'm jealous."

"You needn't be. I put them in a drawer in the writing desk and forgot all about them."

"That won't happen this time." He already had the box open and we both helped ourselves.

He said, "I got assorted creams. Without anything to wash them down, I thought it would be better than caramels."

"Much better," I agreed. "But we'll both be sick if we eat too many."

"At least we won't be hungry."

After we'd eaten several, he placed the cover on the box and slipped it beneath the settee. We used my handkerchief to wipe our fingers and settled back. As the time passed, we started to get edgy. However, at least we could forget our stomachs and concentrate on the lobby and the gentlemen who passed through.

I was just about to get my gloves out of my bag when David gripped my arm. I almost cried out from the pain, but I knew he didn't realize how tight his grip was. I couldn't have believed anyone could have gained entrance to the niche without my seeing him, but someone had. *The chair was occupied.* The potted palms hid the face and torso of the person, but I could see the shoes and, above them, trouser legs, so I knew it was a man.

I could even see him shift his body to one side so he could get his hand down the side of the chair more easily. I had deliberately thrust it down as far as I could. Finally he shifted his body so that he was seated in a normal position. We could see the envelope being held up.

I didn't realize I was so tense that I had moved to the edge of the cushion, as if ready to jump to my feet and dash across the lobby. Not until David, in a protective gesture, extended his arm until he had it across the front of my body up near my shoulders, making it impossible for me to move. His other hand released my arm. Then he put his arm around my back and got a firm grip on my shoulder. I couldn't move.

The next thing we saw was the flurry of papers as the person threw them from him. The envelope followed. He stood up then and strode angrily into the lobby.

At first I was so shocked, I couldn't believe my eyes. Then my mouth opened and I screamed, "Papa."

At least I would have screamed the name had not David's hand pressed firmly against my mouth, smothering my cry. I struggled to free myself from his grip, but he was too strong.

Papa's face was livid with rage. He'd been thwarted in his demand for blackmail money. He was the one who had been blackmailing my aunt all these years. He must have felt it was his due after what had happened to Mama.

I ceased my struggles once he exited the lobby, but David didn't release his hold on me. Nor did his hand move from my mouth.

"I know what you're thinking." He spoke in a low tone of voice, but there was a hardness to it I'd never heard before. Perhaps a touch of anger. I looked up at him. His eyes regarded me sternly.

I again tried to struggle free of him so I could reply, but my efforts were futile.

"You've known your father all your life," he said. "Think of how long you have known Wanda and Calvin—and Kate and your aunt. Also, Hester and Zeffrey. Only a matter of days. Think of what we found in the envelope. Calvin knew there was no money in it. Perhaps Wanda knew also. That's something we have to find out—and we will if you'll just be patient. All I ask now is that you not condemn your father without a hearing. Do I have your word on that?"

I'm sure my eyes flashed the anger and frustration I was feeling because of his refusal to let me confront Papa. And I couldn't even reply with his hand held firmly over my mouth.

David said, "We have to talk this out sensibly. If you'll behave, just nod your head and I'll let you go."

I nodded my head as much as I could, which was very little since his hand was so big and so strong. He trusted me, though, for his hand released me. My veil had become torn when he covered my mouth with his hand, and so the first thing I did was to drape it over the crown of my hat, eliminating an untidy look.

"All right," I said weakly. I did feel spent from my struggles. "What can you say to convince me Papa has not been collecting money from Aunt Emma all these years?"

"First of all," David replied quietly, "did you see the letter which supposedly arrived at Linden Gardens yesterday?"

"I could have. Calvin offered it to me. I had no desire to read it."

"You should have. Something might have revealed it was spurious."

"What do you mean?"

"That letter could have been written at Linden Gardens yesterday while you were in the village. Or perhaps sooner. Its envelope could have been one in which some other correspondence came, addressed to your aunt."

"It could have, but you don't know for certain."

"Neither do you. So give your father the benefit of the doubt."

"What could have brought him here?"

"I don't know yet any more than you do. But I may know before the day is over."

"How? Please, David, tell me how?"

Tears clouded my vision. I tried to blink them back. David took his handkerchief and used it to blot my tears away. I nodded appreciation at the gesture.

"You know I'm using the services of a private detective agency," he said.

"Yes."

"I told the agency to spare no expense. Which means there is undoubtedly more than one man on the case."

"Why would there be more than one man?"

"Have you forgotten I'm really trying to solve three murders? I want to know everything about anyone even remotely connected with them. I want to know about the relatives of those people."

"How long have you had detectives on what you call the case?"

"Over a month. Though things didn't really seem to warm up until you came to Linden Gardens."

"How could I have changed things?"

"The idea of getting you there might well be to do away with you. Have you forgotten the rockslide?"

I thought a moment. "If that was an attempt to murder me, why wasn't a second attempt made?"

"I would say the opportunity hasn't presented itself."

"David, you're talking in riddles."

"I'm sorry. I must ask you to trust me. I must also ask you to risk your life."

"How?"

"By going back to Linden Gardens. We still have no proof the three deaths in that house were murders, not accidents."

"Whom do you suspect?"

"Without proof, I can't say."

"You weren't reluctant to point out my aunt as the possible murderer in your notebook."

"And when I lost the book, I almost lost you."

"I wonder if Kate read it."

"That's something we'll have to find out."

"There's so much we have to find out."

"Yes. Including what's behind these two trips you made to New York City."

"I wonder who got the first envelope I put in the chair."

David encountered that with, "Don't you wonder if it had real money in it or slips of paper cut to the size of bills?"

I nodded. "I do now. But it doesn't make sense."

"Neither does murder."

"Three," I said.

"I believe the second and third victims were killed because they found out something that would have exposed Libby's murderers. Therefore, they had to be done away with and it had to be made to appear accidental, just as Libby's death was."

"But what motive?"

"Greed."

I challenged that with, "Mama didn't want money from her sister. She loved Papa and was happy with what little they had."

"Were you?" David softened his words with a smile.

"I suppose I wasn't," I said sadly. "It didn't take me long to find out life with Papa was beautiful."

"With your aunt?"

"Dreary. And, all of a sudden, it's scary."

"You're going to have to draw on some courage. That is, if you want to find out if your mother was murdered and by whom."

"I do. Just as I want to learn who murdered your sister and Libby."

"In that case, I'm bringing you back to Linden Gardens. I'm sure they expect you to come back."

"*They?*" I questioned.

"Hester, Zeffrey, Wanda, Calvin, and Kate."

"How could Hester be a suspect when she can't get out of a wheelchair?"

"We don't know that she can't. We've just been told she can't."

"Is there a way of finding out?"

"We'll devise a way if we have to."

I slipped my hand through David's arm and smiled up at him. "I'll do whatever you say."

"You'll be in danger."

"I'm still angry that a trick was played on me by someone in that house."

"You mean the envelope containing no money?"

I nodded. "So I'm willing to risk the danger."

"Promise me you'll forget your anger. They mustn't know we opened the envelope beforehand. Naturally, you will have to relate in detail your father's reaction when he found there was no money in it. You'll also have to pretend indignation that you weren't taken into the confidence of whoever made up that envelope. Be sure to mention you are heartbroken at learning your father has been taking money from your aunt all these years."

"Do you think they will believe me?"

"We have to gamble on that. One thing more—tell Wanda and Calvin you wish to speak to your aunt and question her about the whole thing."

"What if she admits it?"

"Accept it."

I was stunned by his reply.

He took my hands and squeezed them lightly. "Trust me. Remember—you must play a game. That mansion shelters some very clever people. You must outwit them. The best way is by pretending innocence."

"How do you suppose they will react when I mention there was only paper in the envelope?"

"Whoever did it will say it was felt your aunt had been blackmailed long enough."

"Should I remind them of Hester and Zeffrey?"

"No. I have an idea they're being watched by the agency I hired. I also believe they know a great deal."

"Are they the murderers?"

"We may know before the night is over. Now let's get to the station or we'll miss our train."

We did miss it and had quite a wait for the next one. It was almost midnight when we arrived at the depot, which was in darkness. To my surprise, the horse and buggy were parked where David had left them. He explained that he had told the hostler at the village stable to come and get it and bring it back by late afternoon for the train we had missed.

David rounded the green, which was deserted at this hour, and stopped the animal at the horse fountain. While the animal quenched his thirst, David lit the lamps on either side of the seat. After consuming a moderate amount of the water, the horse gave a few vehement shakes of his head, signifying he'd had enough.

As we started on our way, David said, "Tom's a dependable chap. He undoubtedly checked to see if the buggy was still at the depot after the afternoon train departed. When he learned it was, he brought the animal back to the stable, and fed and watered it."

"David, does anyone in town know your real identity?"

"The only ones to whom I've revealed it are you and Reverend Lawrence Gates. I call him Larry."

"How did you happen to get acquainted with him?"

"When I rented the home I own—coming here under false pretenses as I did—Reverend Gates paid me a call and told me he knew the young lady who owned it. I invited him to share a glass of sherry with me. He didn't know I was the one to whom he sent the telegram about Nora's death. We got acquainted over the sherry. I sensed that his interest in Nora was more than friendly, and as the evening wore on, he revealed his love for her. The final letter I received from Nora disclosed her interest in a man of the cloth, as she expressed it, though she didn't identify him by name. She probably thought I would be amused since she was such a spirited and independent young lady. I suppose she gave no thought to the fact that I was just as aware that she was a warm, compassionate person. She mentioned your aunt in several letters and her growing concern about her. She was as struck by her changing moods as you were, though I think she got her out for a few drives. Now that I have a better picture of

Linden Gardens, I believe Nora found out something that
cost her her life."

"Do you think that was the case with Libby?"

"No."

"Then why was she killed?"

"I would rather not say just now. As you know, rumor
was that she had loved not wisely but too well, poor
child."

"With my uncle her supposed lover. Wanda insinuated
that."

"That rumor could have been started to blackmail your
aunt."

"You're not blaming Papa for that, are you?"

"I'm not blaming your father for anything. And don't
you—until all the evidence is in."

"I'm sorry," I said contritely. "It was a stupid question."

"You're tired," David said. "It's been a difficult day for
you. And it isn't over."

"It must be after midnight," I said.

"Yes," he agreed. "That isn't what I . . ."

He didn't finish the statement because our attention was
diverted by a light in the distance. As we neared it, we
could see it was a lantern that was being moved back and
forth slowly to attract our attention.

David slowed the animal, proceeded cautiously, and
called out a command for it to halt once we reached the
figure half concealed by the bushes at the side of the road.
David relaxed once he saw the gentleman. He held the
reins of a horse with his free hand. The horse was almost
completely concealed by the bushes. In the dim light I
could see the man was of middle height, probably in his
early forties. He was wearing a riding habit and must have
been riding hard for he seemed a bit out of breath when
he addressed David.

David said, "This is Tom Zaleski, the private detective I
told you about."

"How do you do, Mr. Zaleski." I wasn't startled by his
appearance, but I was concerned it might mean something
had happened to my aunt. However, I relaxed once I
learned his mission didn't concern her, though I should
have realized that since he had no entrée into Linden
Gardens.

Mr. Zaleski acknowledged the introduction, then said he
had some fresh information that David should know

about. Before he revealed it, he blew out the flame on the lamp.

"Just in case someone should come along, sir," he said. "I was at the edge of the village watching for you. I didn't dare approach you there lest someone else was also waiting for you."

"What is the news?" David demanded impatiently.

"It concerns Hester Innis. She can walk."

"Are you certain?" David's surprise matched mine.

"I am, sir," he replied. "The area behind the house is a wilderness. I got there in a roundabout manner and hid out all day. I've been there before, but Zeffrey has always drawn the shades at nightfall. Tonight, they either got careless, or they have other things on their minds. As soon as darkness came, light streamed from the windows at the rear. I lost no time belly-crawling across their yard to the windows. I inched upward until I could see into the room. It was the kitchen. Hester Innis was moving about—on her feet—preparing a snack for the two of them. Zeffrey sat by the table, smoking his pipe and talking."

"Could you hear what they were saying?"

"Some."

"Tell us," David demanded impatiently. "I have a feeling time is closing in on us."

"I don't know about us, Mr. Martin. But I fear for the young lady. I don't think she should go back to that house."

"Why not?"

"The window was open a bit from the bottom," Mr. Zaleski said. "Zeffrey cackled something about she'd go the way her mama went. She had to because she was as snoopy as her mama."

I said, "Mama must have found out something."

"Apparently," David answered quickly, then asked Tom another question. "What else did you hear?"

"Hester said that if she—meaning Miss Abbott—ever learned Eric von Linden wasn't the father of Libby's unborn, they'd never get another cent out of Emma."

"Then my uncle wasn't the father of Libby's child!" Anger rose within me at the thought of what those two evil people had done to my aunt.

David placed an arm around my shoulder. "Steady, darling. This is no time to let our emotions rule our reason. I agree with Tom. You must not go back to that house."

"I must." I spoke without the slightest hesitation. "My aunt could be in danger."

David said, "I think they will use your aunt to do away with you."

"In heaven's name, how?" I was aghast at the very thought of such a thing.

"Hypnosis," he said. "Remember telling me about that ornament on the table in that strange room your aunt supposedly finds so comforting?"

"Yes," I said.

"She is attracted to that room, sir," Tom said. "I learned that."

"So much so," David commented, "she doesn't realize what happens when she goes in there."

"Are you saying Wanda hypnotizes her—with that small circular mirror?" I asked.

David nodded.

Mr. Zaleski said, "It makes sense, Miss Abbott."

"I can't believe it," I exclaimed. "Wanda has been so devoted to my aunt."

"That would be Wanda's way of putting it," David said. "When your aunt is really a prisoner in her own home."

"What about the three murders?"

"I wish I could answer that question," David said somberly. "To be able to point the finger of guilt at the murderer would end the danger to you and would free your aunt of whatever is troubling her."

"Are you saying that whatever is troubling her is connected, in some way, with those deaths?"

"We know that. Though we know only what you have been told by Wanda."

I thought a moment. "Oh no," I exclaimed as I realized what he meant.

"What is it?" David asked, though I was aware he wanted me to speak the thought aloud so I would convince myself.

"My aunt believes she is responsible for those three murders. She committed them while under hypnosis."

"You're not quite right, Celeste," David said.

"What, then?"

"Your aunt has no awareness of having been hypnotized."

"You mean she was deliberately hypnotized and told to murder three young women?"

"That's it. Then she was brought out of it. The victims lay before her and she believed herself to be a murderer. You told me she stated she had no recollection of suggesting you take that walk."

"And Hester made things worse by making up horrible stories about her."

"We have to prove all this," David said. "And the only possible way is for you to return to that house. I can't let you do it. Even if the three murders go unavenged, I won't risk you being the fourth victim."

"I have no intention of being the fourth victim," I said quietly. "You forget one thing. Libby, Mama, and Nora were not suspicious of anyone in that house."

"They must have had suspicions or they would not have been murdered," David reasoned. "I believe Libby was in league with her aunt and uncle. I also think there was more to it than that."

"Her pregnancy?" I queried.

David said, "You know the French saying—*cherchez la femme*—find the woman."

"In this case," I said, "it's *cherchez l'homme*."

"Who else could it be but Calvin?" David mused. "He's devilishly handsome now. What must he have been like seventeen years ago?"

"We're getting a lot of suspects," I said. "I never thought of him as Libby's seducer. I suppose because he is the one who first hinted at Libby's indiscretion. Wanda went into more detail."

David said, "So they're working together."

"If my uncle is innocent of any indiscretion with Libby, they must be," I said. "I'm not afraid of them."

"I am," David said.

"No matter what argument you use," I said, "you'll not dissuade me from going back there. There is another saying I thought of—'Forewarned is forearmed.'"

"You're not dealing with amateurs," David said. "They've killed three times and got away with it."

"Why do you suppose Libby was killed—if she was carrying Calvin's child?"

"I can only give a guess that as beautiful as she was, she was a simple country girl. However, if your aunt had adopted her, I believe he probably would have wed her—though her life with him would not have been a happy one. When he goes to New York City, he spends freely on both wine and women. At least, those are the reports I've received regarding him."

"They're true, sir," Tom said quietly.

"Have you had him followed?" I asked.

"Everyone in that household has been watched—except your aunt, who hasn't gone anywhere in the past month except to your graduation ceremonies."

"Did you get a report on either Calvin or Wanda placing an envelope in that chair at the hotel?"

"No," David said. "And I have a confession to make. It's something you may as well know. Tell her, Tom."

"It was one of our men who retrieved that first envelope you placed in the chair."

"Not Papa?" I exclaimed.

"No, Celeste," David said. "Forgive me for not taking you into my confidence sooner, but I felt—and Tom agreed with me—that the less you knew, the less danger you would be in. That has all changed now."

"What was in the envelope?" I asked, too relieved and thankful to learn of Papa's innocence to feel any annoyance toward David because he'd kept me in the dark.

Tom said, "I believe the same thing as was in the envelope you delivered today—strips of paper."

I gave a bewildered sigh. "It doesn't make sense."

"It does, Celeste," David said kindly. "That's why I'm worried. You see, they had you deliver the first envelope so they would have an ace in the hole. They didn't know how intelligent you were. It didn't take them long to find out, once you took residence at Linden Gardens. Their motive was to divert any suspicion from themselves in case you became doubtful the three deaths were not accidental. I'm not going to say Calvin wasn't concerned when you told him the envelope was gone. Though I'm certain he doesn't know I've been having him watched. I insisted on the utmost discretion. Anyway, think back to your reaction when you observed your father's anger at opening an envelope that contained nothing but empty strips of paper."

I nodded. "There's another question that comes to mind. Why did he go there?"

Tom spoke up. "Zeffrey mailed a letter yesterday. However, on his way he stopped at the tavern and had a few drinks, which I bought. I picked his pocket to see to whom the letter was addressed. The name on it was Mr. Jonathan Abbott, your father. Naturally, I have no idea of the contents of the letter, but it must have concerned something about his going to that hotel and to that particular niche and finding an envelope in that chair. Or a letter that would pertain to you in some way. That's mere supposition, Miss Abbott. I replaced the letter in Zeffrey's pocket and bought him another drink."

"Poor Aunt Emma," I said. "How those people have deceived her."

David nodded. "Let me take you to my place. You can go back to the city in the morning. You'll be safe there. They won't dare harm you because they will know you no longer trust them."

"But we won't have any evidence against them and they will still have a great and destructive influence on my aunt."

"You are not her guardian," David said.

"Mama was killed trying to save her."

"So was my sister," David said remindfully. "I still don't want you to go back there."

"Why would they want to kill me?"

"For a reason you never thought of. You are the only heir to your aunt's fortune. With you out of the way, they can assume complete domination over your aunt. However, if you leave, they can turn your aunt against you. You know she hasn't been friendly."

"Indifferent would be a better word," I mused.

"I only hope her mind hasn't been harmed by such frequent hypnosis," David said. "Of course, during your growing years there wasn't occasion for them to put her under their spell, though they did do it on occasion."

"Why?"

"She signed checks she has no knowledge of signing. They were made out to cash. Your father's name was in the checkbook as the recipient."

"Papa would never take money from Aunt Emma," I said indignantly.

"Though I've never met him, I'm certain he wouldn't," David replied.

"Where did you learn that, Mr. Zaleski?"

Tom said, "We have ways of finding out things, Miss. We found that out. We have a very good informant here."

"Who?" I demanded.

"That I can't tell you. At least, not yet."

I looked up at David. "I am more determined than ever to return to Linden Gardens. You must trust me."

David thought a moment before he replied. "Very well. But I'm going in with you. I want to see both Wanda and Calvin. I'm certain they will be up and waiting for your return, though by now they may be getting a little worried."

"That I wouldn't return to Linden Gardens?"

He nodded. "They gambled that when you saw your father's anger at what you thought was a joke played on him when he wanted cash you would return to Linden Gardens, heartbroken and disillusioned. However, if you confronted him, he could show you the letter he received and you would know there was something quite amiss at Linden Gardens."

"I wonder what their next step will be," I said.

"It frightens me to think of it," David replied.

"Me too, Miss. It's a dreadful risk you're taking."

"Perhaps. But I assure you I'll be cautious."

"Just remember—with you out of the way, they will have free access to your aunt's fortune. They can even have her sign a will while under hypnosis. After that, she might be victim number five."

"I don't intend to be victim number four," I said. "Let's not delay any longer."

"She's right, Mr. Martin. I suppose I might as well call you that now."

"You might as well," David said. "Though I'll not divulge it at Linden Gardens yet. Even though they may know my true identity, they don't know I've had them under surveillance."

"There's one thing more, sir," Tom said. "And I'm sorry to say I can't enlighten you much on it."

"What is it?" David asked.

"Naturally I kept your house under surveillance from the time you left. I had an assistant up here because I was watching the Innis place and I also went to the Inn. However, at midday I rode to your place. My assistant was hiding in the forest where he had a view of both the front and rear of your place.

"A male rider—a man of the cloth, sir, since he wore a white collar—drove up in a buggy. He had a package. He rang your doorbell, and when there was no answer, he propped the book against the doorknob.

"He was just returning to his buggy when Calvin Rosby rode up and dismounted. The two men talked awhile and the minister motioned to the door where the book was still propped. Rosby nodded reassurance, as if attesting to its being safe there. The minister got into his buggy and left. Rosby mounted at about the same time, apparently having been told by the minister you weren't at home.

"Though he started off, he rode in the opposite direction. Before my man could retrieve the book, Rosby returned. He took the package, slipped it inside his coat—it would have been a bit too bulky for his pocket—and he rode off. Sorry, that's all I can tell you."

"A package," David said thoughtfully. "The minister would be the Reverend Lawrence Gates."

"We've not had him shadowed," Tom said apologetically.

"No need for that," David assured. "You've done well. Thanks for intercepting us. The news isn't good, but we know two things. First, Calvin is not the dutiful secretary he seems to be; second, he's worried."

"I wonder why he went to your home?"

"Since he knew I was away, it was probably to try to search it for any evidence Nora might have left behind."

"Don't you think he'd have done that before?"

"Not when the death wasn't regarded with suspicion."

"But he didn't search it today."

"He probably wanted to see the contents of that package, and his presence in the vicinity had been witnessed by someone."

Tom's horse neighed restlessly. Tom said, "That's all the news I have, sir. I'd better be off. Good night, Miss."

He seemed almost to vanish into the forest. I heard the sound of the horse's hoofs as he made his departure, but there wasn't a sign of animal or man.

David smiled at my perplexity. "He's been here only a month and he knows every trail. Where there aren't any, he makes them. He's furious with himself that he didn't see the person who started that rockslide, which was meant to kill you. I imagine it was either Calvin or Zeffrey."

"It would have to be," I reasoned. "Let's get going, David. I want to uncover these imposters as soon as possible."

"How do you propose to do it?" His arms were around me, gathering me close as he asked the question.

"I don't know. But do it, I shall."

"Be careful, my darling. You know I love you."

"That's why I'll be careful," I replied. "I need your love."

Our lips met and our kiss was passionate and demanding.

"Must you go back there?" His lips left mine just long enough to ask the question. "It's you I want and need. Not revenge."

"They're evil people, darling. We must put an end to their killing."

He tried to draw me onto his lap, but I pleaded with him to let me go. He did, though unwillingly.

"I want you as much as you want me, my love." I spoke as he smothered my face with kisses. "But not this way. It would be cowardly of us to turn our backs on my aunt. She's a timid lady and helpless against those who are controlling her."

"Yes." His voice shook with emotion and his hands fumbled as they sought the reins. He tugged on them a few times. The horse got the message and continued on its way. I remained on the far side of the seat. I dared not even slip my arm around David's. I had never known passion before. And I suppose I still didn't know its depths. But I wished we could just go in and tell my aunt the truth about her supposedly faithful employees who had used her these many years. I wished it so that David and I would be free to fulfill the love we had already declared for each other.

◆ Eleven ◆

Wanda and Calvin awaited my return, just as David said. If they were surprised that he entered the house with me, they gave no indication of it. David had warned me just before he turned into the drive that I must wear a very woebegone expression when I entered the house, the result of my discovery that papa was the individual who had been bilking Aunt Emma out of sums of money for years—according to them.

I must have done rather well, or perhaps it was because I knew I was walking into a trap. At any rate, Wanda exclaimed in dismay at the sight of me. Calvin looked quite handsome in a maroon velvet suit.

"We were terribly worried something might have happened," she said worriedly.

"Something did, Wanda," I said dully.

"I hope you weren't involved in an accident," Calvin said. "You're very late. Did you miss the train? Or did you loiter in the village."

"We missed the train," David said.

"It was unavoidable." I addressed Wanda. "The gentleman who picked up the envelope was my father."

I marveled at Wanda and Calvin's superb acting.

"Your father," they exclaimed in unison, their features a mixture of incredulity and dismay.

I nodded. "It was such a shock I lost all control. I embarrassed David."

"I don't understand," Wanda said.

"I had hysterics," I replied. I shook my head mournfully as if I were viewing Papa again, tearing up the strips of paper. "I couldn't believe my eyes. I wanted to rush over and demand to know why he would stoop to blackmail."

David placed a protecting arm around me. "I thought it would be wiser for Celeste not to confront her father. I in-

185

sisted she come back to her aunt's. At least until she got over the shock of what she had seen."

Wanda said, "Well, at least now we know who was getting all that money through the years. I find it as difficult to believe as you, Celeste."

Calvin spoke with compassion. "Had we known who it was, we'd have done our best to talk your aunt out of your playing the role of messenger."

I said, "I'm glad I went. At least now I know the truth about him."

Wanda said, "We'll never let you go again."

"Never," Calvin affirmed. "He got enough this time to take care of him for a while. And if he got the other envelope, he shouldn't need any more for a year."

I lowered my eyes and nodded agreement. I didn't dare look at David, but I wondered if he sensed the trap closing in around me. I was beginning to have second thoughts about my ability to outwit these two. If Hester and Zeffrey and Kate were in with them, that meant five who were against me. Kate hadn't put in an appearance. I assumed she had retired.

I said, "Has my aunt retired? Or didn't she leave her bed today?"

"She's in the master library, awaiting you."

My surprise was genuine. "It sounds stupid, but I've never been in it. Will you lead the way, Wanda?"

"Certainly."

There was an awkward silence as the four of us stood in the entrance hall. I knew Wanda and Calvin expected David to take his leave.

He thwarted them by saying, "Do you mind if I go also? I've never had the pleasure of meeting Mrs. von Linden."

"Of course, Mr. Lathrop," Wanda said. "Though it's very late and she may not be alert."

"I'll understand and I shan't stay long," David assured her.

"Thank you."

Wanda slipped her arm around my waist and guided me along the hall. David and Calvin followed. She opened one of the double doors and led us into a large room furnished with oversized upholstered leather chairs. There were matched divans facing each other before a fireplace on one side of the room. A fire burned in the grate. My aunt was seated at the opposite end of the room, before a second fireplace. The light from the fire flickered across her pale face. She was in a black lace Watteau gown underlined with pink. Her slippers were black satin with a pink rosette decorating each toe. She looked very delicate and helpless in the large leather chair.

Wanda addressed her first, mostly in an effort to gain her attention, for she seemed not to pay the slightest heed to our entrance.

"Emma, you needn't worry any longer. Celeste has returned from New York City."

My aunt didn't seem in the least worried, but she did perk up at the mention of the city. "Did you deliver the envelope?" she addressed her question to me.

I replied affirmatively, then introduced David, though using the name Lathrop. "I already told you he leased the house beyond this one."

"Did you?" she asked.

"Yes, Auntie. You told me you knew the family who used to live there. Martin was their name."

I wanted to mention Nora's name, but Wanda gave me a cautioning look. I nodded understanding. She didn't want Emma to have one of her spells.

David acknowledged the introduction, then said, "Celeste, I think you should tell your aunt who picked up the envelope of money you placed in the chair."

I said, "It was Papa."

Aunt Emma nodded. "Oh, yes. Jonathan made many demands on me through the years. I gave him all he asked for because it was my fault you had to grow up without a mother. It was a small way to repay him for what I had done to you and my sister."

"What did you do to your sister?" I asked.

"What did I do?" she asked.

"Yes, Aunt Emma. What did you do?"

"I killed her."

There was no acting in my expression of shock at her admission of guilt.

"I killed Libby too. She was carrying Eric's child. I couldn't bear it."

Wanda glanced up at the portrait over the fireplace. So did I. It was that of a distinguished gentleman with a slender mustache on his upper lip and a goatee on his chin. His features were Nordic and his hair was blond. He had very blue eyes, which held a look of warmth. Though he was thin-lipped, there was a hint of a smile at one corner of his mouth. His chinline was firm and the tilt of his head, proud. I could understand Aunt Emma's grief at the loss of a gentleman whose portrait gave an indication of his compassionate nature.

"I fooled Jonathan today, though," she went on.

I pretended ignorance and said, "How did you do that, Aunt Emma?"

"I put paper in the envelope instead of money. Usually Calvin makes up the envelope, but this time I wouldn't let him. I wouldn't let him because Jonathan was playing the role of rake. I didn't mind giving him money so long as he behaved. But to covet the wife of another man—no. So Jonathan will get no more money."

"I understand, Aunt Emma," I said dutifully.

"I hope—now that you know what your papa is like— you will live here. I will see that you lack for nothing. Wanda and Calvin will be your good friends—as they are mine."

"If you still want me, Aunt Emma." I think it was fear that made me act out the role so well.

David's features were inscrutable. I wondered what he was thinking.

I said, "Thank you, David, for coming with me. You must be as weary as I. I'll walk you to the door."

"I'll go with you," Calvin said.

And he did, even though he must have known David and I were more than friends. Particularly since David's arm enclosed my shoulders and his eyes adored me every step of the way, as mine did him.

At the door, David kissed my cheek and told me he would be over in the morning and we would go for a drive. I told him I'd be delighted. I stood outside until he drove off. I moved back into the house reluctantly. I was heading for the stairs when I heard Calvin turn the lock in the door and throw the bolt. The sound seemed to portend my doom.

Wanda called to me before I started my ascent of the stairs. "You look very weary, Celeste. I think a glass of sherry might help you relax."

"It would take more than a glass of sherry to ease my pain," I said.

"Please, my dear. Even a few sips would help."

"It will do you good, Celeste," Calvin said.

Rather than antagonize them, I acquiesced and we went into the parlor. The fireplace wasn't lit here and the room had a chill.

Wanda saw me draw my suit coat closer. "The wine will warm you, dear."

Calvin poured three glasses. He raised his to me and said, "To a new beginning for you, Celeste."

I thanked him and sat down. I didn't feel like taking even a sip, for suddenly I was terribly weary. However, I did take two sips and then stood up.

"It does taste good. May I bring it upstairs? I'll finish it before I retire. I'm exhausted. Both emotionally and physically."

"Certainly," Wanda said. "I must get Emma to bed also. She wouldn't go upstairs until you returned."

I said, "She seems so listless."

"Hasn't she been that way almost since your arrival?" Wanda asked.

"Yes. Even the first day. And yet when she came to my graduation exercises, she seemed alert and happy. At least, she gave the appearance of enjoying her day."

"She did," Wanda assured me. "And she will again. Just be patient. Perhaps now that she knows you are aware that it was your father who was demanding large sums of money from her through the years, she will feel more at ease. Particularly since she will no longer give in to his demands."

All I said was, "Papa fooled me." I felt like a hypocrite, but I had to play the game. Hopefully, as well as they.

When I reached my room, I found I was trembling. Some of the wine spilled onto my hand. In my haste to right the tilted glass, my elbow struck the archway leading into the bedroom and the entire contents spilled onto the rug. It was just as well. My stomach was too jumpy for an alcoholic beverage—especially since I'd not eaten since breakfast. At the thought of food my empty stomach started to churn. Yet I was too nervous for any kind of nourishment.

I undressed, washed myself, and gave my hair a hasty brushing. I uttered a weary sigh when I got into bed and stretched out full length. I was aware of a raging headache, but it didn't seem to matter. I knew I would go to sleep in spite of it. Everything was over with. I had no more worries. David would come tomorrow. That was my last thought. My beloved David. I tried to speak his name aloud, but my lips wouldn't move. I didn't even realize I'd been drugged.

It seemed as if I kept hearing my name being called over and over. I tried to shut it out, but I couldn't. It wasn't being called loudly, but it was my name. Or was I dreaming? That was it. I had dreamed it. Was I awake or was I still dreaming?

How could I tell? By blinking my eyes. I blinked them. I was awake. Now that I knew that, I listened. All was silence and once again I told myself I had dreamed that I heard my name called. Only I hadn't dreamed it. Someone really was calling my name. Who? Who would be calling me in the still of the night? My room was pitch black. I looked in the direction of the archway. There was dim light coming from somewhere.

My name was called again. This time I recognized the voice. Aunt Emma! Of course. Her room was across the hall. She must need me. Kate must have slipped out again as she had on that other night. I pushed the covers off me with an effort and sat on the side of the bed. My feet felt around for my slippers. I found them, but my coordination was poor and I couldn't get them on. I was too tired. No matter. I could walk around in my bare feet. I had done it as a child. I still liked doing it.

The important thing was to get to my aunt. I felt for my negligee, managed to get it on, but my fingers were all thumbs and I couldn't button it, so I folded it close to me. I started from my room, but had to catch hold of one of the posters on the bed. I was so weary I was reeling. How could I help my aunt when I couldn't stand on my own two feet? I forced myself to concentrate on what I had to do. Get to my aunt. She needed me.

Moving in a rather stilted fashion, I got as far as the archway and leaned against it for a few minutes. I had to, because in the dim light that slipped into the sitting room from the hallway, the room seemed to be reeling. I'd never had such a feeling before.

Suddenly, reason flashed through my brain. The wine! *I'd been drugged.* I remembered that neither Wanda nor Calvin had touched theirs. I'd taken only a few sips downstairs, but it must have been very potent. I was grateful my elbow had struck the archway and spilled the rest of the contents from the glass.

Now that I realized what had been done to me, I forced myself to concentrate. I had to pull myself together. My brain was sluggish and so was my body, but I had to go to my aunt. Perhaps they were harming her. If so, there was little I could do but threaten them. I could warn them David was wise to them. Tell them he had had private detectives watching them. Reveal his true identity to them. Then I recalled they probably knew that. There were few things I could do to frighten them.

I steadied myself and continued my progress to the door leading into the hall. I had only to cross it to reach my aunt. There was a lamp burning dimly on the table outside my door. My aunt's door was closed. I saw another lamp burning farther down the hall near the stairway.

I also saw a figure there. Aunt Emma! She saw me at the same time and called my name again. It was pitiful the way she called it. As if she hated to waken me. I suppose she did. She was a timid soul, despite her wealth. Timid because she was so filled with guilt. And what had she to feel guilty about? Had she murdered Libby? I couldn't believe she had murdered Mama or Nora.

I moved slowly toward her. Not until I reached her, did I notice the slack lines of her face. Her arms were partially outstretched and her palms were raised and slightly extended.

"Come here, Celeste," she said.

"What are you doing here, Auntie?" I asked.

"I'm going to push you down the stairs."

I was stunned to hear her reply. Yet, though her words were threatening, her manner wasn't.

"Why would you want to do that?" I asked, more to humor her than to get an answer to such a question.

"I must do it," she said. "I must do it. I must do it."

She kept repeating her statement as if she were trying to convince herself. Then I knew. She had been hypnotized. She had been ordered to push me down the stairs. I also recalled having read that a hypnotized person could not perform a violent act if it was not in his or her nature to do so. Certainly my aunt was not a violent person.

I said, "I will go to the head of the stairs. You put your hands on my back and push me so that I will fall down."

She made no move to do so. I said, "Come, Auntie. You must get closer to the stairway."

I took her hand to guide her there, but she held back and emitted helpless little cries.

"Push her, you fool." The voice was a hiss.

"My aunt won't do it, Wanda. It isn't in her nature to murder." I kept my voice as calm as possible. The cold marble floor had helped to alert my senses.

"It will be done." Wanda came out of the alcove where the dumbwaiter was located. She was holding a lamp and raised the wick as she spoke.

I addressed Wanda. "You and Calvin want to be rid of me. I know everything. So does David. We know you are the ones who stole money from my aunt for years. You also committed the three murders."

"You can't prove anything," she snarled.

"Why don't you bring my aunt out of the hypnotic trance you put her in so that she would say what you wanted her to when I questioned her about Papa? Go on, Wanda. Or don't you dare?"

"I'm not afraid of you," she jeered. She set down the lamp, clapped her hands once, and said, "Wake up, Emma."

She needed to say it only once. My aunt blinked her eyes and seemed suddenly shocked to find herself so close to the stairway, her arms outstretched, with palms extended. She cried out in fear and covered her eyes. "I almost pushed you down the stairs. Now you know, child. I do these things and don't realize it."

"You pushed no one down the stairs, Auntie," I said. "Calvin did. At least, I imagine that's what happened, though perhaps Libby, Mama, and Nora were dead before they were found at the foot of the stairs. The marble stairway was what they used for their alibi."

"No, my dear. I did it. I was standing here all alone each time a body was found dead at the foot of the stairs."

"Calvin and Wanda set the stage, Auntie," I said. "You did not kill Libby."

My aunt's eyes begged forgiveness. "I hated her because she carried Eric's child."

"You were told you hated her because of that. It wasn't Eric's child. It was Calvin's."

"Calvin's?" My aunt looked incredulous. "Calvin's?"

"Don't believe her, Emma," Wanda said heatedly. "She has been in league with her father for years to bilk you out of your fortune."

"Papa and I never wanted any part of Aunt Emma's fortune," I retorted. "It is you and Calvin who covet it."

"You talk too much," Wanda said. "Your mother did also."

"And Nora?" I asked.

"She found out something that made her dangerous."

"To whom?" I asked.

"To your aunt," Wanda said. "We have protected Emma all through the years. We knew what she did. We found her at the head of the stairs each time a death occurred in this house."

"A murder occurred in this house three times. You and Calvin, assisted by Hester and Zeffrey, were a part of the conspiracy."

"Hester and Zeffrey—who lost their niece?" Wanda scoffed.

"Libby became a threat when she realized Calvin wouldn't wed her unless my aunt adopted her. I imagine she did her best to persuade Aunt Emma to do so. Didn't she, Auntie?"

My aunt's eyes were beginning to lose their vacant look as she became more and more aware of the conspiracy that had taken place in this house for years.

She said, "Yes. At first, she got on her knees and begged me to adopt her and then adopt the child she was bearing. If I had known Calvin had fathered it, I would have insisted he marry her. I would also have dismissed him. I never suspected him."

"He probably suspected that is what would happen. He liked this life too well to jeopardize it."

My aunt continued her story. "I remember it now so well. When I refused to heed Libby's pleas, she demanded I adopt her. She said I owed it to her. I told her I owed her nothing. That she had violated the sanctity of my home. However, I offered her a modest sum of money that would support both her and her baby for a year. She spurned it and told me I would regret it."

"That sounds like a threat," I said.

Wanda snickered. "Calvin told her to say that. She worshiped him and did and said anything he ordered her to."

"He didn't care about her, did he," I said.

"She was a beautiful child, but not bright," Wanda said. "Intelligence doesn't run in her family. You met Zeffrey and Hester."

"Where is Calvin?" I asked.

"Where is Kate?" my aunt asked.

"Sleeping," Wanda said. "We made sure of that."

"You mean you drugged her as you did me," I said.

"It didn't seem to work very well on you," Wanda replied.

"I dropped my glass—fortunately."

Wanda's smile mocked me. "That's a matter of conjecture. Asleep, the blow on the head wouldn't hurt as much."

"So that's how you did it," I said. "Struck each victim on the head. Then threw them down the stairs."

"And never a suspicion was cast in our direction." Wanda spoke with pride of their murderous accomplishments.

"How do you propose to do away with us?" I asked.

"Us?" My aunt was still trying to grasp the meaning of what was going on. "Wanda, are you serious?"

"About murdering you and your niece? Yes."

"And I did not murder Libby, my sister, and that dear Nora Martin?" my aunt asked.

"You did not," Wanda openly admitted, then turned to me. "We know David is her brother."

"You steamed open the letter he wrote me."

She nodded. "You suspected Kate." When I made no answer, she said, "You did know the envelope had been tampered with, didn't you?"

I nodded. "David and I went to Papa's flat and we steamed open the envelope you gave us. We knew it contained nothing but papers. How did you lure Papa to the hotel?"

"We had Zeffrey mail a letter that Calvin printed. The note contained detailed instructions about an envelope that would be concealed in a chair in the hotel lobby and that would contain news that might cause him to question the wisdom of allowing his daughter to continue to live at Linden Gardens.'

"No wonder Papa was so angry."

Wanda laughed the throaty laugh I had thought so attractive when we first met. Now I considered it ominous.

"I asked where Calvin was," I said. I was merely stalling for time. I knew he was in the house somewhere, if not concealed in the alcove where the dumbwaiter was.

I saw a movement behind Wanda. I hoped she wouldn't notice that my attention had wavered, but she was clever and turned quickly. It was Kate.

"What are you doing here?" Wanda's voice was a snarl.

Kate said, "For years I've been watching you and Mr. Calvin. I feared for my mistress's life. I suspected the two of you when Miss Celeste's Mama and poor Nora Martin were found dead at the foot of the stairs. No one questioned their crushed skulls because of the marble stairs. I did. Because on the evening each of them was found dead, you drugged my milk. I wouldn't drink it tonight, sensing it was also drugged. I knew you and Mr. Calvin were frightened. I heard you both talking about Nora Martin's diary today. In it she said that Hester Innis could walk. Nora had told you and Mr. Calvin that she was going to the constable with the information because she felt that Ruth Abbott's death had not been an accident. She didn't believe Libby Innis' death had been either. She made the mistake of confiding in both of you, believing Hester and Zeffrey were somehow responsible."

"Why did you kill my mother?" I asked.

"She saw the checkbook with checks made out to cash. Your father's name was written on the stubs. Your mother knew he didn't get that money. She confronted us with the information and told us she was going to tell your aunt about it. We saw to it she never got the opportunity. She also suspected Hester was up to something, and never believed Eric guilty of the charge Hester made against him. She was beginning to convince some of the townspeople, so we had to do something."

"You'll do no more killing," I said quietly. I believe I was more revolted than frightened by this woman.

"Not after tonight. We dictated a will today that Emma wrote and signed. Calvin and I witnessed it. As well as Zeffrey. In it, we receive everything."

"While she was under hypnosis," I said.

Wanda made no answer. Her hand touched her waist and her fingers closed around something. When she withdrew it, I saw it was a slender dagger.

"This was the property of Eric von Linden. It will appear that Emma used it to kill you because you learned she had committed three murders."

"I'll never confess to such a thing," Aunt Emma exclaimed indignantly.

"Of course, you won't," Wanda said. "You'll be dead from a bullet wound. Self-inflicted, of course. Have you forgotten the double-barreled derringer your husband gave you when you moved here? You'd never have the courage to use it."

"You'll not lay a hand on your mistress," Kate said, making a lunge at Wanda.

The two women grappled for the knife.

Kate tried to wrest the weapon away from Wanda, but Wanda was strong and twisted free of her. Kate made another lunge and a shot rang out. Aunt Emma screamed and backed to the wall. Kate and Wanda fell to the floor. There was blood on both their chests.

I looked beyond the light to see who had fired the shot. A figure came into view. It was Calvin. When he saw both women on the floor, he gave a shout and then a moan.

"Mother," he cried. "Mother."

Wanda had fallen on top of Kate, whose eyes were open. Her arms and feet moved as she tried to get free of Wanda. It was difficult to see who was wounded.

Calvin lifted his mother and clasped her to his bosom. He spoke her name over and over. His love for her was obvious. He was her son. I wondered which of them had hatched such a diabolical scheme. Neither Aunt Emma nor I dared move. Nor did Kate, who seemed all right. Calvin still held the gun, and though his attention wasn't on us at the moment, if we moved, he might shoot and kill again. It was obvious that the bullet he had fired had killed his mother. Her body was limp in his arms.

The sound of footsteps echoed through the downstairs hall. Calvin set down his mother's body and stood up.

His eyes were deadly as he said, "I will kill you, Celeste. Then I will shoot your aunt. A self-inflicted wound, of course. She killed my mother, who tried to take the gun from her."

"You must be mad," I said.

"Calvin." It was David who spoke. He was holding up a lantern. A perfect target. Tom Zaleski was with him, also holding a lantern.

I screamed, "Calvin has a gun."

He aimed it at David and fired.

Another gun fired simultaneously. Calvin leaned against

the marble railing. The gun he held fell from his hand, but he used both hands on the bannister to support himself as he moved along the hall to the stairway. He moved to the center of it and looked down at David and Tom, who were at the bottom, looking up.

Calvin tried to smile, but it was a grimace. His knees buckled and he fell forward, toppling down the stairs. It was horrible. Both David and Tom started up and stopped Calvin's fall. They carried him down the rest of the way and placed his body on a bench in the hall.

David ran upstairs and embraced me. Kate was already ministering to my aunt, consoling her with softly spoken words as she led her back to her room. Tom went outside. Apparently there was someone there, for I heard the hoof-beats of a horse driven hard. Someone had gone for the constable. Tom came back, still holding the gun he'd used.

At last, the true story of Linden Gardens would be told. A tragic story of horror and greed. But a story that had come to an end.

That was a night of terror. One not easily forgotten. Though once the truth was known, the villagers revealed they were not without compassion. They came to Linden Gardens—most of them to pay their respects to my aunt and offer an apology for the manner in which they had treated her; only a few came out of curiosity. A morbid curiosity, I might add. Kate and I lost no time in showing them to the door, though our manner was courteous.

I am going to dwell briefly on that night so that you, my reader, will know the answers to the questions that puzzled me. Questions not only about my aunt, but about each resident of the household.

As you can guess, my aunt took to her bed following the dreadful events she had witnessed. Dr. Carney arrived in good time, along with Constable Lyons. After a brief examination of the two bodies, Dr. Carney informed Constable Lyons that both were deceased.

The good doctor, after being assured I had not been injured, then went to my aunt and Kate. Wanda, in attempting to stab Kate, had stepped into the line of fire and took the bullet meant for Kate. A bullet from a double-barreled derringer fired by her son. That was a secret they had kept well. Certainly they were devoted to each other. They were just as devoted to the cause of obtaining the fortune of Emma von Linden, their employer. Their first ploy was to destroy her mind and self-confidence through hypnotism. Once under Wanda's spell, she was told to do or say certain things. Then, when Wanda brought her out of the spell, she had no recollection of having been accountable for whatever had happened.

So determined were they to gain control of the Von Linden fortune, they would allow no one to stand in their way. They could be patient because they had lived in the lap of luxury while waiting for millions. However, there were also two heirs who had to be disposed of. First, Mama. Then, me.

Aunt Emma informed me it was Wanda who had suggested she send for Mama. Wanda knew the death of Eric von Linden had had a depressing effect on her. The false information she had been given that he had fathered Libby's unborn child further unsettled her. I asked her if Eric had ever brought up the subject of divorce. She replied in firm tones—"Never." Nor had he ever been closeted in the library with Libby. It was true he had been guiding her in her reading, with my aunt's approval. But it was to my aunt Libby read, not my uncle. My aunt also denied she had attemped suicide following Nora's death.

Mama's death had been hastened when she discovered the check stubs with Papa's name on them. Of course it was Calvin who had taken the money. Among his effects were found several checkbooks. Through the years he had stolen many thousands of dollars from my aunt. Attorney Luke Aarons stated he never questioned them, fully aware of my aunt's generous nature. He also admitted he never questioned Calvin and Wanda's sincerity. I couldn't blame him for that. They were consummate actors. I never once doubted their loyalty to my aunt until David and I steamed open the letter in the apartment I shared with Papa.

We learned a great deal more from Hester and Zeffrey once they realized we knew about the game they had both been playing. They knew Calvin had been responsible for Libby's condition, though they did not know Calvin had murdered her. At least not at first. They admitted they had their suspicions later, but since she was dead, they had no desire to alter their situation. They received money from my aunt, who believed it had been she who had killed their niece. Hester said it was Wanda who had concocted the evil story about Eric that she had repeated over and over.

Wanda and Calvin convinced my aunt she should say nothing about Libby's death. They insisted she had had a mental lapse when it happened. The truth is Wanda had hypnotized her, then told her to push Libby down the stairs. After the dire deed had been done by Calvin, my aunt was brought out of her hypnotic state and saw the body of the young girl at the foot of the stairs. It is small wonder that she had spells of melancolia. The same was done with Mama. And Nora. Though, in Nora's case, Wanda took a vacation so as not to be on the scene when Calvin murdered her. However, she was not gone for two weeks, as she told me. It was a mere matter of two days, according to Hester and Zeffrey. After all, my aunt had to be brought out of her hypnotic state.

Poor Nora went to see Hester. Just as everyone else did, she walked in. Hester stated that since it was a rainy day, she didn't expect anyone. The heavy rainfall also prevented her from hearing the carriage approach—or the door open. She was walking from the kitchen when she and Nora met face to face. Nora was first astonished, then angry. She said she was going to tell Wanda and Calvin. If only she had gone to the constable's office. But it wasn't to be. As soon as Zeffrey returned from my aunt's, Hester revealed her carelessness. He returned at once and informed Calvin and Wanda. The four of them worked closely together.

Reverend Gates came into possession of Nora's diary shortly thereafter. Apparently, when she left Hester's, she returned to her home, possibly to pack for her stay at Linden Gardens while Wanda "vacationed" for a few days as an alibi. Her absence would lessen any suspicion directed toward members of the household when a third accident occurred there.

Nora entered her discovery in the diary, and on her way to Linden Gardens she stopped by the rectory. Reverend Gates was absent, but Nora left her diary behind. Whether accidentally or intentionally, we will never know. In any case, the discovery she had noted in her diary was the reason for her death.

Yes, Hester and Zeffrey freely confessed to their part in the nefarious plot. They were so frightened when they learned what had happened to Wanda and Calvin, they didn't even need the threat of prison to force them to talk.

As for Kate, she informed me that her manner had changed toward me so that Wanda and Calvin would not think we were suspicious of them. She had not trusted them for years and had developed the habit of eavesdropping.

She had learned a great deal, but she knew my aunt would never take her word against Wanda's. Nor would the constable. Or Dr. Carney. I could certainly understand her reasoning so far as he was concerned—though he did apologize to me later. I told him I understood. He could have behaved no other way and still upheld the ethics of his profession.

Tom Zaleski had struck up an acquaintance with Kate when she went into the village on a shopping expedition. He did it so graciously she could take no offense. When he learned a little more about Calvin, he gambled and took her into his confidence after my arrival there. I shall be eternally grateful to her, for had she not been in the house that night, I'd not be telling the end of this story.

My aunt is well now and quite certain she has nothing to fear as to her sanity. Also, her manner is becoming cheerful. Certainly, she will never be lonely again. She attends services at the church and is beginning to take part in social activities.

As for the shabby trick Wanda and Calvin played on Papa, after he left the hotel, he returned directly to the department store and went to the general manager. Papa showed him the letter he had received and related the result of his following the instructions. He asked permission to go to Linden Gardens the following day. He received it. Thank goodness everything had been explained by the time he arrived.

He never knew about the death of Libby. Zeffrey explained that. Instead of mailing Mama's letters, he turned them over to Calvin. Just as he and Wanda had steamed open the one David delivered to the house, they also had steamed open Mama's letters. They were mailed only if there was nothing revealing in them. In one, Mama had voiced her suspicions of Wanda and Calvin after she had occasion to write a check for Aunt Emma and discovered Papa's name on the check stubs for having received many thousands of dollars. Nor were my letters to Papa mailed.

Not that they contained anything incriminating regarding Wanda and Calvin, but if Papa heard nothing and my death occurred suddenly, it would be further evidence of my aunt's mental instability. Especially since Papa had been against my visiting her.

It was Zeffrey who almost killed me with the man-made rockslide, on Calvin's orders. My aunt had been hypnotized before telling me to go there. Small wonder she had no recollection of it. She'd also been hypnotized before telling me I was to make a journey to New York City. She was either drugged or under hypnosis almost the entire time I was there.

What Wanda and Calvin had said was true. Wanda had hypnotized my aunt and dictated a will for her to sign. Attorney Luke Aarons found it. She had no recollection of having done it and so it was destroyed.

I have saved the best for last. This is my wedding day. I am waiting for Kate to come in and place my wedding veil on my head. The ceremony is taking place at Linden Gardens. Reverend Gates will perform it. Aunt Emma asked Papa to please let her have it here. He kissed her cheek and acquiesced. There is no longer any ill-feeling between them. Papa knows what Aunt Emma went through. He is so grateful I am alive, he can shut out the rest, especially once he learned the truth. And he thoroughly approves of David.

A soft tap just sounded on my door. It is Kate. She enters beaming and picks up my veil which is stretched full length on the bed. She puts it on and I turn for her approval. She nods and I kiss her cheek.

"Get on with you, she said. "Your papa's waiting by the door."

"Your wedding will be next, Kate," I said. "Tom Zaleski told me last night."

Her eyes glowed. "In a week, Miss Celeste."

"It's worked out well for all of us," I said.

"Better than you know. Since your aunt refused to prosecute, and they've been ostracized by the townspeople, Hester and Zeffrey sold their place and moved away."

"Good. Is David downstairs?"

"No," she replied. "He's in the garden awaiting you, along with Reverend Gates and the villagers. They've come from miles around. They know there'll be good eating and drinking and dancing."

"There will be," I assured her.

And what a glorious August day it was for a wedding. David and I left the festivities early. We are traveling to Virginia so I may see his ancestral home. That is where we will live. Papa will visit us from time to time, as will Aunt Emma, and we will return their visits. Kate and Tom Zaleski will assume the responsibility for Linden Gardens after their wedding day.

I no longer shudder when I think of what happened at Linden Gardens. Had I not gone there, I'd not have met David. It was he and I who put an end to the horror that exists there. In doing so, we brought Aunt Emma out of the shadows.